Sedating Elaine

Sedating Elaine

DAWN WINTER

ALFRED A. KNOPF

NEW YORK

2022

THIS IS A BORZOI BOOK
PUBLISHED BY ALFRED A. KNOPF

www.aaknopf.com

Knopf, Borzoi Books, and the colophon are registered
trademarks of Penguin Random House LLC.

Library of Congress Cataloging-in-Publication Data
Names: Winter, Dawn, author.
Title: Sedating Elaine: a novel / Dawn Winter.
Description: First edition. | New York: Alfred A. Knopf, 2021. |
    "A Borzoi book"—Title page verso.
Identifiers: LCCN 2021004110 | ISBN 9780593320549 (hardcover) |
    ISBN 9780593320556 (ebook) | ISBN 9781524712198 (open market)
Subjects: GSAFD: Black humor (Literature)
Classification: LCC PR6123.I5775 S43 2021 | DDC 823/.92—dc23
LC record available at https://lccn.loc.gov/2021004110

Front-of-jacket photograph © Antonio Jarosso / iStock / Getty Images
Jacket design by Janet Hansen

Manufactured in the United States of America
First Edition

FOR CHARLES.

"Muw forever"

Sedating Elaine

1

ELAINE PATTED her furry mound as if it were a dog's noggin and said, "Good girl." In a shaft of the day's declining light she lay on the bed in a dramatic—almost poetic—recline, head sunken amongst the pillows, body heavy and flung apart, a golden glow upon her face. Outside, a fuzzy drizzle fell, as it had fallen all day, intensifying the mugginess of the bedroom, dampening the sheets, thickening the smells. Praised enough, the mound was gently stroked in an absent-minded way, pubic hair slicked, then boinging back up as the hand brushed over it. The room was finally still and quiet; all the buzzing and muttering and squelching was over, and both women fell into separate places of contemplation. For Elaine, it was a feeling of sleepiness, drained as she was by the repeated pulses of ecstasy. For Frances, this was nothing but a brief period of bodily respite because Elaine was finally—though never permanently—satisfied. She sat on the edge of the bed with her hands on her knees, aware that behind her Elaine was petting herself in the strangely self-congratulatory way she was accustomed to after sex—as if her vagina alone had done all the work—but Frances' mind was already elsewhere. Normally by now she would be covering herself—joggers, shorts, bathrobe, beach towel, bedsheet, anything—following her outstretched arm in the direction of a cold beer, but today she didn't move, and suddenly, in a moment of uncharacteristic perceptiveness, Elaine's hand paused mid-pet as she said, "Are you okay, babe? Is something wrong? You're just sitting there."

"I'm fine," Frances said.

But Frances was not fine. All day she had been troubled—more troubled today than yesterday, but not as troubled as tomorrow, as is the way with problems we think we can ignore, wishing them away, but they refuse, and grow, double, quadruple. In a strange way it had been useful to have the distraction of a dilemma, something else to focus on throughout the day as Elaine whittered and bored her with stories and thoughts and endless enthusiasm. A letter had arrived which had so occupied her mind, she had managed to survive the whole ordeal—brunch, shopping, drinks, the movies—so utterly consumed with worry that Elaine might as well not have been there. It said a lot about Elaine that she had not noticed anything was wrong. Even as they had tumbled through the door and Elaine had scooped up Frances and spun her round, because Elaine seemed to live in a permanent Lindy hop, Frances' eyes had landed repeatedly on the letter, propped up against an empty picture frame on the hallway sideboard, so that as she went round and round, looking over Elaine's shoulder, she saw it repeatedly, like a message flashing before her: "You're fucked. You're fucked. You're fucked." She was amazed—proud, even—that she had managed to concentrate enough to have sex but, to be fair, her body and tongue were so well trained she could have done it semiconscious. She had done so many times before.

Elaine poked Frances with her big toe. "You don't seem fine," she sagely observed. "What's wrong?"

Oh, where to begin? Frances sighed theatrically. She most certainly was not going to confide in Elaine about her problems, not when Elaine was a problem in herself, another issue Frances had been trying to "sort out." Elaine was of course completely unaware that Frances had been thinking of dumping her, that she had in fact tried many times, but somehow it always went wrong. They would meet in a pub or a park and Frances would steel herself, take a deep breath, and say the words, "Look, Elaine, we need to talk," but Elaine either mocked her or changed the subject or—worse still—took it as a joke: "I know, it's about time we did something else with our mouths," then suddenly they'd be kissing, and a short while later they'd mysteriously appear back at the flat, lurching in bed, and Frances would be left wondering what the hell had happened. But she knew the answer: She'd heard of men being led by their cocks and here she was being led by her clit, brainlessly and helplessly, like a shopping trolley dragged about. This fact made her bubble in self-hate, self-pity, and she resented Elaine even further for causing it. "Just back off, will you," she often wanted to say, but before she knew it, her groin would be overheating, as if it had been plugged in for too long and needed to expel some energy, and then she couldn't remember what she'd been saying. *I'm at its mercy,* she thought glumly, looking down at it. She laughed when comedians and frustrated husbands complained about women having low sex drives. They'd obviously never met the likes of Elaine.

Sitting on the edge of the bed, with the letter in the hallway and Elaine behind her, Frances felt imprisoned in the situation: no way out, no help, no suggestions. She owed money to a dealer for drugs Elaine still had no idea about. And although this was a dealer she had known for many years—one she would even say she liked—everyone has their limits, and he had evidently grown impatient. The debt had been slow to accrue but accrue it had, and over the past few weeks he had sent messages, left voicemails, and generally probed her to commit to repayment. Only one thing to do: She ignored him. She didn't have the money. And the longer she ignored him, the more threatening the messages became. Not that he wanted to—she could hear it in his voice when he said, "Don't make me do this"—but he had a reputation to uphold, she supposed, and quite possibly owed the money onwards, to whatever boss was above him in the complex hierarchy drug dealers operated in. Then, today, she had received the letter, if it could be called that: a scruffy note which simply read, "Remember, I know where you live," hand-delivered without a knock at the door or a word uttered through the letterbox. She'd scoffed when she first read it—it seemed so overdramatic—but very quickly the truth of the fact sank in and her incredulity was replaced with this horrible, haunted dread. He knew where she lived. She put it on the sideboard where it blended in amongst the pile of junk mail and was better hidden than in the wastepaper basket, which Elaine frequently emptied as part of her efforts at homeliness, a gradual filtering-in of herself, like leaving her toothbrush behind or buying slippers for the both of them. And throughout the day Frances had imagined it there, waiting for her, full of threat, and now she thought of it again as Elaine hummed and the rain smeared the window with fat, clownish tears. Elaine poked her big toe into Frances' right buttock again and she leapt up, as if bitten, and started pulling on some discarded and dishevelled clothes from the floor.

"Where are you going?" Elaine whined.

"We don't have any beer."

Elaine watched with her typical head-tilt of amusement as Frances struggled to get arms in sleeves and legs in trousers, a hurried little dance resulting in much hopping and stumbling. "We have wine, you know," she said. "I brought some with me— it's in the fridge. And there's that ginger beer from when I last stayed over."

"I want a real beer." Frances stood up and quickly brushed her hair. "No bother—I'll be back in a little while."

As she turned, Elaine was still smirking, shaking her head side to side in fondness at her girlfriend's quirkiness. Frances stepped out of the bedroom into the smell of a sumptuous, garlicky stew coming from the kitchenette, suddenly and deeply wishing she could just sit alone with it, a chianti for company, and a spliff as fat as a frankfurter. She stuffed her feet into her boots. "Funny Frances. Don't be too long," Elaine called as the door to the flat swung shut.

Frances sprinted down the five flights of stairs to the ground floor, then swept out through the door, the wind barging into her like a spirit, blasting her hair, jacket, and shoulder bag outward as if ready for flight. The end of spring, and the weather was its usual calamity, pleasant one day, wild the next, newly formed leaves no sooner yawned into life than ripped from the branches by a morning storm. People dressed with the eccentricity of uncertainty: shorts, raincoat, trainers. Or Wellingtons, T-shirt, sunglasses. Unopened umbrellas carried with trepidation in a gale, hoping there would not be a spot of rain lest a jousting match begin, but no worry, suddenly the sun appears, and they all become hot and foolish, umbrella dangling from a hooked arm or shoved, with a jumper, into a carrier bag. You'd think they'd all be used to it, as this was the constant quandary of true British weather—in any season, on any day, at any moment—but instead there existed a state of befuddlement and tardiness, forever caught off-guard by whatever happened next, as if weather had never happened before.

Frances cupped a cigarette with her hand and attempted to light it. With a well-timed flick of her thumb in a brief lull amidst the gales, she succeeded and inhaled three times, deeply, in quick succession. Bliss. Then she strode round the corner and pulled out her phone.

"You're alive, then," Dom's voice answered. "Wise of you to call."

"I got your note," she said bitterly. "Dom, you've known me for years—was it really necessary? I'm well aware of how the land lies."

"Hey. I can't make special allowances for you, you know that. This has been going on too long. I don't want it to be this way but you're not helping me. You're not helping yourself."

She sighed. "Where are you?"

"You got something for me?"

"No, I need something from you."

He scoffed, "You're unbelievable."

"I know. Just a twenty-bag of bud. Last time, I promise. Where are you?"

"Getting in my car." A brief silence followed. Then, tetchily, "Okay, fine. Jesus, the shit I take from you. The usual place in fifteen."

"Thanks, Dom."

"Yeah, whatever."

He hung up.

The usual place was a metal bench in a tiny nook set back from the main road where a few bedraggled flowers and a bin for dog shit was somehow supposed to form a vista of relaxation. The road

was only a few metres away; buses stopped, stinking up the pud-
dles, growling to be underway, and cyclists slid along cautiously
beside them, one foot on the pavement. She was early, so she sat on
the frigid bars and smoked. A small plaque was screwed into the
back-rest, if it could be called that. Frances knew what it said: IN
MEMORY OF JANE HOPSON-SMITH. She often wondered, as she sat
here, what Ms. Hopson-Smith had done in life to upset her rela-
tives so much that they doomed her name to this place where flies
buzzed by the bin and cigarette ends poked out between the petu-
nias. The traffic moved off. She watched expressionlessly as cars
and taxis sloshed by, and she wondered what Elaine was doing—
not a caring thought, more a sense of fretful inescapability, like
wondering what work the next day would bring. She might still
be in bed, waiting, stroking, preparing to go again. Frances shud-
dered and lit another cigarette. Finally, Dom appeared, hurrying
as usual, arms straight and stiff, as fists plunged into pockets and
shoulders hunched up to his ears like a vulture. He raised his eyebrows once in greeting and sat down beside her.

Dom was the type of person who had never learnt how to be
friendly but in spite of this had managed to cultivate a certain
appeal. Not quite charm, more like when you pat your lap and a
cat shuns you, making you want it even more. His name was con-
nected to a myth, an urban legend: Apparently he kept a huge collection of guns stored in an old wine cellar, laid down in rows and
rows amongst a few hundred bottles of Dom Pérignon. She didn't
know his real name and she'd never dared ask him if it were true.
His eyes, though tight and low and almost always looking at the
ground, lit like flares exploded behind them. She supposed he
was handsome, in a way, attracted as she was to the darker side
of life, and she liked how, when he smoked, he exhaled through
his wide mouth and long nose simultaneously, so that it engulfed

him. It made him look like a young dragon, still learning its drag-ony ways. She couldn't help wanting to be kidnapped or whisked away by someone like him. She could turn the bottles of cham-pagne and live in the cellar, like a little Gollum. It sounded quite peaceful.

He pulled a small carton of orange juice from his pocket, stabbed the straw into it, and started sucking. They finished their respective indulgences in silence and after a couple of minutes each lobbed the remnants—dog end, scrunched carton—into the litter bin, then they sat with their elbows on their knees. Dom produced a small bag, which he slid into her jacket pocket.

"You've got a fuckin' cheek, you know that?" he said.

She nodded in reply and looked around. Having procured what she wanted, she wished she could get up and walk away, or better still, vanish in a puff of smoke. But a conversation had to be had. It was unavoidable now.

"I'm sorry," she muttered. "I don't know how it happened. It just got out of hand."

"That's exactly how it always happens, you fool." He shook his head and glanced sideways at her. "It's not like I can show you special treatment. Not any more than I have done already. Why should anything be different for you? I know you think because we know each other there should be other rules, but you're wrong, okay? We're not mates. I haven't got your back. You're not fuck-ing special, and I've covered for you enough, just to bide you some time, but I've had enough now—get me? I'm done waiting. I want my money. I fucking need it."

She nodded and looked at the floor like a scolded child.

"Two grand," he said. "You've got until next Saturday. That gives you just over a week to get it. Capiche?"

She nodded again. It seemed futile to plead for more time, to say she didn't have any money, to ask for him to understand: He'd given her weeks already, he knew she didn't have any money, and he completely understood. But it was her problem, and it was for her to figure out, and figure out quickly, or else.

"Look," he said. "You know I like you. I know you. You're okay. You're cool. But if I don't get it, I'm calling Betty, and her and the Ladies will pay you a visit. You know what I'm saying?"

She nodded. She could not know it, but he did in fact go easier on her than anyone else, purely because he mistook her for being several years younger than she actually was, taking pity on her smallness, her vulnerability, her lowered eyes of a desperation tinged with hope, as if searching for dropped coins. Such an appearance certainly had its advantages even if she didn't realise it. Other customers would have had their genitals burnt in a straightening iron by now, such was Betty's speciality.

"Right, well." He stood up and tapped her foot with his shoe. "Don't take the piss, okay? Not anymore. I'll be calling each day, and you can avoid me if you like, you can hide away and pretend you don't hear me, but if I don't get my money, they're coming round, you hear?" She didn't need to nod this time. He said, "Good," then he was gone.

She felt relieved because it was over, yet she knew he meant every word. And she had met Betty once a few years ago, at a similar location to this and for similar reasons. Betty had been drunk, bragging about how she and the Ladies had clamped a cold hair straightener between a woman's legs, then tied her thighs together and switched it on. "Burnt her flaps so bad they stuck to it," she'd yelled. "Bitch screamed like a whore on hump day."

"You're fucked up," Dom had said.

"Got you the money, didn't I?"

After this, Frances had found it difficult to forget Betty.

She dove into the off-licence and grabbed two four-packs of beer. The rain had ceased, and the shop windows and coats of the customers were drenched with steam. The sun had vanished behind the mishmash of houses, and streetlights blinked with uncertainty. She joined the small queue and wondered what to do. She had no savings. The bank would hardly help her; even if she lied about the reason, she'd been overdrawn for years and clearly lived hand-to-mouth—they'd refused her several times before. She had no family to ask for help, no one to turn to. Frances was the sort of person who accumulated incredibly short, intense relationships that ended explosively, beyond repair, way beyond salvaging a friendship. And it would not have mattered if she did have friends or family; none of them would have known about her debt, because she wouldn't have told any of them: It was way beyond shame, simply unthinkable. Some secrets become so normal in ourselves it does not occur to us to share them. She stepped forwards in the queue. Her drug and alcohol use had for a long time dallied on the line of social acceptability. In the eyes of her employer, her colleagues, her so-called friends and even her ex-girlfriends, Frances smoked some weed and drank some booze, more than most, perhaps, but not cause for concern. People, Frances had discovered, tended to excuse even the most blatant of hints when it came to substance abuse—red eyes, the waft of old whisky, unexplained exhaustion, grey skin—because they didn't want to see it, as if it were a contagious problem that acknowledgement would pass to them. So people either saw nothing or said nothing, or both. And to be fair, they were not witness to the troubling times; they might see the fourth glass of wine during dinner but they did not see the vodka at three a.m. She did not drink to quench a physical craving but to quell the edginess, the vividness, the feeling she'd always had that she couldn't cope. She remembered a game she had played as a child, squinting until her vision was blurry, seeing how tightly she could squeeze her eyes and still be able to read, the strange feeling of security that came from it, a sort of distance, a disassociation with reality. Eyes wide open in adulthood, it seemed her senses were too sensitive; sights and sounds startled her, the very essence of being human seemed to be just too much, too raw. It was as if she were missing some protective layer of epidermis everyone else seemed to have been born with. She marvelled at all these people walking around each day, getting on with life, and she wondered how they managed it. So she still sought the squinting game; a few drinks in and she felt it happening, felt herself sinking back in her brain, some bare and basic part taking over the levers of her words and actions whilst she observed as if through a telescope. From here, she was safe, she could even absorb the minutiae, the details. She could cope with them, feel them, appreciate them. The shimmer of water, the angles of walls and buildings, a kingfisher shooting above a sugilite stream. Inebriated, she was not overwhelmed by them; she was as calm and remote as an orbiting moon. But this—all of this—was impossible to explain to anyone, so she chose to be unknown rather than misunderstood, which of course meant she was both.

What to do? There were the short-term loan companies which seemed all chummy and helpful but turned into a vicious Fagin the moment you owed them a penny. She could ask, again, for extra shifts at work, but they always said no—the place was struggling enough; she should just be grateful to still have a job, as they continually told her—or she could look for work elsewhere, but there wasn't time, not anymore. The shop door beeped loudly as another customer entered, and the horrible noise suddenly sparked an appalling idea. It was in fact such an unthinkable thought, such an abhorrent suggestion, that Frances felt herself physically backing away from it, as if it had appeared in the air before her, as if she wanted to hold up her hands and beg, "No, please, there must be another way." But there wasn't. She was out of time and out of ideas. She paid for the beers and skulked slowly home in a new and unexpected rain, the bag swinging from one hand, a can clutched in the other, a perfect picture of resignation.

Elaine greeted her at the door wearing a face of concern and nothing else.

"You were gone a long time." She furrowed her brow. "Where have you been?"

"I got talking in the shop."

Elaine's brow shifted to an isolated raise: "You got talking? Pull the other one. Funny Frances doesn't chat, we all know this."

Frances brushed past her to the kitchenette, opened herself another beer, and stuck the rest in the fridge. Elaine sauntered back to the bedroom, leaving the door open.

"Do you want a beer?" Frances called.

"I wish you'd tell me what's wrong," Elaine yelled back. "I can tell, you know. I'm not stupid."

How ironic that she finally had Elaine's attention yet was, because of her decision, no longer in a position to ditch the woman. And she realised now, almost laughing, that she should have dumped her after sex, when Elaine was dozy and compliant. Just slide her out the door—"Off you go, bye-bye now"— and toss her clothes out after her. She had never thought of it before, and now it was too late. In the kitchenette she downed her beer and leant against the oven. She looked around the place— the mottled sideboard, the lumpy cushions, shelves full of shells and magazines, books piled upon the floor within arm's reach of the sofa—as if it all were a beloved's face she would not see for a long time, as if she were going to war. She thought of luxurious freedoms—an empty bed, space to stretch out as she read, bowls of soup alone with her wine—and in her mind she waved them all goodbye. The train of possibility departed; farewell, dear friend. Then she downed her beer, poured two vodkas, added ice, squeezed lemon juice, threw in some tonic water, and stirred them with the handle of a used teaspoon. Back in the bedroom, Elaine was sitting up with her legs crossed like a yogi, facing the open doorway. Another person might have looked spiritual and lovely in such a pose, but Elaine looked obscene. Why did she seem to be perpetually peeling open? Frances often felt like she wanted to fold her back in and zip her closed. She handed her the drink and stood back, almost out of the room.

"Elaine," she said, and prayed for a sudden miracle to intervene. It didn't. "Would you like to move in with me?"

Elaine swallowed. Then, slowly, as if the question were gradually permeating the layers of her mind until—*ping*—making sense, her jaw dropped, eyes widened, brow lifted. She stayed a moment in this prolonged gormless pause then said, "Oh my God. Are you serious?"

Handed a get-out—the chance to pretend it was a joke, carry on as before, find some other solution—Frances said nothing, then heard her voice sombrely reply, "Of course."

Two broken glasses and a squeal later, Frances found herself on the living room floor. Elaine had leapt from the bed and launched herself—as if falling down stairs, all arms and legs waving—out of bed and straight at Frances, whose smaller size and unpreparedness meant she was unable, as ever, to defend herself against the sudden onslaught of a hyper Elaine. The nude body wriggled heavily on top of her as frantic pecking commenced; her chin, her cheeks, her neck, her lips. "Yes, yes, yes, yes, yes," Elaine squeaked between kisses. "Yes, yes, yes, yes . . ."

This was worse than Frances had expected, and she had expected something ridiculous. Pinned beneath Elaine's behemoth weight, smothered by her girlfriend's strangely masculine bulk—now, apparently, cohabiting—she felt helpless. Her mind flashed back to many nature programmes where a poor animal—an antelope or mouse or sparrow—would be caught and held for a few gratuitous moments before the jaws came in for the kill. Elaine reared up like a praying mantis.

"When? When shall I move in?" Her voice sounded deeper than normal, as if she were slightly choking. Tears trembled in her eyes. "When? When?"

"Um." Frances gasped for breath. "As soon as possible, really. I suppose."

And Elaine looked down upon her from way up there, the undersides of her breasts glistening moistly, then she smiled, and laughed, and said, "I love you, baby," before swooping down, open-mouthed, hungry again.

FRANCES HAD, with naïve optimism, assumed Elaine would need some time to pack, little appreciating that Elaine had been waiting and hoping for this moment and as such had already planned for the occasion just as a would-be bride plans her wedding cake (five tiers, gold frosting; Elaine could practically taste it). She was living with her parents, which Frances for some reason saw as a little bedroom with a few clothes and nick-nacks, not realising that Elaine had her own private annexe with a garden, terrace, and driveway. She was aware that Elaine "came from money"—if she

hadn't, this whole absurd situation would never have occurred—
but she was not aware how much, wealthiness being an abstract
concept to Frances, practically fictional. She assumed Elaine's
parents owned something like a comfortable four-bed semi with
rectangular flower beds and a wooden patio set. She had no idea
about the paddocks, pool, and pagoda. In Frances' mind only lot-
tery winners and the royal family lived like that, and besides,
Elaine spoke with an almost common accent, dropping *t*'s hither
and thither. Elaine had always been very closed-lipped about her
background, and so Frances was somewhat surprised the following day, when, at about eight p.m., just as the hangover had begun
to wear off, Elaine turned up with a standing lamp and a Kitchen-
Aid mixer.

"Elaine?" Frances squinted at her, as if she were a stranger.
"It's late—what are you doing here?"

"Ta da! I'm moving in. You did say right away, and it's the
weekend, so why not? Take this, will you"—she held out the
lamp—"and budge aside; this thing weighs a ton." She heaved
the mixer into the flat.

Frances stood still, holding the lamp and watching whilst
Elaine bustled in and out, bringing up boxes and dumping them
in a pile in the living room. "There's no rush," she started to
say, but Elaine didn't hear her; she hummed and chattered and
plonked kisses on Frances' forehead as she passed. Frances felt a
growing dismay as the boxes formed a mound, then a mountain,
obscuring her view of the television from the bedroom.

"I won't be able to start unpacking 'til tomorrow," Elaine said,
opening a few, peeping inside, rummaging around. "I need to go
home tonight to talk to my folks. They are not happy about this,
I can tell you."

"But they haven't even met me yet. How can it be a problem?"

"Baby, that *is* the problem."

She pulled out what looked to Frances like a black snake that had swallowed a lot of marbles. "Anal beads," Elaine said, waggling them about. "This is my box of tricks. I'm taking it straight to the bedroom," and Frances watched, aghast, as Elaine struggled to lift it, then carried it off with a wink and a chuckle.

Oh, dear Lord, thought Frances. She followed her through to the bedroom, where Elaine had already opened a drawer and was looking at the mess inside as if to say, "Really?" She opened another and was greeted by a similar sight. "Honestly, babe," she said, closing them both, "you keep the flat so tidy on the surface but behind every door there's a disorganised shambles—it's like you're living inside a metaphor of yourself." She patted Frances' cheek as she brushed by her again. "We'll have to reorganise some of the cupboards to make way for my things," she chirruped.

Frances was still holding the lamp. She caught sight of herself in the bedroom mirror. She looked like a sort of shell-shocked soldier, standing to attention, lamp at arm's-length. She carried it to the hallway and shoved it into a corner, then approached her girlfriend.

"Elaine, you can take your time, you know. I didn't mean you had to move in right away, this instant."

"I know. But I don't see any point in hanging about. I want to be here, with you, and it's so exciting. We're roommates now! Tomorrow we'll have to celebrate. I'll buy us some champagne, shall I? And get us a takeaway, and we can spend all evening in bed— how does that sound? You never know, maybe we'll make our way through that box in there," and she winked again. *She's only joking*, Frances reassured herself, *Please, please tell me she's only joking*.

Elaine put her arms around Frances' shoulders and looked

down at her, smiling. "It's going to be like a dream come true," she said, then she kissed Frances' nose and gave her the look—the slight tilt of the head, narrowing of the eyes, a lift to the edge of the mouth—to which Frances quickly replied, "God, Elaine, I'm so tired, I'm sorry."

"No matter." Elaine kissed her again. "You'll need your rest. I'd better be going anyway and face the fallout with the 'rents. You're going to have to meet them soon, you know. Mummy will need to know her princess is living in a way she is accustomed to. They'll want to check you're not a serial killer or anything."

"I know," Frances said.

"I'll be off now but I'll see you in the morning. Sweet dreams, sweetpea," and she blew a succession of kisses. "Love you."

Frances stared at the boxes, already emitting an Elaine-smell into the air, and the mixer, which took up two-thirds of the kitchen sideboard. It was only a small flat, but it seemed to have shrunk, swamped as it was with so much Elaine. She wondered where on earth all this stuff was going to go. Straight out the window, ideally. Then she went to the bedroom and stood in the doorway, staring warily at Elaine's box of tricks on the bed, as if it contained an awful and unpredictable trickery, like a macabre jack-in-the-box was about to leap out. She slowly stepped forwards and lifted a flap with the tip of her forefinger, peering inside. She immediately wished she hadn't: a huge multicoloured tangle of shafts and leads and ropes and pointy things and circular things and the stench of rubber. She closed it, dumped it on the floor, and slid it into a corner with her foot. Then she turned to the wardrobe, opened it, reached at the back, and pulled out a differ-ent box: small and wooden and engraved with a heart. She sat on the edge of the bed.

In amongst the other items was a champagne cork, dated in

Biro—almost two years ago. She sniffed it but it smelled of nothing now. She clasped it in her palm and closed her eyes, as if saying a prayer, then, returning the cork, she carried the box into the hallway and opened the airing-cupboard door. Reaching inside, she felt around to the left, beyond the dustpan and brush and a broken broom, where she knew there was a little hollow. She kissed the box and slid it inside. Hidden. Safe.

She wandered back into the living room and faced the towering boxes. The deranged face of a Furby poked out of one, staring at her. She had the eerie feeling that her home was not her own anymore. It was not a nice feeling.

A spliff and a bowl of stew—smoking with one hand, spooning with the other—the bowl snug in her lap; she sighed. Dom had messaged twice already and she had replied that all was in hand. She ate her meal slowly, like it was the Last Supper, relishing every mouthful. It was not to be a permanent arrangement—heaven forbid—and soon she'd be free of her for good, but in the meantime, she sensed not doom exactly, but some difficulties heading her way, and she savoured each drag, each flavour, all the more because of it. A trial was imminent, and it was called Elaine.

2

LIFE HAD A HABIT of getting out of control whenever Frances made a decision, and she usually had no idea how it happened. Like the time she decided to take driving lessons and found herself in an affair with the tutor, fucking for the whole two hours down a muddy lane, him tilting the mirrors this way and that, until a year later, when the wife found out, and Frances realised she'd spent hundreds of pounds effectively paying for sex because she sure as hell hadn't learnt to drive. And like when she decided to take evening meditation classes and accidentally burnt the hall down when she flicked a cigarette and it went sailing, unnoticed, in through the open window. She always found herself standing and staring at what was unfolding before her, watching the disaster, the fallout, the flames, knowing it was her fault but unsure quite how or why. And so it was now, with Elaine moving in. It had somehow gotten out of control, and all she could do was watch.

She had, with unfounded optimism, presumed Elaine would be like a rent-paying pot plant, taking up a corner. She recalled the command in the classroom during colouring-in: Do not go outside of the lines. She assumed Elaine would instinctively obey this, and stay within the boundaries pre-set by Frances, keep herself neat and tucked away. It would still be Frances' home, Frances' flat; Elaine would exist in designated areas, a drawer here, a shelf there, that was it. Surprise turned quickly to despondency: She'd had no idea that Elaine had so much stuff, nor that the stuff would appear *en masse* the very next evening, nor that rapidly the day after that, more boxes would arrive, only to be enthusiastically emptied, many items—often ghastly—held aloft as if not seen for decades. What could she do but watch as these were then carried around and placed on shelves, critically observed, moved, rearranged, Elaine tapping her forefinger on her chin, scrutinising. What could she do but flop on the sofa, eating Cutie clementines and drinking lager, a dumb audience to the performance, which continued into the afternoon. Occasionally Elaine would say, "What do you think about this painting? Here, or here?" and in response she shrugged or gave a bemused thumbs-up. She had tried being diplomatic about it—"We probably need to both get rid of some things, to make space, it won't all fit"—but it had been met with shock and confusion.

"What? Why? There's plenty of room."

"I don't think there is, Elaine. Look." And Frances had pointed demonstrably at a bookshelf, collapsed at one end through weight, now propped up by novels rather than supporting them.

Elaine ignored her. She had quite astonishing levels of optimism. "You just have to think creatively," she'd said, balancing a piggy bank atop a chopping board atop the cooking books in the kitchenette. "This is both of ours now," she said, and Frances wondered if she meant the pig or the flat.

She meant the flat.

Frances watched the relocation of her toaster to make way for the anvil of a KitchenAid and realised she did not have a lodger but a common-law partner, and as such her possessions were being shoved aside, budged over, to squeeze in and accommodate Elaine's bizarre assortment of clothes, cuddly toys, books, tools, beauty products, and collections. She had never noticed before that Elaine was this jumble of a person. During dating, people keep themselves so tucked away, presenting only snapshots of themselves, their true wonders and weirdnesses kept under wraps. It is only after moving in together that these rise to the surface and we can see what we are really dealing with. That Elaine could, potentially, wear a Panama hat, a Disney Princess costume, and vibrating love-eggs all in one go both amused and disturbed Frances. That she had childhood toys in one box and sex toys in another was also a little odd. The Furby—called Edwin—had taken up residence on a shelf in the bedroom between *Anna Karenina* and *Kitchen Confidential*. Frances' most prized and precious shells, once lovingly lined up in ascending size order on the kitchen windowsill, now were piled up higgledy-piggledy to make way for a floral cake stand. The box of horrors remained on the floor by the wall, concealed by shadow, slightly open in an increasingly menacing manner. Frances began to feel hemmed in, as if every item unpacked and rehomed was a brick in the walls of Elaine being constructed and cemented around her into a vast, inescapable maze.

And there had been an unsettling moment as she watched Elaine unpack her clothes. She had been standing behind her, next to the bed. There was just something in the way Elaine hung them—lovingly, smoothing them, like she thought they might purr—that made Frances want to snatch one of those cashmere cardigans by both arms, wrap it round Elaine's neck, and choke her. She imagined pulling it tighter, she heard the dry sound of the fibres straining—she hated those fucking cardigans—and saw Elaine's feet dancing about on their heels until reduced to tiny, flinching spasms.

"We can share drawer space, can't we?" Elaine had been saying. "I don't mind wearing your knickers." But Frances hadn't replied. Elaine looked back over her shoulder and smiled. "I'm so glad you asked me to move in. It is about time, isn't it?"

"Yes," Frances replied, snapping out of it, sweating. "About time."

Elaine, stepping forwards, looked through her fringe and grinned mischievously, and whispered, "Someone looks a little frisky?" and she swept down like a gannet. The cardigan hunched on its hanger, as if to say with a shrug, "Missed your chance."

It had been a frightening moment because she could see it so clearly and, for a moment, it was only Elaine's superior strength that stopped her, aware that if she didn't succeed she might find herself chasing Elaine around the flat with a kitchen knife, jabbing at the air behind her as she fled, Elaine laughing and leaping over boxes and waving her arms in the air, thinking it was all a game. They had been dating for three months and Elaine sensed nothing odd or unnerving about Frances because Elaine was stupidly, foolishly, hopelessly in love, and as such heard warning bells as the chimes of a future wedding. It wasn't that she was unintelligent per se, just that love makes a mockery of us, turns life into a cartoon of talking deer and sunny glades. Frances kept waiting for her to calm down. She forgot that, not so long ago, she had been the same, giddy in love and full of romance and poetry, the glory of a sunrise, the beauty of another's eyes, etcetera, etcetera, etcetera. She did not see the similarities, because to be loved, rather than loving, was so incredibly tedious. Even before Elaine had moved in, it had been annoying as hell. When they were apart Frances' phone filled up with messages and photos and missed calls. On date days she couldn't walk two steps down the road without Elaine's hand reaching for hers, as if she mustn't cross the road alone. And when Elaine stayed over, Frances couldn't so much as wash up a spoon or make coffee without Elaine suddenly appearing behind her like a giant, groping shadow. Even in the shower, while Frances was trying to have a quiet, blissful orgasm, Elaine would come bursting into the bathroom declaring she needed a piss. All the signs were there that living together was not going to be fun for Frances—she should not have been surprised. And because Elaine was oh, so in love, she misinterpreted much of Frances' behaviour: To her, Frances was a coquette, a tease, an imp; she thought the reluctance was a game, the moodiness a fake. Dear, sweet Funny Frances, who worked too hard and was ever so complicated: What she needed was more love, more affection, more squidges and squeezes. "What could I do?" Frances imagined herself saying to a jury. "My hints were like cruise missiles." And they'd jointly—sympathetically—nod their heads, explaining, "Some people don't understand hints, my dear."

Several beers later, when the flat was looking its most chaotic and horrendous, Elaine clapped her hands together and said, "There! All done!"

Regret was pointless but Frances felt it nonetheless. Now there was nothing left to do but squeeze past the bicycle, step over the tortoise-shaped pouffe, and survey the wreckage. The place looked ransacked; she half expected a burglar to appear from behind the sofa. Elaine clasped her hands to her chest and looked around, sighing. Then, just when Frances thought it couldn't get any worse, Elaine said, "Shall we go for a run? Or shopping? Get some housey bits together?"

"To put where?" Frances wailed, looking around.

Elaine laughed.

"I can't run now," Frances said, holding up the empty beer can.

"Then let's go out shopping. Come on—it'll be fun."

It had all happened so quickly, Frances hadn't even had time to talk about the rent, and as they stood in the drizzle looking at a stall in Camden, the awful thought dawned on her that Elaine might think she was moving in for free, just for the pleasure of her company. She huddled down inside her anorak, sweltering inside, with a chilly, wet nose. She knew she must rectify the situation immediately, but it was difficult finding the opportunity, what with all the fun they were supposed to be having. Elaine spoke gleefully with the stall holders. She told everyone that they had just moved in together, and Frances stoically suffered the congratulatory smiles and expressions of people who didn't really care. Whenever she could—whilst Elaine was busy talking—she wandered away a little, hands in pockets, and let the crowds shunt past her, taking strange pleasure from the occasional shoulder-barge.

"Are you having fun?" Elaine said, linking her arm.

"I'm tired," Frances replied.

Elaine rolled her eyes.

Being tired was an excuse Frances clung to for a variety of reasons. Being tired pardoned lack of enthusiasm, lack of arousal, lack of interest. Initially, Elaine had been concerned. She thought it sounded like a thyroid problem. Frances said she doubted it was. Since then it had become a word Elaine mimicked whenever Frances said it.

"I'm tiiiiiiiired," Elaine whined back at her. "I'm Fraaaaaaances and I'm tiiiiiiiiiired."

"Shut up," she said, and Elaine hugged her, laughing.

Frances was remembering a similar shopping trip—long

before she had met Elaine—a day that had been full of genuine fun, when she and her beau had held hands and bought coffee from one of these stalls, sipping from cardboard espresso cups, still giddy with the wine from lunch. The memory seemed tragic and pathetic now as she walked arm-in-arm with this woman who stopped to sniff candles that stank of candyfloss or strawberry, and an old, familiar pain occurred in Frances' chest, the pain of memory, of what had been and could not be again, the feeling of missing someone, so terribly like disappointment, as if you are repeatedly letting yourself down. When Frances turned her face away from a vial of vile-smelling so-called essential oil, Elaine looked at her and said, "You really are tired, aren't you? Shall we go and sit down somewhere?" and Frances nodded and allowed herself to be led away. "Come on," Elaine said. "My poor little Frances."

The pub was as exuberant as Elaine herself, full of late-afternoon merriment and the voices of many crowds, many couples, many friends, crammed around tables or standing in tight circles, holding the working week at bay with another round. Frances and Elaine found two vacant seats at the bar, removed drenched jackets, and ordered a couple of ales. Frances wondered if Elaine might get drunk enough to pass out before bedtime. She was optimistic. Elaine was clearly in the mood for celebrating.

"I put a bottle of bubbly in the fridge before we came out," she was saying, "I thought we might have it this evening."

Small mercies, thought Frances.

Elaine put her hand on Frances' knee in a way which felt both dominant and adoring, and there it stayed the whole time Elaine sipped her drink, read the menu, ordered crisps. She kept it there as she tore open the packet with her teeth, the way men rip into a condom. The warmth of her palm sank through the denim and seemed to spread itself into bone and skin, creeping its way up Frances' leg to her groin.

"Elaine, we need to talk about money," Frances said.

Elaine licked a moustache of foam from her upper lip and said, wide-eyed, with sincerity, "So that's what's been bothering you."

"Yes. Well, yes and no. But, yes, we do need to talk about it."

"Baby, you should have said. You know you can talk to me about anything." The hand squeezed, fingertips clawing into the nerve of her inner knee, sending a jolt high into her thigh. "I'll pay whatever," Elaine said. "I'm happy to. How much do you need?"

Frances paused then said, "Could you do . . . two grand? By next Saturday? That's when the next rent is due."

She winced inwardly, waiting for some hard questioning, but Elaine just sipped her drink, shrugged, and said, "Yeah, no problem. What about after that? Is it two grand a month you need?"

"Um." Frances scratched behind her ear. "Yeah. Yeah, it is."

"You pay four grand a month for that shitty little flat? No wonder you're always skint."

"I'm including bills," Frances quickly said. "Council tax, electric, gas, insurance. All that."

"Yeah, no worries. I'll set up a standing order, that alright?"

Frances frowned. "Is that okay?"

"Of course. I want to pay my way. I'm not a freeloader," Elaine laughed.

Frances stared at her. She couldn't believe how easy it had been. She clearly could have said any amount; Elaine didn't have a clue. Frances had expected this sudden expense to be at least an inconvenience, an adjustment, but Elaine just drank her beer, completely unperturbed, looking slightly bored, if anything. "Your job at the charity must pay better than I thought," Frances said.

Elaine wafted her hand dismissively and said, "I have lots of money."

Frances' eyebrows raised, then settled themselves down, and suddenly she was enjoying her beer. She wanted to probe further, but what did it matter? Betty and her straightening irons vanished from her thoughts. The letter from Dom disappeared. She smiled, felt unburdened, carefree. Elaine hooked her arm round Frances' neck and pulled her in for a kiss that tasted of cheese and onion. The knee, at liberty, felt an equal sense of relief.

"Feel better now?" Elaine said.

Frances smiled back at her, momentarily full of goodwill and joy, almost—but not quite—loving her.

AFTER SEVERAL DRINKS, and in the light of several berry-scented candles, Frances decided the flat looked much better. *It has a sort of bohemian artistic beauty,* she thought dreamily. Shadows cancelled out many objects and the flickering glow softened others. Sitting on the windowsill, smoking whilst Elaine was in the shower, she was drunk enough to observe it all with detached carefree and careless humour, which actually stemmed from a very real sense of disbelief. But this disbelief—like so many other emotions—was numbed now. Pleasantly, welcomingly, tipsily numbed. And she exhaled out the window, looking down at the evening street, darkened by the rain that had finally moved on, and flicked the ember out on a wide cascade. Then she put the radio on and poured herself another glass of champagne.

She had already messaged Dom. Just two words: SORTED. SATURDAY. He hadn't replied. She felt, as people often do when they have rectified one problem and not yet realised the extent of a new one, rather pleased with herself. That was, until Elaine appeared berobed from the bathroom and took her hand, saying, "Come on."

"What's going on?" Frances said.

"The bedroom, silly. Come on."

Clutching her champagne glass, Frances was walked through the cavern of candlelight to the dark, tousled bed. She stared drunkenly at it, as if she didn't know what it was. The pillows still bore the dents of their heads. The sheets, all twisted and wrung, looked to Frances like piled limbs. Elaine sat her down on the edge of the mattress. Elaine was not drunk, Frances now realised. Merry, but not drunk. And when she was merry she was also most tireless. She turned to the box by the wall. With her back to Frances, she started rummaging.

Frances finished her drink quickly and put the glass on the floor. When she sat back up again, her head spun, and as her vision settled she was greeted with the sight of Elaine walking towards her, waving a double-ended dildo like a medieval torturer would his implement of choice. "I bought this for us," Elaine said, "as a treat."

Frances swallowed and said the only word appropriate to the circumstances: "Fuck."

COLD WATER. Blissful handfuls of it, splashed on her face and neck. She looked at herself in the bathroom mirror, still catching her breath. Her face and body looked red and sordid. The water dripped from her jaw into the sink and she snatched up her toothbrush. Down her right temple was a scratch where Elaine's fingernail had dug in as she clung there; it was accidental, Frances knew that, but she examined it closely now like it was evidence of abuse. "Don't move," Elaine had panted. "Don't move." A point-less instruction; Elaine's hands were massive and muscular, and, clutched between them, Frances' head was a small and fragile object, like a premature egg.

She dabbed at the wound with a washcloth, then slunk over to the kitchenette, glancing in the bedroom on her way to make sure Elaine was still asleep. She was. She had in fact rather con-veniently commenced snoring within moments of finishing, one end of the toy still protruding from her, as if she had died birthing it. Not quite knowing what to do, whether to take it out or leave it in there, Frances had covered Elaine in a sheet up to the shoulders and crept out as quietly as possible. She went to the window for a cigarette. Eyes half-closed, she smoked. On the sideboard stood the empty champagne bottle beside its discarded cork. Frances picked it up and smelled it: a sweet, musky fragrance, retaining the essence, the spirit, of the product. She threw it in the bin. Then she walked to the airing cupboard.

She carried the wooden box to the sofa and sat down, balancing it on her knees. She was still a little drunk; her hands were clumsy and uncertain as they opened it. For a few moments she just looked inside. *An entire person lives in here,* she thought to her-self, *like a genie, she lives in here.* And she almost said the name, almost whispered it aloud, as if to conjure or release, but she dared not, fearful of failure. *She's in here, but she's not,* she thought. *Aladdin was lucky; there's nothing I can do to free her.* Then she reached in and took out the dried cork, held it again to her nose, although she knew no scent remained, and that all taste had long since vanished.

Two years ago they had popped the bottle of cava, calling it champagne, as a joke, pretending, as they often did, to be rich and posh. "Congratulations, dahhhling," they said to each other.

The bottle had been cheap but it didn't matter; they drank with the unfounded certainty that it was to be the first of many, future celebrations were surely to come, and there would be time, when they were older, for Bollinger and Lanson; for now cava would do nicely. They toasted each other, themselves, their love, and said, smugly but not caring that they were smug, "To us, and our first night together." Not strictly true—they had spent countless nights together before—but this was different, they said. They lived together now, they were a proper couple. They talked into the night about the future, suggestions and ideas, nothing huge. Plans do not have to be big when your little world is charmingly new. They finished one bottle, then two, then danced around singing Queen until a neighbour complained.

"I'm having such a good time—"

"I'm having a ball."

Later, Frances sat on the floor with her head on that sweet, beloved knee and listened to the reassurances that they would always be together, that she was adored, that this was them, set, forever. "I love you, my little pet," were the words she had heard as her head was stroked and her shoulders caressed. They made love on the sofa, sucking warm cava off of each other, laughing at the tickling trickles sliding down each other's breasts, pinning down wrists and draping fingers across skin. Oftentimes this was enough for them—they didn't plough and plunder to climax, they preferred to hold back and exist, daily, on a heightened edge, always eager for each other. It was not denial, but, rather, a choice to exist amongst the rolling, charging waves instead of being periodically flung ashore. The next morning, Frances had awoken early and left her slumbering love, curled like a calla lily in their wild bed, as she wandered around the rooms of the flat and looked at how her life had doubled. Two washcloths, two towels, two toothbrushes. Two dips in the sofa, two chocolate wrappers in the bin, two empty glasses on the sideboard. Doubled. Gloriously doubled. Her heart, enormous, twice its normal size. She kissed her love awake and said to her, "I thought my heart was something small and hard like a stone, but now I see it's a balloon. A big balloon heart." They made love. It was beautiful and it was the beginning.

And now this. She put the cork back in the box and closed the lid. She did not wish it hadn't happened, but often—such as now—she wished she had no memory of it. All the drinking and drugging was for this purpose, holding memories far away at bay and making those which arose easier to deal with. Trying to keep the past in the past, always aware that it bleeds into today.

Elaine stirred as Frances slid into bed. She made a small grunting sound and something thudded to the floor. Then she rolled over and flopped an arm over Frances' tummy, and whispered that she couldn't feel happier.

3

Frances could not feel worse.

It was Tuesday. Two days had passed since their shopping trip and, rather than settling down, life had continued to feel strange. Her familiar old habits and routines seemed another lifetime ago, and as she increasingly felt less and less like herself, Elaine was becoming more and more . . . Elaine. This is the problem with cohabitation—there is no escaping personality; in fact, it becomes condensed, compounded, exaggerated. A once barely noticed slurp suddenly becomes a deafening guttural sound, some slop caught in broken plumbing between two twenty-foot speakers, drowning everything out. Frances had been in need of some respite, and as the flat was now a place to escape from rather than to, she had started going out, at all sorts of times, trying to find a little peace: a jog, a sudden letter to post, an excuse to go to the shops; anything would do. She had lingered later at work the previous evening until King, the head kitchen porter, ushered her out with his broom, wielding it like a sword, barking, "What you doing? Go home, Puppy." She had always liked work but now found herself actively looking forward to it. But quite frankly, anywhere that wasn't home would do.

Midmorning in a normal London café. Her shift didn't start for several hours and she would normally—previously—have spent this time cooking or reading, but Elaine had taken the week off "to settle in." It could have been any café, on any street—who knows if it was by chance or design that she found herself here again? In every respect an unremarkable place, much the same as any other: low chairs, high prices, pretentious in its urge to be rustic. Artsy paintings of coffee beans on the shabby-chic walls next to massive images of toiling Kenyans, bent over, beaming at the camera as if they hadn't a care in the world. The hiss and gargle of the coffee machine, the slide and crash of the till, the queue of people, headphones in, eyes down, shuffling like a chain gang. A long line of bar-stools along a bench by the window, where students sat and watched the shapeshifting crowd. Frances didn't exactly like it here; it was bittersweet with memories, and the students who gathered in noisy groups, drinking cappuccinos whilst catapulting balled-up sugar packets at one another, frightened the child within her who couldn't help seeing them as her old high school bullies. But she couldn't quite bring herself to be a morning pub-goer, so she sat at the back by the toilets, where there were a few dimly lit sofas, tables coiled with cup-marks, fat serviette dispensers poised to catch the tears of weeping women. Occasionally a cleaner would amble by, swishing a mop side to side as if reliving a long-dead dream to become an artist, thudding chair legs with each movement, like they were to blame.

Was it any wonder her mind wasn't right? Steam from the coffee machine, steam from the coats, and outside the muggy drizzle that had returned despite the forecast for brightness. A stifling, damp heat within and without, and up there, Elaine, sprawled about everywhere, both figuratively and literally. Was it any wonder that Frances was exhausted? Was it any wonder that she felt a little odd? Was it any wonder that she felt she was choking, she couldn't breathe, she was stuck, trapped? It didn't matter where she went or when she would go, she could not escape this sense of suffocation, like a stuffing inside her. Was it any wonder that as she watched a woman in sloppy flip-flops come in shaking an umbrella—the squelch of each step, the batwing flap of the umbrella—she suddenly knew she must do something about Elaine. She simply couldn't go on like this.

She felt hounded in the flat, humped around every time she dared bend over to pick up a bag or the junk mail: Always, there came Elaine and her great groping hands, grinding against her and feeling around. *I'm not going to last another night of it*, she thought, staring into her cup. *I'll kill her, I swear*. And Elaine seemed to be having such a jolly time. She had, after all, found herself in a very advantageous position, one that Frances had never even considered: Here she was, living with the person she loved, the flat filled with her crap, sex on tap, suffering zero financial hardship. Of course she was enjoying herself. Of course she was bouncy and happy and talkative. Of course she was in the mood to sing "Three Little Birds" from the moment she awoke. Nuzzling the back of Frances' neck, tonguing her tired and vulnerable ear, "This is my message to you-oo-oo," whilst Frances closed her eyes and clenched her fists and tried to remind herself that every little thing would indeed be alright. Any niggle of guilt was soon eradicated, turned into self-pity, because she alone was suffering, because she alone lived with Elaine.

But she could hardly kick Elaine out; she hadn't even received the money yet. Elaine had set up the standing order, and payment—or "rent," as they called it—was due to arrive on Saturday, which might as well be years away. No, she couldn't break up with her now—she was going to have to wait until Sunday, at least. She counted on her fingers the days until Sunday. Five days. Five whole, long, Elaine-filled days.

Really, she reasoned, blowing on her coffee, *she just needs stifling. Sedating. Calming the fuck down.* Frances imagined going home to silence, Elaine unconscious on the sofa, a book on her chest, as if she'd drifted off whilst reading. She imagined the relief of the quiet, the lack of questions, being able to move freely around her home without Elaine sniffing up behind her like a bloodhound. *And sleeping,* she thought with a sigh. *Imagine going to bed at night and just being allowed to sleep, unpestered, untouched, unmolested.* Because this was how it felt now, under constant threat of attack. Elaine's tongue had been useful but Frances had quickly tired of it. It just wasn't worth it, all the kissing and touching and Elaine's body and Elaine's breath and Elaine's smell just for a few minutes of zinginess. And, to make matters worse, now that they lived together, Elaine scarcely bothered with clothes at all, she just walked around naked all the time, which made her seem even larger and to sprawl even further, as if zips and buttons had been reining her in all this time and now flesh came bursting out in all its orgasmic freedom. Bulbous boobs, big bush, a broad stomach with a bit of a pot belly, especially as she stood with her hips thrust out and her hand on her waist. A simple mathematical face, triangular nose, round eyes, curved, sarcastic mouth. And her thighs. She had runner's thighs. The muscles bulged as she walked, twitched as she stood, and could clasp almost any item— a cup, a book, a head—in their incredible grip until the only option was to tap out. Frances felt both repulsed and fascinated by those thighs. She was, in truth, both repulsed and fascinated by Elaine. Coaxed and poked at by those huge hunter-gatherer hands,

Frances' face would mutate from disgust, to confusion, to bewilderment, to awe, to incredulity, round and round, expressions shuffling like a deck of cards. It was like living with a huge teenage monkey, grabbing and fucking wherever she could. Even the early mornings—always Frances' most special and sacred time of the day—were now spoiled by hands that crept beneath the covers, landing—first attempt, with a surgeon's precision—on a breast, or buttock, or thigh, and gripping on as if to say, "Where do you think you're going?" Frances set her alarm earlier and earlier. She'd arrived at the café as the shutter was being lifted, like a battered wife in a moment of respite.

She bought another coffee and returned to her sofa, wondering where the line lay between consent and abuse, what exactly you called this muddy area of resentful tolerance, worn down by pushiness and persistence and inevitable, eventual arousal. It seemed to her that with consent, like anything else a person wished to extract from another—be it money, forgiveness, personal property, anything at all—all you had to do was chip away for long enough and you would get there in the end. Consent not so much volunteered as exhaustedly submitted, as a bargain, in exchange for a bit of peace. Up there, in the bed, Elaine lay in waiting. She knew that no nastiness stemmed from it, and sighed at her own tragic magnetism. "I can't get enough of you," Elaine often whimpered, head down, eyes up, tongue out, the words slobbered and mumbled as she lapped like her gums were swollen. "Hngeye cang geh enguff of ngoo." And she clung on with those two massive hands as Frances looked to the heavens beyond the lampshade and let it happen, the terrible orgasm betraying her. Frances tried to picture Elaine differently now. Glassy-eyed, drugged to a limp oblivion, and she pictured coming and going as she pleased. She could shower in peace. She could lie in. She might even be nice to her, stroke her clammy forehead, bring her drinks, which would sit, untouched, on the bedside cabinet. A suitable drug should be easy enough to procure; sedatives of all varieties were Dom's speciality and he usually had them ready at a moment's notice. Now she had promised him the money, he might be willing to help. In this way Frances might survive the rest of the week without resorting to violence. Then she could pay Dom back and finally be rid of Elaine once and for all.

The idea settled quickly, changing from daydream to plausible possibility within three sips of coffee. *Well, why not?* she thought. *Why not do it?* She raised an eyebrow at herself. *I could. I could drop a little something into her food. It would be so easy.* Swiftly, almost excitedly, the idea changed from possibility to decision; there seemed to be no alternative. It was best for them both, given the circumstances. A few minutes later, finishing her coffee, she even nodded, as if she had been told this was unavoidable and categorically must be done. She put the empty cup down with a feeling of acceptance: Sedating Elaine was the only way forwards. It was unfortunate, but that was how it was. She could imagine Elaine finding out, walking in as Frances crushed pills into her lemon squash, and Frances heard herself wailing, "Well, what was I supposed to do? It's not *fair.*"

As with all breaking points, there was more going on with Frances than there seemed. She could not say precisely when, but at some point during the aftermath of heartbreak, she had fizzled out and become numb. Senses quelled with beer or bourbon, emotions exhausted, sleep-deprived and rolling through repetitive days, she felt sort of . . . flat. It had been about a year since the break-up. She had of course raged at the time—inwardly, at least—the ravaging, passionate depression of the jilted. The phone calls and accusations and the hurling of a clay cat, which had split into three neat pieces—head, body, tail—Super Glued back together sometime later as she sobbed on the sofa. But at some point all of this emotion had reached if not a conclusion, an end, at least, not so much healed as devoid of energy. Like a boxer at the twelfth round, sweat-drenched, arms as wobbly as winter branches, her emotions had stumbled off, and there, in retreat, they had become stuck. She could no more find the gusto for anger than the boxer could strike a knock-out with an upper-cut. *I'm done*, she had thought, when the moment came. Yes, she remembered it now: She had been standing on a platform, wait-ing for a train. It was during her phase of going on excursions to desolate beaches or dismal cities, taking photographs of herself looking half-mad and wind-swept, which she would then send, confrontational in their misery, to her ex-beloved. "Look what you have done," her frenzied hair seemed to say. But as she stood on the platform, the rage quite calmly slipped out in a downwards motion, like she'd expelled a very wet and easy infant, and she found herself staring at the tracks, her rucksack like a boulder on her back, her legs inexplicably weak beneath her. *I'm done* was the single thought, followed immediately by the knowledge—sudden, like a brilliant new idea or invention—that she could simply wait for the next train speeding through, and step off the platform. *Bam.* It would be over. The temptation was great. But she was not one for impulsive gestures or making a mess, and the train whizzed through unhindered, and so this flatness filled the space where rage had previously occupied, and there it had remained. It was largely thanks to this benumbed and drugged feeling that she had managed to tolerate Elaine for the previous three months, much like tolerating a persistent electrical hum. But the noise and smell and presence of her had interfered with it, ruined it, and she needed that numbness back, because she needed peace, and the two had become synonymous. It was imperative to feel nothing, or else risk feeling everything. The booze and weed were not enough alone. But with Elaine sedated she might quickly get back there again, untroubled, undisturbed. Coping.

She bought another coffee and took it back to the sofa. And it was then that she realised, sipping, *I could put it in her cinnamon latte.*

Cinnamon latte, for heaven's sake. Even the woman's drinks were ludicrous.

FRANCES ROLLED through the kitchen door shoulder-first, tying her apron, head down against the burst of steam and barrage of noise, demands being bellowed, jokes being yelled, orders being questioned, dumb waiter being slammed, the radio blasting out some crackling heavy metal, and the dishwasher clattering open and closed, open and closed, which was where she headed to now. Weaving her way between the chefs, repeating the mantra "Behind you, behind you, behind you," she arrived at pot-wash, where her drenched and dead-eyed colleague ripped off his apron, said, "All yours," and left. The pile was at its usual rickety, teetering level. Pots, plates, pans, utensils, all in various states of congealed mess. Those weren't the worst ones, though. The worst ones were already soaking, having usually arrived with a grin and quick, "That one's caramelized, sorry," chef-talk for *burnt.* She turned the water temperature up, her bare hands underneath. Gloves prevented you feeling grease; only skin could feel if a plate was really clean. And after so many years working here, she had developed what they called "asbestos hands." It seemed even the flames of hell couldn't burn her now. Just another part that lacked feeling. She pulled the hose over a stack of twenty or so plates and got to work.

It was the kind of old Italian restaurant that seemed to have been there for a hundred years, and it showed. Both food and servers were stylish and authentic with a quirky, rugged edge, so the place was popular enough to stay afloat but could never afford to redecorate or modernise. It struggled against the tide of chain restaurants nudging ever closer, as all small family-owned places did these days. It was a strain they tried to hide upstairs in an ambience of relaxed yet fun hospitality, customers greeted with smiles and charm, informed about specials and recommended wine, given equal portions of banter and professionalism. But downstairs, in the kitchen, the strain was evident within the steam and curse words as the chef patron—a normal human being outside of the kitchen, if by random chance anyone ever saw him there— was hourly crazed and infuriated by a lack of orders or incorrect food or running out of a dish or having too much left over. "What the fuck are you doing?" was regularly bellowed across the counters during an unexpected rush. "Where the fuck are the people?" was cried when no tickets came in. The poor man was despairing. He had been despairing for several years. But he'd be damned— or so he said—before any fancy piece-of-shit restaurant that didn't even make its own pizza dough was gonna put him out of business. Mopping brow with tea towel, hands on hips, he'd announce this to the chefs as they prepped, again, in the dead hours, and yelled it at them again during a sudden rush. "Those cunts won't take us down!" he'd shout, and they'd all respond as one: "Yes, Chef!" Thus the chefs and the restaurant as a whole maintained a weary but strong integrity as the underdogs of the battle, where their reputation and unique food were their only weapons, and it should have been enough for a clear win if the fight had been fair, but they were outnumbered and outmanoeuvred, and the enemy had them surrounded; all they were ever really doing was holding them at bay. Still, it kept the kitchen team loyal and strong, despite the unpredictable hours, because no one had the heart to leave and because they were all proud to work at Gabe's House, including Frances.

She had been a kitchen porter since she left school, not because she couldn't do better but because she loved the job, and with her share of tips the salary was better than many expected, enough to keep her afloat, anyway. She didn't care that it was hot, she didn't care that it was dirty, she didn't care about the hours; it was loud loud loud and it kept her thoughts from dwelling on herself. The hours were unpredictable and unsociable, which suited her unsociable personality. In fact, these guys were the closest thing she had to friends, ticking as many of the criteria for friendship as she personally required; they listened to her and joked with her, and when her heating broke, the sous chef called his brother-in-law, who fixed it for free. There was none of the drama and hassle of real friendships, no obligations to go to the cinema or attend birthday parties, because none of them had time for such things anyway. So it was perfect for Frances; she had the benefits of friendship without all the maintenance and, most importantly, none of them had time or the inclination to ask her probing questions. They didn't care about her past, her parents, her problems. They bantered about the Italian sausage and flicked towels at one another. It suited Frances nicely. It was enough.

And she was regarded as the best KP, barring King, obviously. Valued as a hard-working and trustworthy soldier in the battle, maybe not on the frontline, but strongly bringing up the rear. King had asked her once or twice, "You don't wanna be a chef?"

as if it was that easy, because it was: There isn't a kitchen in the world that won't spot a semi-capable KP and try to swap their scourer for a Sabatier, and Frances was evidently more than capable, but always she shook her head side to side and said, "No, King, it's not for me." She worked at a frantic pace with a methodical process, dunking plates, soaking pots, scrubbing pans, slamming them into the huge dishwasher, wrenching them out as soon as it finished, still gushing, like reaching into a fiery waterfall. She knew the timing of the dishwasher precisely; she'd have the next load ready to go the moment it had finished. There was a satisfaction in it. She even liked the smell. It didn't matter what had been cooked, the smell was always the same, a meaty, pungent smell, slightly sweetened by sweat and washing-up liquid, which lingered in her hair and up to her elbows. The long hours passed quickly and, within the chaos, she found an almost meditative peace.

King had been at the restaurant for decades, minus a few absences at Her Majesty's pleasure. He was a heavily tattooed bodybuilder who sang opera and gulped down egg whites from a huge bowl set aside for him by the chefs when the yolks were taken for crème brûlées. He took his job seriously: No smear or smudge or mark allowed, glasses gleamed, cutlery shone, and if a chef returned a plate with the tiniest remnant of cheese on it, King would bellow at his KP, "What the fuck you doing to me? You tryin' to make me crazy? Eh?" and glare with such fury, they could only mumble, "Sorry, King," never entirely sure if he was serious or not.

"Unbelievable, that's what this is. Clean it again!"

"Yes, King. Sorry, King."

No one knew what he had done time for. It seemed irrelevant. Despite the bulk and roar of him, he was not really an angry man.

None of them were. Bellowing and slamming was just part of kitchen life, to be heard, to keep momentum, to push on through the continuous physical and mental focus that is a restaurant dinner service.

Today, it was busier than usual due to a new early-week special. Frances scarcely had time to think about Elaine or her plan or anything else. Then, a couple of hours into her shift, King walked past with half a side of beef on his shoulder. "King," she shouted, "I need to ask you something."

"Okay, take your time," he said, glancing at the beef.

"Sorry. Sorry. I know it's short notice, but could I swap shifts with someone, or take some holiday? I'm sorry. Family emergency. I only found out today."

"Ah, Puppy, what you doing to me?" He shrugged the beef up on his shoulder. "You tell me this now?"

"I know, I know, I'm sorry."

"What's going on with you?"

"Just family stuff. Sickness."

He clicked his tongue in his cheek and said, "Look at me, I'm holding this cow, I don't have time to fight with you. I'll talk to you about this later," and he went to leave.

"Please, King," she begged. "You know I never ask for time off."

King rolled his eyes because this was true. She didn't like to give such short notice but what choice did she have? On the bus ride to work she had texted Dom and asked for his help. He had replied that she had a nerve. She said she knew she did, but could he help, just this once—she had the money coming, after all. He'd agreed with one word: OKAY. Off the bus, she lit a joint and rang him as she walked the five minutes to work. She told him, briefly, what she needed, which he said wouldn't be a problem—he could get his hands on something that evening, in fact. "But you've got to be careful with this stuff," he said.

"What do you mean?"

"Too little or too much and it's not going to be fun."

"That's fine. Just get it for me, will you?"

"No, listen to me—you don't want to wake up in some random place. Or, if it's for someone else, you'll need to keep an eye on them. It's a little unpredictable, how people react to it at first."

"Like what?"

"I can tell you the rough dose but you'll have to feel it out to begin with. Might make you nuts, might not work at all. Plus some people feel really sick on it. Others go a bit crazy."

"It sounds fucking dreadful."

"Nah, nah, it'll do the trick, no worries. Someone I knew, their cousin took it, didn't wake up for three days straight. Didn't remember a thing. He said it was like being in stasis."

"That's more like it."

"But like I said, it can be a little unpredictable at first. Everyone reacts differently. The right amount for one person won't be the right amount for someone else."

"Okay."

"So, is it for you or someone else?"

She hesitated, then said, "Someone else."

"I'm not going to ask why," he said, which was clearly a way of asking why.

"Good," she replied. "Don't. I can pick it up tonight? After work."

"Usual place. Midnight."

"See you then."

Whilst she had not been thinking about Elaine during her shift, she had been distantly mulling over this conversation with

Dom, and had concluded she should stay at home, ride out the coming days until she got the money, keep an eye on Elaine, and hopefully get some rest herself. A less scrupulous person would have called in sick, but she respected King too much to leave him in the lurch while she drugged her girlfriend. The oddness of this did not pass her by, but she chose to ignore it. It was all about timing with King. Had he been joking around with one of the chefs or standing outside smoking, his response likely would have been, "You take time off when you're dead, Puppy. Living is for working and working is for living. Now fuck off—I'm busy." Stopping him beneath the weight of beef as he hurried past, heading for the door, was not in fact bad timing, but perfect timing. His own idea of politeness did not allow him to pass by without responding, and she knew he'd soften at a little pleading and "family problems." And she knew the beef was heavy. Frances had played him, and she had won.

"I'll change your shifts," he shouted now, waving his free hand in the air. "It's fine, it's fine, it's fine, I work overtime anyway, overtime are my normal fucking hours in this place. I'll change your shifts, you work less hours this week, but I can't give you all time off, Puppy, you can't ask me like that, here today, you need to give notice, you know that. But look, it's fine, it's fine, I'll sort it out for you, an easy week for Puppy," and he shunted off as Frances shouted, "Thank you—I owe you one," but he just waved his hand in the air again and vanished through a door.

Frances felt responsibility keenly. Responsibility in her job. Responsibility for her home. And responsibility for Elaine's wellbeing once she drugged her up. That she should care enough to feel such responsibility but still go ahead with her plan was, of course, also odd, and again she noticed the oddness, and again chose to ignore it.

The rest of her shift went quickly, as always. As she was finishing up, King stopped by her and said, "Oh. Puppy. Got some old carrots for you. You want them?"

"Yes, please."

"In that tray over there by the blender, okay? What you use them for, anyway? You got rabbits?"

"I do what I can with them, that's all."

The truth was, she turned their leftover vegetables into soups and stews, but didn't want anyone in the kitchen to know that she cooked, no matter how basic the meal, or else suddenly there would be no excuse. "Oi! You! KP, you can cook, we know it! Peel this ten kilo of potatoes! Now, Puppy!" And so she would be dragged from her isolated little world by the sink and shoved into the heart-poundingly-insane world of the chef. As far as they were concerned, she lived off takeaways and noodles, and long may they believe so.

ON THE BACK SEAT of the near-empty bus she put her feet up and closed her eyes, immediately entering the restorative semi-slumber well-accustomed users of public transport are apt to find in an instant, a skill they have honed. She dozed, eyes jumping open with the occasional jolt of brakes or lurch of accelerator. Outside, the rain fell like crystals, flashing in the streetlights and headlights and trickling down the windows. The strip light in the bus was purple, the sky outside was the dim orange of night, the colours of life all a muddle and peculiar; it was easier to keep one's eyes closed and avoid the strangeness than sit there as part of it. She did not quite dream, but the sound of passengers getting on and off entered the same space until she could picture them perfectly without opening her eyes, imagining what the old man with the cough looked like, the drunken woman, the two girls who whispered. When she opened her eyes again, a man with a single bead of sweat, or rain, dangling from the end of his nose had taken the seat in front and had turned around, watching her.

"You looked very peaceful," he said.

Streetlights flashed across his face. The droplet didn't fall, but clung there and wobbled. He smiled at her, all teeth in the purple light. Frances drew her jacket tighter around her, and he said, "I'm just saying you should be careful. Your bag is on the floor and you look so obviously vacant and indifferent. And lovely."

She gathered up her bag in her arms and slid across to the other side of the bus, feeling exposed and tired. The man smiled and turned away, looking out of his window. She stayed awake the rest of the way.

Dom was late. By the time he arrived she was drenched and tired, and almost tempted to cancel the whole thing. He arrived in a black coat with a fur-lined hood, said, "There you go. Two drops. No more to start with. See how it goes," and handed a bottle to her. "I'll add it to your tab," he said with a smirk. Before she could say anything, he had turned and was gone. She suddenly felt very alone in the world. She would have liked him to stay a few minutes and talk to her, about anything, or even just sit in silence and smoke. She realised she was afraid, the sort of fear that creeps in so stealthily from such an unclear place that it takes a while to notice it is there at all. Just his company, his cigarette smoke, even his slight threats, would have given her a sense of normality. She put the bottle in her pocket, picked up her bag of carrots, and headed home. Hopefully Elaine was already asleep.

4

It was the next day, and it was hot. The sun had risen, undisturbed and unfiltered, into their bedroom at five a.m., announcing that summer was suddenly here. Forecasters heaved sighs of relief: That yellow orb was like a crystal ball to them, clear, high, predictable pressure, straight, unwavering, uncomplicated sun. People would no longer curse them; in fact, they'd temporarily become good guys, even heroes. For once, they didn't have to use the cloud/rain/sun symbol that equated a bewildered shoulder shrug. It wouldn't last forever, but for the next few days, at least, they could hold their heads up high and smile at the dinner table with their families because of a job well done.

Elaine was tying her running shoes and Frances was leaning against the wall.

"Are you sure you don't want to come?" Elaine said, looking up. "It's beautiful outside. It'll do you good."

"No." Frances smiled. "You go. I want to cook."

Elaine stood up and jogged on the spot. "Funny little Frances. Who wants soup when the sun's shining? Only my Frances, that's who." She kissed Frances' forehead, and Frances smiled, again, saying, "Well. Have a nice run."

"I won't be too long. Ten K or so."

"Take your time. Enjoy it."

"Bye. Love you!"

Finally the door closed.

Elaine had not been asleep when Frances returned from meeting Dom. She had, in fact, made a point of sitting up, waiting, two glasses of wine poured. The night had been long and hard. Frances' first thought on waking was to get to the café, get the process started; Elaine was a fussy eater, but she couldn't resist a cinnamon latte. But before she had the chance Elaine sprang out of bed, gay as a mascot on a cereal advert, announcing, "The sun's out! The sun is out!" and that she was going for an early run. "Come on!" she chimed. "Let's go together, in the sunshine. It feels like a holiday!" But the prospect of some time in the peace and quiet was not to be missed. Frances almost didn't mind that the latte would have to wait; as long as Elaine was out, she was happy. But Elaine dithered, choosing her running gear, changing a shoelace, playing with her hair, answering her phone, as Frances stood in the hallway by the wall and waited. Now, at last, she was gone, and Frances was alone in her flat. It felt very still, very static, without Elaine's presence. It felt once again hers and hers alone.

She wandered to the window with a pre-rolled joint between her fingers and looked down. The shiny top of Elaine's head appeared, bent over as she fiddled with her watch, then her earphones. It was almost laughable, Frances reflected, how completely unaware Elaine was. Unaware that she might be spiked at any moment, unaware of how she made Frances feel, unaware of the little lies and deceptions occurring daily around her. Off she jogged without a care in the world. It was as if they were experiencing two completely different realities running in parallel, which of course they were, but only Frances was aware of it. *Her life is not what she thinks it is,* Frances thought, watching Elaine disappear. Then she opened the window and sat on the ledge, smoking.

In truth, she was a little relieved. Call it nerves or conscience, she didn't feel quite ready. When it came to the crunch, she wasn't sure she had the guts to go through with it at all, no matter how badly she wanted to. Just knowing the stuff was in her bag was, for now, enough. She could use it at any time. An impromptu trip to the café would not seem out of character, day or night. She could always act impulsively. *There's no rush,* she told herself, exhaling slowly, eyes heavy, *no rush.* She could always be good and change her mind, pour the stuff down the sink. She had options, and options always give the illusion of power.

ONIONS, GARLIC, CHILLI. They hissed and sizzled in the pot as she chopped the carrots one by one from the bag. How she loved making soup! The simple act of transformation, from ingredient to meal, whole hard globe of onion turned to delectable translucent slivers—it was like sorcery. The freedom of flinging in herbs, the earthy colours of turmeric, paprika, coriander, and the fixability of almost any mixture, learning from experience how to balance flavour, season blandness, and sweeten or spice up as one desired, turning each pot of humble beginnings into a bowl of absolute comfort. Glimmering noodle soups, sweet onion soups, garlic soups, bean soups, and any number with an egg plopped or poached inside. Like so many people who struggle, Frances sought solace in food. It had long been her escape, ever since she was a child heating up tinned cream of tomato on the stove, sprinkling in broken crisps as makeshift croutons. For some people, the comfort is in the eating. For others, in extravagance, lobsters and caviar and fillet steaks. For many, the reassuring control of denial. But for Frances, the real pleasure was in the cooking. Enveloped in the scent of roasted garlic, cloves plump and pouting to be plucked, she found more relaxation than most do in the hottest, headiest rose garden.

She stirred all the ingredients together and added stock. Carrots bobbed to the surface in a cluster. She turned the heat up, brought it to a boil, then left it to simmer.

What with the sun and steam, the flat felt stifling, so she opened all the windows and let the fumes and fury of traffic drift in. She listened to it a moment, peeling an orange, then sat on the sofa and ate, relishing the tear of segment from segment, a minute act of violence. Head back, heels up on the coffee table, she chewed loudly with her mouth open, because she could, because she was alone. She lobbed the peel in the direction of the bin. Outside, on the street, a woman squealed—the sound reared up through the window, high above a distant siren—and it suddenly felt like Elaine was right: This was a little holiday, and she could do what she liked. Sticking a fingernail between her back teeth, she picked out a piece of orange flesh and flicked it across the room. Then, looking side to side, as if checking that no one was there, she slid a hand down inside her trousers and closed her eyes.

Adrienne. Frances allowed the name, the face, the person, to enter her mind and body. *Adrienne.* Impossible not to love a woman who smells and feels so cool, natural, unfathomable, like a beautiful relic at the bottom of the sea, permeated by minerals and miracles. So many times they had lain here in a multitude of knots—limbs and hair and fingers—letting the chilly midnight air rush upon their nakedness, encouraging them to tangle tighter. From the sofa to the bathtub, toe-sucking 'til the water chilled, and then to bed, where night became timeless. Stumbling down the sleeping street to buy wine and bacon and chocolate, they giggled in the aisles at their hair, their scent, their so very obvious sex, and they kissed there, knowing security cameras were on them, hands sliding beneath shirts and down the backs of underwear. Frances tried, now, to picture brutality instead. It had become her slight act of revenge since heartbreak, fantasising hate-fucks she half hoped Adrienne would feel. Clenched eyes, clawing, biting, fisting, binding, anything she could imagine, she tried, using every muscle of imagination to claw the insides of her. She couldn't do it. Since she herself had suffered Elaine, it had become harder and harder to indulge this way. Adrienne's face, pained and confused, churned up no feeling other than sorrow, and she stopped, she gave up, gave in, kissed, apologised, and was received, forgiven, loved again. She remembered the way they lay side by side in a mirror image, stroking and kissing, breath musty with lust and half-drunk merlot. The urgency of the moment, the holding back, never wanting it to end, building to the whisper "I'm close. Shall we stop? I can't stop . . ." And then, a key in the door—slam—and Elaine's voice calling, "Hellooo? Baby? I'm home. Where are you?"

"For fuck's sake," Frances muttered, removing her hand, slapping it on her thigh, trying to catch her breath. "That was quick," she shouted.

Elaine appeared in the living room, sliding her fingers through her damp hair and smiling with a flowering cactus in one hand.

"I only did a few miles in the end—it's roasting. The florist on the corner was selling these outside. Got you one as a present.

Well, us. A house-warming. Something for the flat, for us to nurture together."

She kissed the top of Frances' head, then picked up the orange peel and dropped it in the bin. She peered into the bubbling pot and said, "Carrot and coriander? Jesus, it's hot in here." Frances remained slumped down on the sofa, feet a foot apart on the coffee table, pulse receding resentfully.

"How the fuck do you nurture a cactus?" she said.

Elaine put it on the windowsill and dabbed her forefinger into the middle of the flower in an exploratory manner, just as she did the cap of a thistle or the gap between collarbones, that one permanently probing digit always seeking the centre of things. The flower was a vibrant red. Elaine said, "It's alive, and all living things need looking after." She had a tendency to become whimsical, considering herself both artistic and intellectual. She wore a T-shirt that said SMART ALECS WEAR GLASSES, which she accessorized with a pair of Ray-Bans. Perhaps it was the embarrassment that troubled Frances so.

"You're wrong," Frances said, sitting up, picking her nose. "Cacti thrive on neglect."

"Yes, but the neglect is intentional, so it's a form of care."

"How was your run?"

"Like I said, hot. But otherwise fine. I think I'm getting faster." She slapped her thigh.

Frances enjoyed running, and in the first few weeks of their relationship they had often run together, creating the illusion that they were alike when actually they, like so many couples, had just enough in common to stay together, despite the fact that their differences were huge, both in volume and importance. A shared love of running was focussed on whilst massive clashes in priorities, beliefs, and morals were overlooked. Elaine overlooked them because she loved Frances, and Frances overlooked them because she didn't much care what Elaine's beliefs and morals were. Then, as the weeks passed, running became just another thing that Frances felt was stolen or encroached upon; she suddenly was not allowed to run alone anymore. "Why didn't you ask me?" Elaine would whine if Frances mentioned a pleasant route she'd found along the river.

Frances used to love running with Adrienne. They'd listen to the same playlist and sing aloud to their favourite tunes—"This thing called love, I just can't handle it, this thing called love"—but, increasingly, whenever she ran side by side with Elaine, Frances was gripped with a sort of panic, the urge to sprint off ahead with her hands in the air, screaming. Not jogging but fleeing.

"I might go out for coffee," she said. "I won't be long."

But Elaine stepped in between her open legs and said, "In a little while," and Frances looked up at her, mutely. *Now? Again?* But, what with the spliff still spinning in her head, and the lingering tingling in her groin, and her lack of energy to put up a fight, she remained as she was and watched, like it was happening very far away, as Elaine knelt down before her, unclipping her sweaty sports bra and flinging it away.

INSIDE HER, close to the womb, fingers beckoned. *Over here,* they said. In the darkness they moved with fake coyness. *Come on, don't be shy.* They curled forwards, then released, curled forwards, then released, an action repeated again and again, motioning for obedience, rubbing against a spot of adherence, a place that could not help but obey, nudging the nub, and flickering away reluctance. *Come,* they urged. *Come this way.*

Resistance was impossible; they motioned faster the more you withheld. Wizened witches' fingers, they coerced you with a trickery, a promise, a manipulation you understood but were powerless to repel, eventually succumbing to their wishes. Flickering faster when you tightened around them, dancing their way around each turn; *come, come, come,* they insisted, *you cannot fight it, you will not win, just give in, and come.* Leading you onwards, teasing you to them, flicking you forwards, to the edge, the edge, the edge of yourself, into the fairy tale where the witch always wins, tipping you over, over the edge, down into her well, to drown you with bliss.

FRANCES LAY in her T-shirt and one sock, head against a yellow cushion, staring at the television screen. Her mouth—half-open—gave her a dim-witted appearance. Clothes lay in indistinguishable lumps across the floor. A mauve crotch poked out, panting, from between two magazines. At the end of one very long arm, stretched out straight like a junkie's, Frances held the TV remote, her finger poised as if to switch channels, but she didn't.

She was drunk. Not even caring if Elaine noticed, she had drunk and drunk and drunk. The soup, unfinished, sat thick and tepid on the stove. In between each bout of insuppressible Elaine, Frances had stumbled to the fridge and grabbed beer, or wine, or vodka, whatever came to hand. Elaine had chuckled and said, proudly, "You look fucked, darling." Elaine had paused only to go to the bathroom—to freshen up, as she called it—a courtesy Frances didn't bother with and Elaine either didn't care or notice. It was as if Elaine were on some mission to destroy Frances—that was how it felt. Returning, wearing nothing more than a grin, Elaine rolled and manoeuvred Frances as she wanted her, count-

ing out the rounds. "Round two." "Round three." "Round four."
And so on, as Frances gradually removed her conscious mind
from all proceedings and reduced herself to just an empty, pli-
able body. By the time the final round was over, the cafés had
shut and Frances was immobile, so she missed the opportunity to
begin her plan, eventually forgetting about it completely. But as
she lay there now, eyes glazed at the TV screen, she lodged it in
the back of her mind: *Remember, tomorrow morning, café, latte.*
There must be no more of this. This was the final straw.

"I'm jumping in the shower," Elaine chirruped from the
kitchen sink, swigging a glass of water. "I reek."

Yes, thought Frances dozily. *Like a hot pond. Like algae. Something stagnant.*

"You're welcome to join me."

Frances twitched her arm in a negative response. Elaine
kissed the top of her head as she passed. "You get some rest," she
laughed, and Frances felt the relief at being finished with, no longer needed, surplus to requirements. She heard the shower flick
on, the glass door slide, and water pattering, splattering, in another
room, where Elaine finally didn't want her. She had orgasmed
once, Frances had. A resentful but powerful shudder of release,
void of emotion, just a bodily reaction, like a leg jerking when the
knee is hit. Elaine had several times, loudly, wetly, gripping Frances in place with her two thighs 'til she was done, laughing afterwards. "God, I love you!" she'd yelled, grasping Frances' jaw in
her hand and looking down at her. Now, as she gawped at the television, and heard Elaine merrily singing away about those three
fucking little birds as if nothing had happened, one arm in the
air as she scrubbed her stink-pit, Frances thought: *Tomorrow.*

On TV a small, unremarkable black bird bounced about on
the ground in a forest. She wondered vaguely how the following

days would go. The black bird moved tirelessly, hopping around. She imagined standing in the queue, ordering the coffee, the girl with the reluctant smile saying, "Three fifty," but there the vision ended because after this there was no certainty, no knowing how it would be. She wondered, absently, about the risks Dom had referred to. She didn't much care right now; the imprints of four fingernails remained on her right thigh. Her insides felt misaligned, like when walls in a house are knocked down and rebuilt elsewhere. She was almost out of wine. The black bird suddenly doubled in size and thrust out an electric blue light from its chest, like a flicked switch. It pranced about in front of a bemused female who watched, flicked her head, and flew away.

Elaine had said she wasn't a serial killer, but this was only partially true. Yes, Frances felt responsibility keenly—it was one of the many reasons she drank. Responsibility for her work, her life, her actions, no matter how long ago. They troubled her deeply. Truths within the past troubled her even more so.

Not a serial killer, no.

But one boy, years ago.

The little blond boy with the podgy feet. She still smelt his sun cream, still saw him there, still heard him. Gargled words from behind a sucked thumb. A pause, then the scream, and panicked pigeons bursting into the air. But Elaine wasn't to know. Nobody knew. And all she could do to cope, with all of it—the past, the pain, Elaine, Elaine, Elaine—was to smoke and gulp, smoke and gulp.

·The shower turned off and Elaine quit singing. The remote control fell to the floor. Frances had finished the last of the wine and had fallen into a deep, blank sleep.

5

Sunlight slid stealthily into the bedroom. Around the edges of curtains it felt, fumbling its way across the ceiling, inching over carpet and walls, trying not to disturb. Inevitably, after several minutes, a particularly bold palm of light reached up the bedsheet and touched—ever so lightly—the side of Frances' face. She awoke, mumbling, "Fuck, it's bright," and shoved her head beneath the pillow. There, in the darkness, she semi-slumbered, her mind slowly fizzing awake, the heat around her scalp building, and an awareness of the day—Elaine sleeping, the coffee shop opening, her bag in the hallway, her hangover—roused her to wakefulness.

The impetus was already there: Elaine was asleep on her back, jaw slack, drawn open and inwards, eyelids spasming as she breathed moistly. Clearing the crust from her eyes, Frances observed the rise and fall of her girlfriend's chest, the forefinger of her right hand twitching sporadically, like it was sending an SOS. She crept out of the room on tiptoes, cartoon-like, and went to the bathroom. Wary of making a sound, she didn't flush the toilet, she didn't have a shower, just briefly scrubbed her teeth and brushed her hair, even then worried that the rinsing and spitting might be too loud; her mouth hung directly over the plug hole, low, so that she could dribble the foam straight down. She felt less boozy and much better. She picked up her shoes and put them on in the main hallway on the ground floor as the postman bustled past, saying a cheerful "Good morning," then she stepped outdoors.

Into the brewing festival of sunshine. Summer had arrived with all the demur and subtlety of a court jester; people spilled from buses and tube stations and buildings, a mixture of cheery day-trippers wearing clothes crumpled from two seasons stuck at the back of a drawer, squinting at the sky, and the nightcrawlers wending their way home from clubs, equally as crumpled and squinty. It was not even yet seven o'clock; Elaine would probably sleep for another thirty minutes or so. Frances began to walk up the street, weaving through the people who talked too loudly because sunshine insists on such exuberance, and because they had yet to wither in the permeating heat—it was all new and fantastic. "Incredible," they seemed to say as they peered up beneath a saluted hand. "I thought we'd never see it again." Give them a day or two, a blistered sunburn, and a few sleepless nights, and their attitude would soon change. Frances already pined for the damp, and it was out of a sort of rebellion that she wore shoes instead of sandals.

Months of fickle forecasting resulted in this rush to embrace the certainty of a season. Cafés brought out little tables and chairs and placed them precariously on their tiny piece of pavement in an attempt to look Parisian. A wide turquoise car reverberated its way down the narrow street as bass and beat blasted from its open windows. A soup shop put a sandwich board outside advertising CALIFORNIA ORANGE AND MANGO SMOOTHIES, yellow suns smiling all around it. The drab, nondescript normality of reasonable temperatures was lost to this bizarre playtime. Everything and everyone rejoiced: Summertime! Nationwide the barbeques were being brought out from their spidery abodes, the seaside ice cream shops were stockpiling chocolate flakes, the children were being tricked into believing it was a special day because Mummy and Daddy spent three hours driving to the coast, only to sweat in a deckchair and eat from a cool box. It is not simply the sun itself which causes such a reaction but the promise of days and days of it, at last. National jubilation! And then there was her, Frances, entering the coffee shop, relieved at the semblance of order— clean tables, the hissing machine, the smell of pastries—with a bag full of books and old bus tickets and broken shells and a bottle of drugs.

There was, to her surprise, already a queue, people wanting cold brews and juices and bottles of water. She tried to act as normal as possible. She was just buying coffee, after all; she did this most days. She forced herself to focus on the man in front, a large man by anyone's standards but mountainous compared to her. The back of his T-shirt was dark with sweat and a warm animal smell eradiated from him. She looked down at the feeble flip-flops squished beneath his feet, appearing much too small, as if he were an ogre riding a toy bicycle. As he leant over to look at the goodies in the counter she noticed him entering numbers into a calorie counter on his phone and felt at once disappointed, as if he had let her down, as if his giving into his impulses would have excused her doing the same. Then he was gone, and the girl behind the counter was talking, and Frances was just standing there.

"Good morning," the girl said to her, obviously not for the first time. "What can I get you?"

There was no reason to be nervous, and no need for her now to look down at her hands as she mumbled, "Cinnamon latte, please. To go."

The girl smiled her customary reluctant smile, which seemed to Frances more reluctant than ever, and said, "No worries. Anything else?"

"Yes," said Frances, looking up, confident now. "A double espresso, please."

And that was it. The girl just nodded and hit the relevant buttons on the till. Frances was seized by how easy it was to trick people; the girl had no idea, none at all. *If the rest goes like this*, she thought, *it'll be a breeze.* It was going so smoothly, she even had the correct money in her hand. And if she wanted to, she could just trot home with the coffees right now and give the latte, kindly, lovingly, to her girlfriend, who would stretch awake and be overly happy, and she could forget there was ever any other motive. It was completely possible, she realised. She didn't *have* to do anything.

"Um, hello? Excuse me?"

"What?"

"That's three fifty," the girl repeated pointedly, glancing down at the receipt on the counter before her.

"Sorry."

Suddenly mortified, Frances handed the cash over and picked up the cardboard cup. The tragic line from *Macbeth* came to her as she walked away with it: *Why did you bring this coffee from the place?* She drifted to the table where sugar and condiments were. She could even just leave it behind, she realised. She tore open two sugars and tipped them in. *I could*, she reasoned. *I could just leave it right here on the side, or give it to a homeless person—that would be a nice gesture.* She stirred the drink and looked at the door, open to the sunny street, which led back to the flat and the dozy Elaine. She put the plastic lid on and began to walk towards the light.

"Hey," the girl called. "Your espresso."

And as if waking up, she spun towards the counter. "Thank you," she said. The girl watched her, wide-eyed, with raised eyebrows.

Frances carried both drinks—one in each hand, clutched like grenades—to the back of the shop and went into the toilets.

It is hardly arsenic, she reminded herself. *Calm the hell down.* And she told herself it was not cowardice that made her falter now: No, she had the bravery, the gumption, the guts, as it were, she was sure of it, she had *balls.* Kneeling on the damp floor, she took the lid off the latte and added more sugar, frustrated by her shaking hands. All this ridiculous paraphernalia—coffee cups, paper, stirrer, bottle—just barely balanced on the not-quite-flat lid of a toilet seat: It was very inconvenient. Her leg cramped beneath her; her espresso tipped over and splashed—not entirely, but with intent—over her leg, scalding her. "For fuck's sake," she muttered, and leant back, trying to catch her breath. She couldn't work out what was wrong—it felt like she was about to have a massive seizure—and she saw a flash image of her semi-conscious body being carried out whilst a police officer picked up the suspicious-looking bottle and squinted at it. Gradually the feeling subsided, and she told herself it was just the heat—she needed to hurry up and get out of there, that was all. The cubicle was claustrophobic, like a prison cell. She imagined food being slid under it, a burly prison guard spying on her at night. The prospect—the likelihood—of incarceration was so inconceivable that to toy with it was like a game; she couldn't even imagine Elaine drinking the latte, let alone consider such ludicrousness as arrest, judgement, internment, and grey meals served on plastic trays, so it was funny to ponder it in the same way one ponders what it would be like to get cancer or lose a leg. Did people go to jail for adding a little calming-juice to their partner's beverage? It seemed unlikely. Dom's words about risks surfaced again and Frances realised this was part of the problem; there was an awful lot of uncertainty, and a lot she could not plan for. She really did not know what to expect and could only hope for the best and stay alert. Calmed, she sat up again and reached for the bottle, but the same thing happened: hands shaking, wrung with sweat, and a sense of panic.

And, she told herself, *I have not done anything wrong. Even this very second, I have not, morally, done anything wrong. This is not like before. None of us are perfect. We can all purchase items or substances that are questionable, but does that make it wrong, really, truly, in-the-eyes-of-God wrong? Of course not. I have not done anything wrong. I have not done anything wrong.* She felt her heart begin to slow, but her hands, held out before her, bounced around as if playing with string-puppets. She repeated to herself, *You have not done anything wrong, you have not done anything wrong, you have not done anything wrong.* An odd choice of mantra, perhaps, for a person about to do very wrongly indeed. Nevertheless, she repeated it, out loud now: "You have not done anything wrong."

What an unfortunate time for Adrienne to pop by on one of her visits. The memory was there before Frances could stop it. She saw both hands reaching across the table towards her, in the space between the condiments and the menus; they'd not long sat down, hadn't even ordered yet. Frances was still under the illusion that this was just another date, unaware she was in the last moments of happiness and her life was about to change. She had heard this place did good pâté, which she leant over and whispered to Adrienne in their silly posh-voice, "I hear this place does a good parrrhtaaay," giggling. As far as she was concerned, they'd eat, sharing their food, all plates in the middle of the table—what's mine is yours—drink plenty of red wine, then go back to the flat and make love. It was, in the most wonderful way possible, their norm. No dullness, no boredom, no ruts yet, just the simple joy of routines and habits shared with a beautiful beau whose very presence still delights you. She had let her hands be taken and she smiled. They often held hands across the dinner table, and Frances thought it was cliché but romantic, like spooning in bed and sharing baths, yawningly unimaginative when single, wonderful when in love. She had fallen under the common misconception that it would never end simply because it had happened a lot, and regularity becomes normality, which always brings with it a false sense of permanence. Really, this is the time to be most on guard, and yet it is when we are least so. Even when she looked up and saw Adrienne's expression—unusual, vacant, pleading for some innate understanding without a word being spoken—it did not occur to Frances that bad news could be heading her way. But Adrienne was not of the confused, furrowed-brow type, and Frances held on, like a gymnast to a tightrope, as Adrienne nearly spoke several times but no words came out. Utterly bewildered, saying, "What's wrong?" Frances tried to stand, to sit next to her, to be close, appreciating the seriousness but not imagining even for a moment that it might be about them—an illness, a missing family member, perhaps, a problem they would battle together and it would make them stronger. But Adrienne clutched her hands so she couldn't stand, and shook her head, looking down. Her smooth hair had a halo around it from the light above, like she was wearing a crown. "What is it?" Frances said, and Adrienne took a deep breath. Then she said it: face up, eye to eye, determined, even stern-looking.

"I'm sorry, Frances, but it's over. This, between us, it's over. I'm so sorry. I can't do it anymore. Do you understand? I can't do it anymore."

Later, Frances would be angry with herself for not being loud and indignant, not snapping her hands back, at least. But she didn't, she couldn't; her hands went limp and cold in Adrienne's, her shoulders slumped, and she felt a sinking within, like her heart had dislodged and was stuck in her lungs, suffocating her. Adrienne said some other things, but Frances didn't hear what they were: the usual placatory offerings, promises to be friends, spoken with the desperation and hopefulness of one who has been planning this for a while, has willed it, adjusted to it, and now just wants it out of the way. The pleading look was of course for forgiveness but also a way of asking, "Go easy on me." Adrienne didn't want a scene, not in the restaurant and not in her heart, just a nice simple break-up. Maybe she was already planning their next visit to the seaside, their next lunch out, perhaps she was even hopeful that this very meal might still go ahead, sharing a chicken liver pâté dripping with chutney and sentimentality, sad but new-found friends who would both agree it was for the best. A parting hug in the restaurant doorway. "Let's keep in touch."

Within the drowning, suffocating, slaughtered feeling was a barely contained fury that, if it could only get a foothold past the pain, would reach out and ram a fork in that beautiful eye.

"Look at me," Adrienne said, as if daring her. "You have not done anything wrong. All you've ever been is yourself. Sometimes that just isn't enough. But you tried. We both did. This is where it ends though, okay?" And she had smiled her tiny smile, the one she gave to beggars and hookers as if to say, "Chin up. It'll be okay." Then she withdrew her hands. The fork glimmered. Adrienne stood up. She was wearing the red military-style coat Frances had first seen her in. She hadn't even taken it off, Frances now realised. Adrienne wafted her hand as if to prevent tears, then turned and walked away without looking back. Frances was left bereft at the table, staring at her two empty hands. She stayed there, drinking wine, and wished she had paid attention when Adrienne was explaining. What had she said? What was the reason? Was she fucking someone else? Because that, of course, was what really mattered. Was she fucking someone else?

On the floor now, Frances pushed her fingertips into her quivering eyes. "Fuck her," she whispered, and took the lid off the bottle. Dom had told her to go easy; she added two drops, then an extra one for good measure. She stirred it, put the lid back on, and placed the bottle back in her bag. Then she picked up both drinks and left.

Outside, she felt hurried; plan in action, she could not stop now. She had cups in her hands like many other people did, and she rushed, like them, down the busy street, full of adrenaline and drive. The feeling was a pleasant surprise, considering all she had really done was go out and buy coffee. She even felt rather proud of herself; she had balls, indeed. The drug was in there, mingling with the cinnamon, and it was oddly thrilling that every person she passed had no idea.

ELAINE WAS NOT AWAKE YET but had rolled onto her stomach with both arms sticking out sideways from beneath her, like an extra pair of open legs. The bedsheet was tangled up around her waist, draped in an almost feminine manner across her behind. A full glass of water was on the bedside table and the bathroom door was open. Frances couldn't hear her breathing, nor see any movement at all, not so much as a hair twitching, and she stood in the open doorway and wondered if this is what Elaine might look like dead. She had heard that dead people looked distinctly . . . dead. Not just asleep, but dead. There was an emptiness about them—so people said. You just *knew*. But surely from a distance a sleeping person and a dead person didn't look so dissimilar. She squinted for a moment and saw through her blurry vision a very tragic, elegant figure, like Evelyn McHale, and thought this might be the prettiest Elaine had ever been. What a shame it was she didn't look like it up close and conscious. Blinking, Frances swung the door closed, and went into the living room.

The windows were all closed and the room was stuffy, but she kept them closed so she could think. She put Elaine's cup on the coffee table and flopped on the sofa, staring at it, sipping from her own. She knew this was a bad idea. Not the drugging—the hesitating, the thinking. To see it through she must move in smooth actions, be like mercury, slip over and around doubts and furniture and just get on with it, so it happened almost without her impetus. But Frances had developed a strong ability—practically a skill—to sit very still for long periods of time and do absolutely nothing. Elaine had once observed, "It's like you're a robot that's been switched off. Don't you get bored?" With sudden decisiveness she stood, picked up the latte, put it back down, ate an orange, picked it up again, and went into the bedroom.

She sat on the edge of the bed as if visiting a patient, and for several moments just looked at Elaine, because it seemed the right thing to do. In movies, the villain always looked for a moment at their unsuspecting victim before commencing the act. All she could see was Elaine's back and head; the two arms stuck out facing the door, so from this angle she looked like an amputee. There was a strange, expectant air of occasion; she almost felt like she should make a speech: "Dearly beloved, we are gathered here today to witness . . ." Elaine's skin was very pale, she suddenly noticed, as if she had never seen it before. Not in a pure way, but like she might be ill. What a blessing that would be; a sickly Elaine would be a quiet Elaine, surely. When the drug kicked in, how would she look? Could such paleness become paler? Perhaps she would turn grey. She put the cup on the bedside cabinet and reached out to touch her shoulder, then hesitated, looking at the clammy back, and instead bounced up and down on the bed a little. Elaine stirred.

"Good morning," Frances said.

She had attempted a light, chirpy, sing-songy voice but for some reason it came out as a growl. Elaine spun round in the bed.

"Oh!" she said, blinking. "You're back. Where have you been? I woke up and you weren't here. You know I hate that—it makes me panic."

"Yes, I know. Sorry."

"Where did you go?"

"Just to the coffee shop," and she held up the cup as evidence. "I got you your favourite. A cinnamon latte." She wiggled it side to side as if to tease.

"Oh, you angel." Elaine sat up in bed and knuckled her eyes like a child in disbelief. "Thank you so much." Then she yawned as only Elaine could, wide as a hippo, making that horrendous sound, "Nnnnnnnnnnnnngghhhaaaaaaaaaaaaaaaaaa."

Frances said, "Here's your coffee," and thrust it out. Elaine opened and closed her mouth several times as if savoring her own saliva, and looked around like she didn't know where she was.

"What shall we do today?" she said. "It looks lovely outside. We shouldn't stay cooped up in here. Let's go out somewhere, shall we? We could go to the seaside or a park or for lunch . . ."

Her voice dwindled off in the back of Frances' mind as she rambled on and on. Frances, instead, was becoming increasingly aware of the cup in her hand, which felt like it was beginning to burn her.

"A picnic!" Elaine said. "Oh, let's have a picnic," and she smiled, all dreamy with sunny memories. Just as Frances was about to argue—she fucking hated picnics—she remembered that she could agree to anything, because none of it would happen.

"Yes," she said. "A picnic sounds great. Here's your coffee. Don't let it get cold."

"God, I don't even know if I want it, I'm so hot."

She plonked her arms down beside her, as if to show how exhausted the heat had already made her. Frances, dismayed, held the cup out further and said, "But I went out early to get it for you."

"Oh, I know, and you're a sweetheart, aren't you? But I think maybe I just need water—I'm parched."

Well, this was going horribly wrong. Frances reminded herself that it was likely the whole procedure was going to be full of these little hiccups; the key was to navigate them, to be sharp, to be clever. She said, "Why don't you drink some water first, then have your coffee? I'll be very hurt if you don't drink it. I got it especially for you," and topped it off with a slight pout.

Elaine, *ever* so much in love, leant over and kissed Frances' cheek. "My poor Funny Frances, look how sensitive you are today! Okay, I promise," and then Frances even kissed her. She held the lovey-dovey gaze as long as she could, then left and went into the living room.

+

SHE COULDN'T BEAR to watch.

She had expected Elaine to start sipping, making *mmm* noises and rubbing her belly before slipping into a nice, neat coma, but—unsurprisingly, as far as Frances was concerned—Elaine was not so cooperative; she stuffed the cup between her legs, untouched, and picked up her phone and started texting. Frances, unable to cope with the tension, turned on cheery early-morning children's telly, and repeatedly glanced back over the sofa into the bedroom, where the cup sat ignored between Elaine's thighs. She was visibly, punchably, engrossed in her phone. She was even smiling—she chuckled once or twice—and all the while Frances wanted to scream, "Get on with it!" She couldn't bear to watch, and yet she couldn't stop looking. It was like seeing the tail of a speeding car begin to sway side to side and you knew—just knew—it was going to crash, but you didn't know when or where. Back and forth she looked, from TV to bed, not wanting to look, having to look, trying to be calm, forgetting to be calm, pausing every now and then in little blips of complete surrealness where she just felt stunned. On TV a mixture of humans and animals danced together in a woodland clearing. Frances now opened a window; a wash of noise rushed in amongst the fumes of traffic. She stuck her head outside and inhaled it. She could see why people leapt from buildings. There was an inviting quality to the air outside when you're indoors, in a bind, feeling icky. A sharp stab to her little finger: the cactus on the window ledge. She looked back. Elaine had the cup in one hand, and with the other she continued texting. Frances imagined hurling the cactus at her, pictured it striking her with a squelchy *thwack*, sticking Velcro-like to her face, the red flower on top like a comedy hat. She peeled an orange but it was no use—

her tongue felt like Fuzzy-Felt. Any minute now she was going to have to stride in there, take the cup from Elaine, chuck the coffee in her face, say, "Well, thanks for nothing," and storm out. But then, very slowly, thumb still wiggling away at the phone, Elaine lifted the cup and began to sip.

Relief of reliefs! She might as well have lifted a trophy! Success! Frances wanted to jump, to applaud. She fell back onto the sofa and absently stared at the screen, basking in the deep acknowledgement that a decision had occurred; the step had been taken. And, she reasoned, it was Elaine's step. It was her choice, after all, to drink the thing. Frances hadn't forced her, hadn't put a gun to her head (the image popped up, briefly, then *bang*, back in the room), and so, really, she was hardly to blame at all. In the TV, submerged within the dancing creatures, she could see the reflection of her face, grey, withdrawn, ghostly. *God, it's tiring,* she thought. But at last they were off, and it was Elaine's own doing, and then suddenly she heard a little click—the sound of an empty cup being put down—and Elaine called out, "That was delish—thanks, babe," and that was that. Three little drops, in her system.

Frances looked at the clock. Only a few minutes had passed. The anticipation of drinking was replaced by the anticipation of a reaction, but what did she really expect? Her name to be called, quietly, nervously from the bedroom: "Frances . . . can you come here . . . I . . . I don't feel very well," or, more intriguingly, "What's happening?" Perhaps nothing at all, just the sound of footsteps, bare and slapping, followed by a thump. Or, if she had given a touch too much, perhaps a more comical scene, Elaine appearing beside her, clutching her throat, before crumpling to the floor in little jerky spasms, wide-eyed, staring at her accusatorily: a briefly amusing thought which quickly turned into a frightening one. She had read a book once where a victim of poisoning had projectile-vomited across the room, and she wondered now if she ought to go in there and remove her Turkish rug and tapestry wall-hanging. She would have to learn to be patient. She decided to try. A flyer for a nearby takeaway was on the table, so she picked it up and examined it, turning it over, studying the pictures of doner kebabs. She looked back. Elaine was again on her phone. She seemed absolutely fine.

This was just typical of Elaine. It was like when they went food shopping and she'd bump into someone she knew and would stop and talk to them, leaving Frances standing there awkwardly on the outskirts of their conversation, pretending to smile and listen, reading the ingredients on packets and tins, clicking her knuckles, wishing Elaine would take the hint. Or when they got the tube, and Elaine would always wait until it had completely stopped before she stood up. Or in restaurants, reading every single option out loud—"The fish sounds nice. Oh, but the lamb . . ."—mulling it over, changing her mind, changing it back, laughing at herself for being indecisive, then always—always—ordering the same as Frances. And now here she was, petulantly refusing to submit to the concoction she had swallowed. It was outrageously stubborn.

"You okay in there, babe?" a voice suddenly called from the bedroom.

She looked back. Elaine was holding her phone and looking over at her. "Yeah," she said. "You?"

"Yes. Mummy wants to know when she can come over."

"Oh. Really?"

"Don't say that," she scolded lightly. "She wants to meet you and she wants to see the flat. I can hardly keep telling her it's not that serious, can I."

"No. I suppose not."

There was a pause. Frances turned around and Elaine was still looking blankly at her. For a moment Frances thought a reaction was about to happen, then Elaine said, "Are you reluctant to meet my mother because I can't meet yours?"

"What? Why would you say that?"

"I'm just checking, that's all. I don't want it to seem insensitive."

"It's nothing to do with her. It's nothing to do with my mother."

"Isn't it?"

"No."

"I'd understand if it was. I know it must be hard for you."

"Can we stop this, please. I don't want to talk about it, okay?"

"You never do."

"Okay, so maybe take the hint!"

"Well, what is it, then? Why the reluctancy?"

"Nothing," she sighed. "I'm not reluctant. Not at all."

"Really?"

"Yes. Really."

"She'll love you just as much as I do."

And Frances thought, *I fucking hope not.*

"Maybe in a week or two, alright?" Frances said. "We're still getting settled."

Elaine sighed. "You don't want to meet her."

"Yes, I do."

"No, you don't—I can tell."

"I do, for fuck's sake! I keep saying it, don't I?"

"You sure?"

"Yes!"

What weird world was this, where she was now arguing *to* meet Elaine's mother?

"Okay," Elaine said happily. "I just wanted to check."

Slow minute passed by slow minute.

She kicked aside some of Elaine's books to make space for her feet on the table. In hindsight, she probably should have moved to a new flat after the break-up with Adrienne, get a fresh start. Thirteen months they had lived here together, that was all. Now, with Elaine refusing to sicken in the bedroom and so many possessions, so much *stuff*, all around her, she wondered if this wasn't part of the problem; she hadn't let Adrienne go, emotionally speaking, before Elaine moved in, and now it was all a jumble. The past, the present, and whatever the future was—back there, in the bed—all gradually unfolding. She recalled the day Adrienne had come for her things. Frances had spent the morning wondering how to confront her, to beg, or cry, or shout, or strike out at her, but in the event she did nothing, because she loved Adrienne, and so all she could do was stand by the oven and watch. It had only been a few days since the restaurant incident but Adrienne already looked different, almost radiant, and Frances had thought, *It's because she's got the weight of me off her back.* Adrienne had bustled around the place, gathering the pieces of herself that she'd dotted around, avoiding eye contact or perhaps genuinely not noticing her. *Are you fucking someone else?* Frances longed to say, but she couldn't do it, couldn't bear to hear the response, knowing her righteous indignation would fall flat beneath her heartbreak if Adrienne answered yes. And what if she said no? Would she believe her? At the door, Adrienne held three boxes balanced almost up to her nose, a fortunate barrier to a hug, a convenient excuse to have to hurry, have to go. "I'll call you soon," she said, and they both knew she was lying. Frances watched Adrienne's body as it descended the stairs: legs gone, then torso, then head, then nothing but the sound of footsteps growing fainter and fainter in their familiar way, and then, far away beneath her, the open and closing of the main door. Then silence. She could have rushed to the living room window, she could have looked down and had one last glimpse at the top of her head, she could have leant out and yelled, "I love you," or lobbed an empty wine bottle in her path. She could have run after her, grabbed her, kissed her. But she didn't. She didn't do anything. Stoppered not by pride or acceptance but by a freezing fear and horror at what had just happened because she had dared to hope in a reconciliation, as if "coming to pack up" might have changed to "coming to talk." She had even made the bed and shaved off most of her pubic hair. Oh, the appalling feeling again, heart sinking into her lungs, as she watched box after box appear and saw that Adrienne wasn't even going to sit down for a few minutes. The embarrassment, then; even though nobody knew she had prepared her bed and her body, she felt foolish nonetheless. Hearing the silence which followed Adrienne's departure, she closed the door and she longed to weep dramatically, so loudly and so pained that the neighbours would hear and come to comfort her or call the police, and she longed to make a statement: Adrienne has killed me. But instead she stood there, her back to the door, and discovered she couldn't cry at all, as if Adrienne had boxed up the necessary valve or whatever and taken that away too. Then she'd wandered bewilderedly around the rooms and stared at the gaps of the absent Adrienne-shaped pieces, snatched from their enmeshed life, not so enmeshed, after all, in fact. A line of dirt exposed on the kitchen counter, previously concealed by the cookery books. A creamy puddle where her soap had sat. A faint yet perfect circle where her blue vase had stood since the day she moved in and which Frances had routinely filled with alstroemerias. A huge space the size of a coffin in the wardrobe where her clothes had hung. Her pillow, flecked with smudges of mascara, as if she had ever wept. Frances found a lash on it two nights later and fell asleep looking at it, in the way grieving people do, clutching at the comfort such connection brings: an eyelash, to an eye, to a face, still sleeping there beside you. Her own belongings seemed suddenly out of place, like every item was a twin it had been severed from, now one toothbrush, one comb, one soap bar, one towel. The brutality of the act—being sliced in half—somehow struck her deeper than had the actual break-up in the restaurant, an event which already seemed vague in her memory. Worst of all, the smell of her. It seemed to have permeated everything and she could not bring herself to wash it away, to remove it from the towels and cushions she wrapped herself up in each night as she cried in bed. In the end, after nights of this and a brief, drunken, but very real rage, she had thrown them all away, only to rush down to the bins in the morning desperate to retrieve them, but it was too late—they were gone. Then she had carefully gathered up the random assortment of objects and souvenirs that were the remnants of their relationship and put them in the wooden box of precious things, wrapped in a crumpled piece of paper with an address written on it.

I suppose I assumed that Elaine would fill the gaps, she said to herself, but Elaine could not fill the gaps no matter how much of herself she brought in, because she was the wrong fit, the wrong shape. She was Elaine-shaped, not Adrienne-shaped. And she refused to be moulded, to take baths instead of showers, to drink red wine instead of white, to use a comb not a brush, so it never worked and could never work. She was quite immoveable with regards to her own precious shape. To any outside observer it would be obvious that it was in fact these differences that had attracted her to Elaine. Don't we all attempt to heal a heart by brutally smothering it with some new individual, as if the organ might recover if stifled by another, like a wound beneath an unbreathable bandage?

"She was a bitch," Elaine would sometimes say. "I'd never hurt you like she did."

And whilst this was pitifully, painfully, obviously true, the words brought no solace. In fact, when Elaine went on these little tirades Frances would find herself defending Adrienne, as if the name itself were sacred and how dare Elaine—a commoner— sully it or say a word against her. Hands on hips and oddly warrior-like in her brazen nudity, Elaine would continue, triggered by Frances' lack of agreement, lack of loyalty. "Hate her, babe. Like I do. Hate the bitch. She used you, that was all—you just can't see it." These statements were not so much reassurances as declarations of war.

"You didn't even know her," Frances would retort, in a voice far whinier than she'd hoped for. "You don't know the first thing about her, so just leave it, okay? Drop it."

"I know enough. I know she hurt you."

"I said just drop it."

She didn't want to think of Adrienne like that. She didn't want to hate her. They say love and hate are close together but they are also absolutes, in opposition, and when you are consumed by one, you cannot even entertain the other. True, she repeated the words to Elaine, the three single syllables that Elaine sang down the phone, whispered in her ear, and panted at climax. "I love you," she endlessly gushed and, with a far-away look, Frances would repeat them, a muffled "I love you," picturing Adrienne as she said them so as not to feel she were being unfaithful.

A NOISE came from the bedroom, followed by the bathroom door. Frances tiptoed over and listened: just Elaine, peeing. On the bed were some clothes. Shorts and bra and a T-shirt and from an open drawer poked the rim of a sunhat. Her phone lay open on the bed, a list being written in Notes: sandwiches, Scotch eggs, bananas, white wine. In a moment of entitlement Frances flicked into Elaine's messages: MUMMY, I MISS YOU! I'LL SEE YOU SOON. IT'S A DELICATE ISSUE BECAUSE OF WHAT HAPPENED WITH HER MUM BUT I'M WORKING ON IT.

Frances stepped into her shoes, grabbed her bag, and rushed to the front door. "I'm just popping out," she called, and left before Elaine could respond. *Fuck if she faints, fuck if she collapses—if I stay there a minute longer, I know I'll hit her.*

6

I<small>N THE AFTERMATH</small> of the break-up—when disbelief and horror had passed and flatness was the order of the day—
Frances had woken up one morning and decided she should go to
a doctor. She was vaguely concerned about herself. Like a twinge
in her neck that she'd grown used to and almost didn't notice
anymore, she knew it wasn't right, and in a way she cared that
she didn't care, because she knew she should care. She also knew,
vividly, that a wide range of emotions existed and in its very centre, like a cosy pearl, was calmness. All other emotions sprang out
and darted around it, but the middle should always be still, and
she was aware that she had been flung from this scale altogether.
The flatness could hardly be described as calm; rather, it was a
distinct lack of emotion, an absence of any feeling. She was in an
entirely separate place now, which had no range whatsoever, and
the memories of emotions were recalled like holiday snaps, far
away, over there, belonging to a place and time she couldn't access
anymore. Even Frances knew something was wrong.

The door to the doctor's office had been slightly ajar, and as she raised her hand to knock she overheard a harassed voice within, speaking in the rasped tones of exasperation that come spitting out during stress and impatience and an attempt to whisper.

"I said, I'll get there as soon as I've finished. No, I can't come any sooner. Yes, I know how ill he is. Please don't make me feel bad—I'm at work, I have to work. I told you, I'm across town. By six o'clock, I hope. No, I can't leave any earlier, I have patients, for heaven's sake. What? Is that a serious question? Yes, Mum, she's still gone. Still left me, yes. Yes, the vet. The bastard vet, the guy I knew at school. Yes, still him. I am trying, Mum. I am. What? Well, I sent her flowers. To her work. Yesterday. I don't know, carnations, I think. Well, I'm doing my best—what else can I do? I'll try to get there soon. He'll be okay. Oh, please don't cry, please, Mum, please . . ."

Frances knocked gently on the door, guilty for interrupting, but also aware the clock was ticking on her ten minutes. She heard him say, "I've got to go," and by the time the door swung gently away from her apologetic knuckles she was greeted with the sight of a chubby, scruffy man stuffed in a suit, smiling inanely from behind a desk. "Come in!" he bellowed as she was closing the door. "Have a seat." He gestured at the only available chair, as if otherwise she might have perched on the windowsill or sat on his knee.

Frances felt like a chance voyeur, like she'd just caught him taking a leak. She felt she should apologise for being there, for interrupting him, for troubling him; out of the two of them he looked more in need of help than she did. In fact, he looked like he'd climbed fully clothed into a washing machine, suffered the stain setting, then dried off in the jet stream of a Boeing 747. His face was as damp and creased-looking as his clothes, yet dried skin flaked around his nostrils as if he'd been sick, or sobbing, and despite his self-soothing habit of stroking his tie and brushing his sleeves, resultant trails of thread suggested he was coming apart in more ways than one. Only the top of his head seemed in any way neat and orderly: a scalp as smooth and shiny as a diving dolphin. His red face reddened further as he squeezed his stomach up close to the desk, squinting through his spectacles at the computer screen.

"I'm sorry," he said to her, poking dubiously at keys, tapping the mouse, slamming it on the desk once or twice. "This isn't my normal office, you see. I'm still settling in here, and the computers are so slow, it's a wonder we can get anything done."

She sat down in her crumpled jeans and lightly soiled shirt, wondering if she'd just met a kindred spirit. For a moment they just looked at each other. Then he interlaced his fingers as a signal for her to begin.

He was nice. He listened as she explained about the flatness and lack of range. He nodded and asked questions and ran his hand down his tie several times. He was attentive as she jumped from vague statement to vague statement, and eventually he asked her, "So, has anything specifically happened? Something at work, or at home, perhaps?" And, with the door of conversation thus held open, inviting her in like a welcoming hand, she found herself quickly summarising the situation. It took her less than a minute and she said Adrienne's name seven times, but still it felt insufficient, like saying the *Titanic* sank because it had a dent in it.

"So"—he stroked his tie again—"you're depressed."

"Is that it? I don't even know."

"It would be my diagnosis, yes."

"But it's not like I'm crying all over the place or anything—quite the opposite, in fact."

"Depression doesn't feel or look the same to everyone. From what you've described, and considering what has—ah—happened, I would say yes, you are depressed. We can prescribe something for that and refer you for counselling, if you wish."

"I don't know. What sort of something and what sort of counselling?"

"Antidepressants, and probably CBT. It would be group therapy, once a week."

It was a typical NHS doctor's room: brown floor, little sink on the wall, a lot of big books on rickety shelves, and various anatomical posters with curled corners. Boxes of blue gloves on a windowsill, pressed up against the wonky blinds, through which was the blurred image of a wet and crowded car park. If you didn't have depression before you went in, it seemed highly likely you'd contract it. Frances sighed and instantly regretted it, worried she might seem ungrateful. But it was not ingratitude; she just realised he couldn't help.

"You don't understand," she said. "I can go to work, I can meet people, I can behave like anyone else. And I'm pretty sure I can go to group therapy and sit on a chair and listen and talk and maybe some of it would even sound relevant or helpful, but it wouldn't affect me, it wouldn't sink in, it would just sit in my brain, floating on the surface. Do you see? It wouldn't change this feeling, because it wouldn't reach it. And I don't know how anyone can find or reach me now because I feel like I've dropped off the radar, I'm the GPS signal that has disappeared: blip. And I don't need a pill to bring me up or put me down, I just need to be . . . located. Do you think that happens by sitting in a circle on plastic chairs for an hour a week? In my experience it only happens with love. It's love that finds you, rescues you, puts you back on the map in the world again. And I don't think you can prescribe that. I wish you could. If it could be swallowed down or shot up, I'd take it in an instant."

He sat back in his chair and interlocked his fingers on his belly, elbows spilling out over the armrests. The chair creaked ominously. She felt sorry for him again; it was all too uncomfortable, the narrow chair, the annoying computer, this girl talking in metaphors when all he wanted was a simple yes or no. He observed her expressionlessly for a moment, then sighed, looked away, and quietly said, almost to himself, "Flat is not so bad. I almost envy flat."

"It's awful," she said.

"There are worse things," he said. His eyes seemed to lock on to a space on the wall as he continued. "Like feeling betrayed, abandoned, humiliated, lost. Like everything you knew to be true was a game and no one even told you you were playing it, you thought it was real life, but it wasn't. Then suddenly it's over and everyone's gone and you're left packing away the pieces in the shameful, illuminating light of day. That's worse, I think."

He sighed again, and the sigh seemed to sink in the air, leaving silence behind, a silence he may well have cringed in, suddenly aware of his emotional outburst, but such opportunity for further inappropriate self-pity was thwarted by Frances saying, "That's not so bad."

"Pardon me?"

"I just mean at least it is something, at least there's some fire in it. Someone could shoot you in the face right now and I doubt I'd even flinch."

He scoffed, "Me too."

"And I know what you mean. You talk about abandonment, believe me, I know a thing or two."

And she meant it. Frances clung to the term *abandonment* with the same attachment as others give to *feminism* or *veganism:* a label she not only believed in but felt made up a vital and profound part of herself. Abandoned, as she told it, by parents, friends, lovers; it was a miracle she'd survived such endless, incessant cruelty. But this was because—as is the case with all of us—her perception of behaviour, including her own, was rather inaccurate. Her father had been away working thirteen hours a day, and many people would say Frances pushed friends and lovers away. In fact, so riddled was she with this notion of abandonment, and so dearly she clung to being the victim, it was difficult for her to know what was real and what was not, because the truth was not important or relevant. The numerous times she had dumped, ditched, ignored, or fled people in her life were cleverly swept aside amidst the tide of so-called rejections she allowed to dominate her life. Where was her mother? "Gone," she would say, with a sad turn of the head. There was a strange pleasure in sensing such sorrow in the eyes that followed her, that said, "I'm sorry." After her father died she allowed the word *orphan.* An abandoned orphan. Only a cup of gruel away from a Dickensian pauper.

"Well," the doctor said. "In which case, flat is probably an improvement. Personally, I'd rather that. There's not enough whisky in the world to make me feel flat. Except flat on my face, of course," and neither of them laughed at this sad little joke which was too true and tragic to be funny. "Ah, well!" he exclaimed cheerfully. "What's one to do?"

And for a moment Frances thought he was actually asking. She looked around and shrugged her shoulders, then he seemed to remember he was a doctor, cleared his throat, turned back to his computer, and said, "Have you been taking anything?"

"Like what?"

"Drugs?"

"No."

"Alcohol?"

"The odd jar, perhaps."

"Anything else I should know?"

"Like what?"

"Suicidal thoughts? Self-harm?"

"No."

He knew she was lying on every count but there was nothing he could do about it. When patients walled up like this, you would never get the truth. "What about the antidepressants, then? The counselling?"

Frances wanted to say, "Okay. Why don't you join me?" He didn't seem to be in much of a position to help; she felt bad for bothering him with her petty concerns when his own life was so obviously in decay. Inappropriate as it had been, his humanity had touched her and she found herself liking him. Not as a doctor—in that respect he seemed quite useless; she doubted he should even be working—but as another poor, damaged person. In an ideal world he'd be sitting beside her and they'd both be asking a shrink some very demanding questions about what the hell is wrong with our minds, why do they break, how do we cope? She saw the strain he was under. Making one person's sanity the sole responsibility of another human being did seem a bit much when you thought about it. After all, he wasn't a psychothera-pist, he wasn't a counsellor, he didn't have any real answers for her, he couldn't help in any meaningful way; all he could do was refer her for therapy, which took six weeks to come through, and prescribe drugs that took two weeks to work. This is why help is so rarely sought: It takes too damn long. When your suffering is moment to moment, second by second, what possible use is help in a fortnight? The bottle is right there, temporary relief only a swig away. He looked at Frances as if to say, "God, it's hopeless, isn't it?" but thankfully she ran her hands through her hair and said, "Sure. Okay. Go on, then. It makes no difference, really. That's sort of what I've been saying."

"I'm sorry," he said.

"That's okay."

Eventually, after much typing and tutting, he printed off the prescription. He said the referral would be through in a few weeks—she'd receive a letter. "No drinking alcohol on the pills," he said, because he had to say it, but they both knew she would wash each one down with a glass of booze, because that's what he would do too. She took it, thanked him, and they looked at each other.

In a sudden, impulsive moment, she nearly confessed. She could hold her hands up high: "Doctor, I killed a boy." What would his face look like if she told him? What would he say? It seemed, in that moment, that she could tell him anything and he might understand, might nod in his fatherly way and offer some reassurance, and then, when she left his office, it would be as if it had never happened; there would be relief whilst in his room, then step outside and return to normal. The thought of unburdening herself was so tempting she felt the words "There's something else" form in her mouth. But, after holding it so long inside, she found that it was impossible to confess, impossible to be honest, and when she swallowed the words, the moment passed. The truth had been in there for so long it was like a brick in mortar, in the wall of her personality; it didn't do anything— it just lived there—and she was used to it, even though she knew it had corroded and was the cause of much instability. As they looked at each other, each felt a sense of fleeting recognition.

She stood to leave. Stopping at the door, she said, "You know, I wish you could just hit or hug me."

"Sorry?" He looked up.

"I said, I wish you could just hit or hug me. I can't help feeling it's what people like me really need. One or the other. It probably doesn't matter which."

He leant back in his chair. He seemed for a moment to be seriously considering it. She pictured them standing there, taking it in turns to slap each other around the face. He said, "Eat well. Sleep well. Keep busy. See your friends and family, and get outside, in the fresh air."

They looked at each other again and she wanted to ask, "Is that what you do?"

"Yes," she said. "Okay. Thank you."

Outside, in the car park, she stopped to light a cigarette and found herself standing before the row of cars in the spaces reserved for doctors. Hemmed in either side by glistening bonnets was a grubby Mondeo, parked askew, the licence plate almost unreadable through the coating of dirt. Empty chocolate wrappers and crisp packets and cigarette cartons filled the dashboard, ties were draped all over the place, empty bottles and sandwich crusts filled the footwells. Glancing back, she saw the doctor peering out between the blinds, looking at her. She turned away, and the blind, like a huge eye, snapped shut.

NOW, OUTSIDE OF THE FLAT, Frances headed straight for her haven. There were the cafés, of course, but when walls and noise and people became too much, she remembered the doctor's poorly-given advice and sought fresh air, and as she was often unable to run or walk far, this place had become a favourite.

The duck pond was only a short walk around the corner. She had stumbled across it by accident one day, concealed within a square hedge, with no sign or markings to announce it, it was the sort of place people walked blindly by for years, known only to drug dealers and secret lovers who ushered through after dark. She snuck in now, looking over her shoulder, as if she were having an affair or being followed. She wouldn't put it past Elaine to have come after her, on hands and knees, if necessary, grappling at her ankle. It would have been very typical of her.

It was not a pretty place, despite its origins as an art installation. The boxed frame of concrete slabs had once been a vision of clean lines and clear water which the hedges and the muffled city noises combined to create a place of peace. Now a low water line traced by green slime ran around the dank insides. The high buildings and tall hedge which towered over it meant the small, shrinking pool saw little daylight, and so the water appeared to be black, with a scummy green surface, home to only mosquitoes and a sort of putrid sludge which gathered there. The only hint of past beauty stood in one corner; a rusty sculpture of a mallard with its wings wide open, as if coming in to land. Four graffitied benches bordered each side behind which, in the ever-dark, ferns and mosses and mushrooms grew, quite possibly overseen by an elf or two. In the heat, a stench of metallic dampness lingered, along with a more offensive odour, like sulphur. Frances went to her favourite bench and was immediately affronted to see a couple opposite, across the pond, sitting side by side and nuzzling each other's necks, glaring over at her for interrupting them. Frances folded her arms and stared back; they whispered and giggled. The

tight, claustrophobic space meant they were within striking distance; Frances was tempted to throw one of the many discarded
beer cans at their conjoined head. The front of the girl's top was
untucked from her shorts, and the boy had his hand high up her
thigh, where his thumb kneaded away at the whiteness. Looking
up, behind them, tipping her head way back, Frances could see
her living room curtains. The place looked silent and empty up
there, as all properties do when no one is at the window. It was
very easy to imagine it without Elaine, and Frances found herself
wondering how it was going, if she might be asleep, collapsed,
throwing up, or still cheerfully writing the shopping list on her
phone, wondering where Funny Frances had gone. Buses rum-
bled hungrily away down the road, voices—talking, laughing,
shouting—filtered in, and in the gap between the hedges she saw
the pedestrians rushing by, back and forth, like flashing images,
innumerable, faceless, multitudinous humans.

She had heard that, whilst grieving, it is quite common to
"see" your loved one everywhere, and she hoped for it constantly.
She wasn't asking for much: the sight of Adrienne's hair vanish-
ing around a corner. Her scent left behind as a stranger walked by.
Her smile on a passenger, in a bus going up the road. Anything
would do. The knowledge that she was out there merrily existing,
allowing other people—random people, everyday, unimportant
people—to see her and interact with her was awful, insulting.
Knowing some old anybody could at that moment be caressing
her and kissing her was enough to make Frances want to curl
into a ball. It was not only a question of whether or not she was
fucking someone, but whether or not she was being fucked, being
probed and penetrated as if she weren't precious and lovely, but a
pot of compost you make a seed-hole in with one grubby finger.

The couple were kissing, tongues poking out between the gaps where their lips failed to lock, messily salivating upon each other like they hadn't eaten in months. His left arm dangled around her neck like a scarf, strangely immobile considering all the face action. The girl kept her hands in her lap, on a red duffle bag, only her face turned towards him, the rest of her body towards Frances, as if this were all for her benefit. In between kissing they whispered in the stilted way kids do when they know how to kiss but not how to talk. The newness of their relationship was embarrassingly apparent: he suffering that uncomfortable arm just because it was what he had seen in films, and she suffering him, because she hadn't made her mind up yet. He had a habit of pressing his left hand into the girl's jaw to turn it towards him, as if it were on a hinge; she would turn away again and he would be laughing, joking, like it were a game, but the girl looked increasingly annoyed by it. Frances thought, *That won't last long.* When it is true love, your faces are mirrored, magnetised. She marvelled that Elaine had never noticed any of these failings between them. She was half tempted to bring her down here to observe this couple: "Look—do you see now? Do you notice the clashing, the wrongness? That is us, my dear. You pushing on and me turning away." Then she remembered that she would not have to feel Elaine's hand touching or turning her face, nor any other body part, and she felt better.

She had, for a brief time, taken the antidepressants the doctor had prescribed, mainly because she could see what an effort it was for him to print it, but after a week or two of no obvious improvement, she threw them away. When you know how to get proper drugs—drugs with an almost instantaneous effect—why bother with wishy-washy, soft, sensible prescription ones? If she was going to do drugs she was going to *do* drugs. When the referral came through for group therapy, she went, in as much as she sat in a bar opposite the hall and drank as people arrived. Seeing them all go in cemented it for her: She couldn't do it. For one thing, she would have to enter last, alone, and they'd all stare at her as she slid awkwardly into a chair; some might smile, but no one would speak. The hall would reek of cheesy gym mats and sweaty insoles, it would be echoey and cold, the windows too tall, the ceiling too high. Distance from the door: miles and miles. And they had all looked so normal, so casual, as they strolled in, like they were popping into a library. One man had been holding a Disney store carrier bag, for heaven's sake. She shook her head and sipped her beer. She had scarcely made herself understood by the doctor; how on earth was she supposed to explain herself to this lot? She had finished her drink and left.

Almost-fresh air. Stagnant though it was, it was better than being indoors. The couple had finally stopped kissing and now he was holding her hand and talking to the mole on her disinterested cheek as she stared back at Frances. Frances had the sudden urge to rescue her. She knew that expression well, knew the bored thoughts behind it, knew what it was like to be holding in a tirade of curse words that fought to burst out. No, they would not last. In fact, two weeks later he would be abruptly dumped in front of his friends when he announced she had performed some fiendish—and, as it transpired, fictional—acts upon him. Everyone has their breaking point. But for now, they'd drift on, he quietly salivating, and she unable to put her finger on what exactly was wrong because it was not yet fully clear to her that she just simply couldn't stand him. Frances wondered if perhaps the girl should stick around, tolerate him, marry him. He didn't have the power to destroy her, and that was no bad thing.

+

"HELLO?" Frances hovered in the doorway as if ready to dash back into the street. "Elaine?"

She listened, she sniffed the air, she peered as far into the living room as possible. Nothing. Not a grumble, no smell of vomit, no items knocked over on a dash to the bathroom: It all looked just as it had when she had left. She glanced at her watch. She had been gone only an hour. Despite the fact that nothing appeared to have changed, the flat felt eerie now, as if she had returned knowing it was haunted, and she crept in stealthily, slipping her feet out of her shoes. Perhaps this was the stillness of sleep, perhaps the emptiness of absence, or the hollowness of death. She knew it was of the utmost importance that she behave completely normally, ready to greet whatever she may find with sensibleness and strength, so she was surprised to find herself creeping about like a caricature, slowly pressing the front door closed, leaning to listen with a cupped ear, tippy-toeing across the hallway as if she should have a money bag slung over her shoulder.

She leant forwards, squinting into the gloom, not because it was particularly dark but because it had been so bright outside that she now felt quite blind, and as her eyes adjusted she realised it was also stiflingly hot, the sort of heat which develops a density, so that merely walking through it makes you sweat. She called again, a little louder, "Elaine?" She glanced quickly in the bedroom. The bed was a tangle of damp sheets. No Elaine. She looked in the bathroom. One lace-like web wafted gently beneath the extractor fan. No Elaine. She stood staring into the living room, looking at the back of the sofa, the black TV. She must have gone out. She'd probably come skipping back in soon with Scotch eggs and fizzy pop, all happy and sunshiney, as if nothing had happened. Frances' bag slumped to the floor with a thud.

"Boo!"

Elaine leapt up from the sofa, hands up like bear paws, and she laughed wildly. Frances stumbled backwards and fell into a box full of shoes.

"For fuck's sake," she muttered, trying to haul herself up. "Don't do that to me."

Clutching her stomach as she laughed, Elaine walked round and grabbed Frances' hand. She wrenched her up out of the box and onto her feet as if she weighed nothing. Frances eyed her suspiciously and said, "Are you alright?"

Elaine was wearing a bandana and a pair of polka-dotted cycling shorts, nothing else. Her thighs stretched the material until it turned white.

"Those are my shorts." Frances pointed at them.

"I know. I'm sorry. I can't find my clean running gear. I had to go through your things—I hope you don't mind. But look!" She stuck her thumbs into the suffocating waistband and pulled it a quarter inch from her body. "Look how stretchy!"

"What are you doing?"

"Going running!"

As if to demonstrate, she dashed into the bedroom. Frances turned, following slowly, then stopped in the doorway and gawped as previously unnoticed devastation came into view within the gloom: All the drawers were pulled out and upturned and half the wardrobe had been emptied. "Jesus, what's happened in here?" she said.

"I told you," Elaine replied, burrowing away on the floor, her vast behind poking up from the other side of the bed. "I can't find my clean running gear. It's still packed somewhere. Here"—she tossed a pair of shorts and a top at Frances—"put these on."

"I'm not going," Frances said, "and you shouldn't either. Are you sure you're feeling alright?"

"I told you." Elaine walked round to her and kissed her forehead. "I'm fine. I feel great. Let's get out of here. I want to run, baby! I absolutely must run. I'm going nuts in here."

Elaine was grappling with her breasts, trying to wrangle the bulbous objects into one of Frances' small sports bras, which would have been difficult enough without her jogging on the spot. It reminded Frances of lava bubbling up out of the earth.

"Elaine," Frances said, "I think we should stay in."

"Why?"

"You don't seem quite right."

"What are you talking about? I feel great."

"I just think it would be for the best. It's really hot outside. It's too hot to run, for sure."

"Are you mad? Look, missy, you might have been out already but I haven't and I want to run, and I want you to come with me, okay? We never run together anymore. Come onnnnnnn."

"I want to stay inside."

Elaine paused and raised an eyebrow at Frances. "You . . . want to stay in?"

Elaine's ditzy enthusiasm seemed to home in on Frances with a sudden, fierce precision. She grinned.

"No. You're right." Frances clapped her hands. "Let's go running."

"Yay!"

A few minutes later they were by the front door and Frances was tying her laces, feeling like a babysitter in charge of an excitable child. She tried to think positively; it might be nice to enjoy the simple momentum of running, to feel air in hair, blind in mind, but it was difficult to focus on such things with Elaine before her, bouncing up and down and punching like a shadow-boxer. "Come on!" she cried. "Come on!" Then, unable to wait a moment longer, she turned and bolted out the door. It occurred to Frances that she could probably just stay where she was; Elaine might not even notice she wasn't there. Reluctantly, she grabbed her keys and followed.

Outside on the sunny street, Elaine was performing donkey-kicks round and round in a circle, then put her hands on her hips and walked around doing lunges. She had the rump—and run—of a racehorse: thin, bony ankles disguising a vast amount of strength, upper legs fit to burst through the polka dots, which strained in huge, elongated splats against such sheer bulging power. Frances, on the other hand, ran like a rodent, in many short, fast bursts, close to the ground, little leggies frantically doing their best. She often thought her run should be accompanied by a high piano trill, like when animated mice are being chased.

"Can we keep it nice and steady, and not too far?" she asked, but Elaine hadn't heard her, because she was already across the road.

"Hurry up!" she yelled, her face appearing up and down beyond the traffic as if she were bouncing on an invisible trampoline. Frances wove her way across the road in between impatient cars, full of reluctance, dragging her feet to delay the inevitable. She had only just stepped one foot on pavement when Elaine took off, catapulted by enthusiasm down the crowded street, unable to wait any longer. Frances yelled, "Wait!" and sprinted after her.

For a while they ran side by side in silence; Elaine didn't speak because she was smiling, her mind elsewhere, and Frances didn't because she couldn't—she could barely even breathe. They'd been going only a few minutes and already she was covered in sweat; it ran into her mouth and down her back, her temples tickled with it. Pedestrians walked in their way, dogs and prams appeared out of nowhere, forcing her to leap, dodge, even dash into the gutter. "Can we slow down?" she wheezed. "This is like a fucking assault course." But Elaine didn't seem to hear her; she charged on, arms pumping back and forth, eyes staring off into an imaginary distance. It was all very disconcerting, and Frances wondered what the hell was going on inside that muscular body and tampered mind, and which of them might collapse first. After a couple of miles, just as Frances felt her legs turn to spaghetti, Elaine suddenly vanished—one moment there, beside her, the next only a wall—having darted into a play park so swiftly that Frances had sped past its entrance. She skidded to a halt, looking around for a moment, then walked back and found the gate and went stumbling in, relieved beyond words to no longer be running, taking lungful after lungful of glorious air, her legs solidifying into a deep ache. Her relief was short-lived, however: There was Elaine, swinging from the monkey bars, much to the delight of several small children. *Oh, God,* she thought. Elaine was, with apparent ease, moving her body back and forth from one end to the other, shouting at the applauding audience of chocolate-smeared faces, "Look! I'm urang-Elaine! I'm urang-Elaine!" Frances looked on, stunned. She had to admit, Elaine did look rather long-limbed and at home there, as if this were her natural habitat. Enthralled toddlers on the roundabout ignored their mothers' adoring faces to stare over at her, and children on the swings forgot to keep moving, clutching the metal chains and watching, open-mouthed, as they sat motionlessly, absorbing the sight of this bizarre performance in the Peewee Playground. Some of the larger children tried to climb up to join her but wary parents quickly encouraged them in other directions: "No, let's leave the nice lady alone and go on the slide, shall we? Oh look, an ice cream van . . ." Elaine did not notice; she was having a fabulous time.

Frances stood nearby, catching her breath, as Elaine spotted her and called out, "Frances! Come and join me! You can be an urangu-Fran!"

Frances shook her head. "It's for kids, Elaine. And it's too high. Are you okay?" she wheezed. "I feel like I'm going to puke."

A nearby mother wheeled her pram away.

"I'm fine!" Elaine squealed. "Come and play!"

"Elaine." Frances pointed to a sign which read NO ADULTS OR CHILDREN OVER THE AGE OF TEN. "Come on, let's go."

"Don't be a kill-joy. Come on, Funny Frances."

"I'm going now," and she turned to walk away.

Perhaps she thought this tactic would work, as it does occasionally with kids; parents wander slightly out of sight and the anxious child comes waddling after. But Elaine was not a child, and she was not going to play such a game. Suddenly, Frances felt herself being lifted up from the waist, spun around, and bars appeared before her. Instinctively she grabbed on, yelling, "What the hell are you doing?"

Beneath her, Elaine had hold of her thighs, keeping her raised up in the air. "Play!" she demanded, then stood back, leaving Frances dangling there. "Adults never play. They should! Life's too short to not have fun. We're all just kids inside. Play!"

Frances looked down as if she were being asked to jump out of a plane. "Put me the fuck down!" she yelled.

"Play!" Elaine said. "Go on, swing across!"

"I can't fucking swing across, you idiot—I don't have the strength. What are you doing? Come here and get me down—this isn't funny."

"Oh, it is," Elaine laughed. She had appeared at the opposite end and was swinging there by one hand. "Come on, my darling, swing across to me—imagine you are Tarzan and I'm Jane."

"Elaine, I'm serious. Get me down."

"Don't just dangle! Play!"

"I'm warning you."

"I'm sorry, but it's hard to be intimidated by a girl hanging from the monkey bars with her belly out."

"Get me down!"

The small crowd of children had moved closer to look and were giggling. "Just let go if you can't do it," one of them said. "It's not that high. Don't be afraid."

"Oh, fuck off."

A mixture of giggles and gasps. Two children ran back to their parents.

As she swayed gently back and forth, mocked by miniatures, a breeze upon her exposed belly, Frances wondered if this was her lowest ebb. She despised them all equally in that instance, herself included. Bracing herself, she let go, and landed heavily but with embarrassing ease upon her two feet. The children ran away as if she might beat her chest and come running after them, but she only pulled her top down and sulked off to a bench.

"Where's your playfulness?" Elaine called to her. "Where's your sense of fun?"

"I thought we came out for a run, not to mess around in the Cabbage Patch."

She sat down.

Side effects, Dom had said, but she had not expected this. The exertion and heat were making her feel ill, and as she sat there wiping sweat away with her hand and listening to Elaine laughing with the children, she had a sudden worrying thought: *Did I put it in the right cup?* She tried to remember, tried to recall the details of sitting on the toilet floor, unscrewing the bottle, pouring the drops in. She wished she hadn't been so flustered, she wished she had concentrated, then she might remember. As it was, her doubts were swiftly overtaken by the sight of Elaine charging through the playground, out into a small patch of grass and trees, where she watched in horror as Elaine swept upon a toddler in a red dress, snatching the child up and holding her overhead, laughing. Frances half fell in her urgency to stand, to run, and she barged through the playground, shouting, "I'm so sorry, I'm so sorry. Elaine, put her down. Put her *down*." She arrived and tried to pull the girl away, grabbing at her dress, her arms, as Elaine clung on and on, saying, "Hey, oi, calm down."

"Please," the mother was saying. "It's alright—you don't understand."

"Put her down," Frances snapped, wide-eyed, at Elaine. "Now!"

"Get off, you madwoman!" Elaine swatted Frances' hands away. The girl began to wail.

"Please," the mother continued repeating. "It's alright, it's alright."

And as Frances wrenched the child away victoriously and clung on to her by the waist, she heard the small sobbing voice saying, "Aunty 'Laine. Aunty 'Laine." Arms out, the girl's hands squeezed the air as she reached to be rescued. Elaine covered her hand with her mouth as she started to chuckle. The child's mother was no longer in a placatory mood. "Might I have my daughter back now?" she said curtly.

Elaine's eyes were watering as she stifled her laughter. The woman looked furious. In her arms, the little girl wailed and bellowed for Aunty Elaine. Frances could feel all eyes on her from the playground. In less than five minutes, the two of them had turned a pleasant trip to the playground into a circus show. Frances handed the child back, saying, "I'm so sorry. I didn't think you knew each other."

"Instead you thought I'd stand by and watch total strangers snatch my daughter?"

"God, no, I didn't mean that. It's just, Elaine has been acting a bit out of character today—"

"Yes," Elaine laughed. "I'm the one who has been acting out of character. You're hilarious."

"I've known Elaine since school," the woman said. "I'm guessing you must be Frances."

"Yes," she said, and shook the woman's hand whilst looking at the floor. "Nice to meet you."

"I'll call you," the mother said to Elaine. "We'd better be going home now."

Elaine kissed both of them, and said, "I'm sorry about her—she's not good with children."

"No bother."

As the mother and daughter walked away through the gate, Elaine said, "Well, that was hilarious."

"Can we go home now, please?" Frances said.

"What? We've only run two miles."

"I think that's enough exercise for today."

"Are you mad?"

Elaine's elbows pumped back and forth and her calves popped out on display as she ran. She was talkative now, though, a constant tirade. "You need to embrace your inner child sometimes, babe. Where is little Frances? What did she like to do? You know everything about me but sometimes I feel like I don't even know you. One day we should sit down with cake and tea and you can tell me everything, the whole story." Another mile down the road and Frances knew she was near burn-out—she would fall, she would faint, she would throw up. And the feeling of panic reared up in her again as it had on so many recent runs as she reached out to grab Elaine's top but missed. She couldn't speak. A stitch struck and she gripped her side, bending over, clutching it, running like a hunchback. Elaine's ponytail bobbed intermittently amidst the crowd; she was moving away, rather quickly, talking to herself. A few minutes later and Frances realised she was no longer running with Elaine but chasing after her.

"Excuse me. Excuse me. Excuse me," she panted, knocking bewildered shoppers and dillydallying teenagers out of the way, shouting, "Sorry!" over her shoulder as she went. Her arm shot up in the air as if it knew an answer and she managed to yell: "Elaine! Stop!" but to no avail. Out of breath and in pain, she slowed, and within a few moments Elaine's ponytail had swished its way around a corner, and she was gone.

Frances moved aside and leant against a wall, her hands on her knees, trying not to throw up. The crowd swept haphazardly before her, as if she weren't there. Elaine could be anywhere now. Frances stumbled down a flight of concrete steps and sat on the lowest, away from the street, people's feet moving around behind her, way above head-level, as she waited for the nausea to subside, and wondered what to do. She pulled her phone from her pocket and rang Dom.

"What the fuck is this stuff?" she snapped when he picked up.

He sounded as if he'd been asleep—it took several moments for him to respond. "What?" he said. "Who the hell is this?"

"It's Frances. She's totally fucking hyper, Dom. She's gone nuts."

"Side effects, remember. Calm down. It's just side effects."

He made a horrendous phlegm-rattling sound, and spat. The next moment, he started chewing on something. It was like talking to a cement mixer.

"Well, what do I do now?"

"Don't worry about it," he said, crunching. "She'll soon crash."

"Crash?"

"Yeah."

"Great. And I've fucking lost her."

"What? Where are you? I told you not to go out."

"Dom, have you ever tried putting a rabid giant under house arrest?"

He laughed.

"It's not funny," she said.

"She'll come home—don't worry."

"Let's hope so, hey. Let's hope I don't get a call that she OD'd and is in A and E. You fucking asshole, Dom—why didn't you tell me this would happen?"

"I did. I told you some people go a little crazy to begin with, and I told you to stay in. Not my fault you ignored me and now your bitch is off the leash."

"What am I supposed to do? If she does come back, do I give her more, or what?"

"Nah, no need. She'll definitely crash."

"I don't like the sound of that."

"I'm sorry," he said, "but is this all you wanted me for? You know I'm not a helpline, right? I'm not 'Talk to Frank.' Deal with it yourself." And he hung up.

Frances muttered, "Shit," and stuck the phone back in her pocket, looking around, as if an answer might appear. Elaine ran more than a dozen different routes—there was no point trying to find her. Frances supposed she might as well go home and wait for her there. She stood up and her head swam dizzily. Suddenly a loud bell rang, and beyond a wire fence a door opened and children came tumbling out with all the energy of a mass escape.

Balls and ropes and chasing and squealing: The place filled up with them, the air saturated with their noise. Frances walked backwards and slumped down again, as if bowled over by them, too dizzy to move.

She thought of the seaside, the place she had visited hundreds of times, and of this exact same noise coming from the beach. And she thought of the pier, with its huge red and yellow banner, joyfully proclaiming THE HAPPIEST SOUND IN ALL THE WORLD IS THAT OF CHILDREN'S LAUGHTER. She stared glumly at the children and thought about what Elaine had said, correct in her half-crazed, gibbering way, because Frances never spoke about her childhood; she kept it strictly at bay. Watching, she was full of a difficult emotion, one she struggled to comprehend because envy disguises itself in many ways, as disgust, or resentment, or hate, and as she looked on, she felt all of it, muddled and spun into indistinguishable mulch. She had never been able to abide the thought of pregnancy. Birth, she imagined, would for her be the easy part, like the relief of a huge pustule finally bursting and all the stuff oozing out. But pregnancy, no, no, it would be awful. A head growing, forming, cell by cell. Walking around each day with another brain and heart and two eyeballs in your belly— it all sounded very sci-fi. And she imagined the only thing worse than this would be the responsibility for it. Squealing newborns scrunched on their backs like upturned woodlice: How did their mothers handle the second-by-second strain of loving it, subduing it, keeping it alive? Yet here before her each child represented precisely this continuous, ongoing success, the result of obvious care. Of course they ran about and played games. And as she watched them from what felt like ever so far away, their laughter began to ring a little too loudly in her ears, as if mocking her. "Cunts," she muttered, and a woman passing by looked over, shocked. Then Frances ran. Quickly. Not chasing, but fleeing, as if she had committed a terrible crime.

A TINY NOISE, not quite a groan, more like a stifled sigh. Then another, and another. Frances dropped her keys on the hallway sideboard and slid her feet out of her trainers. The sound came again.

She was relieved, at least for the first few moments. She hadn't expected Elaine to be here when she returned. She'd had images of ringing round hospitals, the police turning up, bloodwork peculiar, handcuffs, and a shameful walk to a waiting car. She'd imagined wandering the streets all night, looking for a sprinting spectre darting between trees, possibly cackling. Or finding her collapsed on the street, or face down in an alleyway, or floating in the pond like a huge Ophelia. To hear these miserable groans was such immediate comfort to her, she sighed, "Thank God," as if now everything would be alright.

Frances walked slowly around the sofa, kicking a few magazines and an empty mug aside, and stood before the TV, facing Elaine.

Her head was resting on the yellow cushion, her hair draped wetly across her cheek. Her face looked like chilled, wet white clay. Frances stepped back, analysing this figure on the sofa, and bumped into the coffee table, toppling some glasses and a few books. Elaine opened her eyes and frowned in obvious discomfort, but whether it was pain or nausea or something else altogether, Frances could not tell. Just a general look of suffering. Frances cleared her throat, and said, "Are you okay?"

A raised eyebrow, a drunk-like wobble of the head: "Do I *look* okay?"

No, she did not look okay. She was still dressed in her running clothes, now drenched and smelling like algae. Her lips were white, her eyes rimmed with a pale, glistening purple. Her knees were drawn up to her chest. The polka dots on her backside looked fit to burst. Evidently, she had crashed.

"Where did you go?" Frances said. "You shot off like a greyhound. I called after you but you kept going, then I lost you. I've been very worried." This last statement was true. The relief to find Elaine here was so enormous it shocked her.

"I don't even know." Elaine winced as she spoke. "One minute I was feeling great, the next, I don't remember. It was like hitting the wall. A couple helped me out—they brought me here in their car. All I could do was lie on the back seat. I barely remember it. They wanted to take me to hospital, but I said no, I wanted to go home. They helped me up the stairs and brought me in here."

Frances glanced around at the mess of the flat and winced.

"They didn't want to leave me here alone," Elaine sighed. "They were so kind." Frances analysed Elaine's face, voice, body, trying to ascertain what had happened, what was happening. She was crashing now; soon she would be asleep. Then, Frances knew what she had to do, so she did it.

"Ohhh," she said soothingly. "Ohhh, oh, my poor baby."

It was now time for the acting to begin, no time for rehearsals or warm-up, straight to the performance, Act One, Scene One. Glass of water brought and placed within reach. Offers of blankets and baths, sleep? Elaine shook her head to all. Bed? She shook her head again, and Frances resisted the urge to fist-pump. Never before had Elaine refused the suggestion of bed.

"Poor baby," Frances cooed.

"Do I have a fever?" Elaine said, slapping her hand to her chest. "I feel like I must have. I'm burning up. I'm a thousand degrees. I'm barbequed. Feel me." Mustering all her resolve and trying not to look too closely, Frances put her hand to the clammy forehead. Elaine stayed slumped, her eyes turned upwards, as if looking beyond her eyebrows. She felt hot, Frances realised. She was sweating globules. Frances didn't know anything about fevers. She went and opened the windows.

"Your temperature is normal," she said, wiping her hand on her leg. "Looks like a tummy bug to me. It must have been something you ate," and it passed through her mind that this might in fact be the case. Elaine screwed her eyes in pain.

SHE STARTED TO DRIFT into a world of daydreams, eyes closing, floating off in between bouts of mumbling, grumbling, groaning, moaning. Knees drawn up and clung to, breathing loudly, periodically saying, "Ohhhhhh," in a deeply worried way, eyelids dropping closed for a moment or two before pinging open again. Every now and then she gripped her stomach and fell completely silent, holding her breath. Frances put an empty bucket beside her and stood there for a second, as if Elaine might oblige. She didn't know what else to do. It was all rather awful, and she wished for this phase to pass, for Elaine to sleep and the flat to be quiet. Occasionally Elaine would rise up onto an elbow and lean over, sweating and spitting into the bucket, her neck straining desperately, a worm-like vein visible beneath the red skin. As her head hovered there in mid-air, her hair straggling down into the bucket, she would spit and spit until patience or opportunity passed, then she'd flop back, breathing laboriously, dipping in and

out of consciousness. The yellow cushion had developed a darkened stain from her head. "It's so hot," she said, pulling at her
clothes, and Frances opened the windows wider. "It's so bright,"
she said, covering her eyes with her hands, and Frances closed the
curtains. By early evening the light and heat had intensified, like
the inside of a clay pot on a hot fire, the terracotta curtains enclos-
ing the room in a stuffy orange light. No breeze came in, and the
room began to smell of them both, a strong, sweet smell, like fruit
long forgotten, now fermenting. All external sounds were muffled
by humidity in the same way they are muffled by snow.

Elaine asked, in a slightly delirious way, for some medicine, the
words slurring off in the request. "Do we have any medshie . . ."
and Frances, genuinely interested, looked through their little
first-aid kit, through the plasters and safety pins and bottles of
antiseptic, as if she might stumble across a bottle marked ANTI-
DOTE. "Who ever actually uses any of this stuff?" she called, pulling out rolls of bandages, but Elaine didn't respond. Elaine was
responding less and less now, it seemed. A sign of progress, surely.
Failing to find anything of interest, Frances called out, "Nothing.
Nature will take its course, I'm sure. Do you want more water?"
Then she opened a bottle of beer and leant against the worktop,
sipping.

Elaine had slumped down on her back, her eyes closed, her
head slumped awkwardly to one side. Frances paused, beer in
hand, and a coldness swept from the crown of her head, down
through her face and body as she thought, *Oh my God. She's dead.*
She put the beer on the sideboard. Her pulse thudded in her ears.

She reached into the drawer by the sink and pulled out a wooden
spoon. Then, like a kid with a stick readying to poke a dead bird,
she slowly advanced. She'd read that human bodies excreted certain fluids when they died. She imagined poking Elaine's stom-

ach and a trail of brown stinking goo pooling out beneath her, or poking her neck and green slime spilling from her mouth. Her spoon-wielding arm was shaking. She watched closely for movement. Nothing. The splattered inside of the bucket came into view, a shallow, foamy puddle at its bottom. She held her breath and prodded Elaine gently in the arm with the utensil. Nothing. She whispered, "Elaine." Poking twice more, a little harder now, she reached out with her other hand to press at Elaine's throat, to feel for the jugular. She hesitated. What could be more horrifying than feeling for a pulse and not finding one? Suddenly you're not feeling for a pulse at all, you're just touching a corpse. Her fingers were a few inches away, then a few centimetres, and as she braced herself, the spoon fell from her hand and hit Elaine in the face, and she snorted awake. Frances leapt back with a startled yelp and Elaine peered questioningly up at her, then at the wooden spoon, which she threw on the floor, then rolled over and instantly fell back asleep.

Frances' expectation of liberation, freedom, joy, did not happen; instead she just felt cautiously relieved, as if the process had ended successfully. She stood staring at Elaine for several minutes, expecting her to stir. When she didn't, Frances got herself another beer, then, moving carefully, leant over and took Elaine's phone from her limp hand.

Because heartbreak causes trust issues that become so normalised they do not even feel like paranoia, but, rather, like an entitled sense of nosiness, Frances had been accustomed to looking through Elaine's phone for a while. It was usually either bland, boring exchanges with her parents or giggly girly drama with her friends. Frances slouched in the armchair, one foot up on the coffee table, a fresh beer wedged down the seat cushion beside her, and unlocked the phone, suddenly greeted with Elaine's screensaver. The pier, two months ago. Frances had drunkenly confessed that the seaside felt like home, and the next day Elaine insisted they go. They had sat on the beach and smoked a spliff before going on the rides, and afterwards Elaine had wanted chips and ice cream, eating both in alternate mouthfuls and giggling. The picture showed them grinning like a couple of idiots with vanilla ice cream around their mouths and the slate sea behind them. She had been happy that day, Frances had. She was always happy there, by the sea. To us all, there is a place on earth where our heart feels right. Same sky, same sun, same air, nothing re-markable or different or even beautiful, but a belonging our heart recognises and nods: "Here." For Frances, this was the place, so much so that she ached for it when she was awake and dreamt of it when she was asleep.

She scrolled idly through the phone and went into Album.

Her and her fucking family, Frances groaned inwardly. The bullshit pictures they sent, the bullshit pictures Elaine kept—there were reams of them. Frances felt like she had seen them all before, so samey they were; the only thing that changed was the seasons. Mummy and Daddy on a coastal trek in coats/shorts/waterproofs, beaming and holding their walking sticks out before them, proud beneath the cloud/sun/rain. Mummy and Daddy in the green/brown/bare garden, looking ruddied and muddied with a trowel in one hand and a glass/cup/mug in the other. And then, Mummy in the swimming pool, drenched in jewellery, laughing at the camera. A few tilted landscapes of the new fitted kitchen. Mummy on a horse, Daddy standing beside her. Frances remembered Elaine's words: "I have lots of money." She began to see the extent to which that statement was true. This was no four-bed semi. The more she flicked through the album, the more she realised that, actually, the house was more than just a house; it was a whole estate. She looked over at Elaine, a slumbering purse of comfort and security. The resemblance between Elaine and her parents was uncanny and unsettling, like she was a Frankenstein of her parents. The most recent pictures seemed to be her mother showing off a new dress. Standing before a mirror, lots of different angles of a flowery knee-length monstrosity. In the mirror's reflection, Frances could see their elaborate walnut furniture, Regency style, and open balcony doors leading to a terrace.

"They aren't rich," Elaine would often say. "They're just comfortable."

Yes, it must be very comfortable to have a swimming pool. So, this was why Elaine could earn a pittance working at a charity, and vote Green, and go on protests, and spend £150 on a shirt she knew with absolute certainty a child in China hadn't been forced to make, whilst scowling at Frances' bargain-bucket clothes. If it all went hideously wrong and her own efforts to improve the world left her broke, Mummy and Daddy would catch her fall. She had the luxury of being able to be good, rather than financially forced, like most were, to be a bit evil. People couldn't all afford to live by the morals they believed in. "You shouldn't buy that," Elaine would often say when Frances reached for the cheap coffee. "People have suffered and been exploited because of that. Don't support it."

"I'm not buying it because I support it. I'm buying it because I can't afford anything else."

"Then don't buy any. No coffee is better than cruel coffee."

"Then why do you drink it when you come round?"

Whilst Elaine lived at home she could afford the uncompromised coffee, but Frances had wondered how she would cope when half her salary was going towards rent. But presumably her parents gave her an allowance—how else could she afford it? Now, she could clearly see, Elaine would never have to make any of these sacrifices; she would never know how it felt to only buy second-hand clothes, to buy the bread full of chemicals and preservatives because it lasted longer, to drink the cruel coffee. Without her parents, Elaine's moral high ground would be sharply knocked down every time a bill came in. But she mustn't sneer; it was this wealth that was going to pay off Dom in two days' time, and it pleased her, in a way, looking at this prim lady in her floral dress, knowing their money was soon to go to a drug dealer.

Frances' own upbringing had been far narrower. Just her and her father, who worked himself to death by the time she was nineteen, absent in his efforts to keep a roof over their heads. A pride in her experiences hid an envy of others—her father missing meals so she could eat, her battered shoes worn through, hair cut with kitchen scissors. She bore it all with the firmness of having survived hardship, and viewed the wealthy as soft and a little underdeveloped of heart, as if all their fortune and money had protected them from emotional strife. They were, therefore, in her eyes, inferior and silly, for this reason. People like Elaine had never had to struggle, and so they found themselves in polar-opposite positions regarding money, where Frances counted the grocery bill to the penny, and Elaine handed her card over without checking or reading anything. This meant that, out of the two of them, Frances felt she was the one with her feet firmly on the ground, despite how prone hers were to floating off as if immune to gravity.

She picked up her beer with one hand and opened Messages

with the other. The latest conversation was with someone called Janine, a name Frances vaguely recalled as a workmate. She sipped and scrolled through the conversation.

E: THANKS FOR YOUR HELP THE OTHER DAY, BABES, YOU'RE A STAR.

J: NO WORRIES! GLAD I COULD HELP. IT'S BEAUTIFUL BTW, SHE'S GOING TO LOVE IT.

E: HOPE SO! BIT NERVOUS!

J: DON'T BE NERVOUS, JUST REMEMBER ME AS BRIDESMAID, OKAY? HAHA.

It was a strange moment for Frances. Here was her freshly drugged and deceived girlfriend, here was the phone containing this secret, and Frances was also the only person who knew everything. Part of her wanted to stand up and scream, "Are you mad? I can't fucking stand you!" But then, just as quickly, and with a sudden wash of relief, she realised it did not matter, she need never face the dreaded question, because Elaine would—for as long as necessary, she now concluded—be unable to ask her anything. And by the time she came around, the debt would be paid and her bags would be packed. There was no reason to panic. She switched the phone off and stuck it in her pocket.

7

WHEN ASKED, Frances would always say she met Adrienne by the bananas, and it was not an outright lie but certainly a tweaking of the truth: They did indeed meet in the fruit aisle of the Asian supermarket, and bananas were involved; however, it was not the first time Frances had seen her. She first saw her several weeks earlier, in the café. Frances had been wafting a sugar packet to and fro, watching customers, making assumptions about their lives based on a bag or book or the way they cleared their throat. She observed so many people in this bored way, it was unlikely anyone should stand out at all; they all blended together after a while, a homogenous repeated image of face and clothing, so when one walked in so full of familiarity and grace, it shocked her. And whilst the familiarity was real, it stemmed not from true recognition. It couldn't, because it was the face of a person she had never known, only pictured, imagined, much like an artist would. It was the fantasy-face of her make-believe mother.

A face dreamt-up in childhood and installed in the memory-gaps of years ago, where a real mother should have been. A mother who was always young and always beautiful, and here she was, standing before her like a reincarnation, a solid ghost, just as she had pictured her. She stared as the woman walked up to the counter and ordered a drink, then stood aside with her hand on her hip, looking around in the self-conscious way attractive people do when they are just being normal but know they are always being watched. She did not see Frances staring at her, perhaps because so many others were, but she was alert and aware of them all; the lovelies of the world sense eyes on them like the rest of us sense danger. Frances was concealed, however, having slid down in her chair behind an advert for bagels. The woman looked at her watch, then took her drink and abruptly walked out, done with that insignificant episode in her life, off to the next, unaware of any tsunamis she had made in the meantime. Frances sat up amidst a surge of incredulity, even anger: She could not just go, just like that, so easily, forever—it wasn't fair, it was unthinkable, it had not been enough—she must look at her, absorb her, analyse her. It was not quite love at first sight, rather an outraged feeling of being owed. All her life she had longed to see her mother's face and here it was, come and now gone in so hasty an instance. What could she do? There was only one option, in her opinion. She grabbed her coat and rushed out after her.

It was not like a movie; the woman's head was not bobbing away down the street through a throng of people, Frances did not have to give chase, it was not raining. No, she was just standing there outside the café, lighting a cigarette, and as such Frances fell through the door and collided into her. The woman didn't even notice; she smoked and talked on her phone, leaning against the café window. An unusual red coat, buttoned all the way up in military style and worn with long black boots, gave her a slightly kinky and intimidating appearance, beautifully contrasting with her soft, supple face. Frances stumbled over to the nearby bus stop, sat down, and watched. She knew, of course, that there was no way this could be her mother, but the fascination remained as attraction deepened, and Frances felt drawn to the woman out of not only familiarity but a pure neediness more mature individuals would recognise as lust. The way she moved, elegantly struggling with bags and phone and cigarette, her hands dancing between each item to steady it or shift it. The way she flicked her hair, then tucked it behind an ear when it fell across her face again. The way she stood, one boot across the other. The way she slid her little finger into her ear and quickly dug, uncaring that the world could see, because her ear was lovely, her finger perfection. It was difficult to tell if her phone call was a happy one; she certainly talked animatedly—frowning one moment, laughing the next—in a way Frances would come to know very well, creating the excitement of having to keep up with her when her words and moods could shift so wildly from one moment to the next.

"Tell him Adrienne called. And to stop being such a little cunt."

What a magical name, Frances thought dreamily. She knew little about her mother, but did know she had been called Anne. It did not take a huge feat of mental hocus-pocus to decide their meeting was fated, even if she must now force it to happen.

She watched as Adrienne hoisted her bag higher, her cigarette clasped in the corner of her mouth, coffee spilling slightly, unnoticed, phone wedged between ear and shoulder, and Frances knew there was an opening here, somehow, to go and help her. She imagined holding the cigarette to the woman's lips, silently standing beside her in a deferential act of servitude. She longed to do it. She looked down at her own clothing, her usual crumpled jeans and muddied boots, and felt the sort of compounded shame made all the worse for realising you should have felt it awhile. Her hands were dry and chapped from work, her hair needed washing. She did not usually care about such things, but suddenly she was angry at them, at her hands, at herself, for not being in a state of affable readiness. Then she watched as Adrienne shrugged her bag again, pocketed her phone, flicked the cigarette into the street, and walked off. Frances was left open-mouthed. It was like the story had abruptly ended, mid-plot. So, what could she do? She had little choice but to follow her.

It turned out that following someone required far less of the ducking behind trees and darting into bushes than Frances had imagined, in London, anyway: Stay back five paces and the crowd conceals you. It was worryingly easy, in fact. She decided to go only as far as the woman's next means of transport—assuming she must be heading for a bus or the tube—but it turned out she was going home, and lived just across the park, so Frances inadvertently followed her to her front door. She lived in a flat above an Asian supermarket, accessed through the sort of inconspicuous side door often overlooked, except when used as a place to plaster up trashy posters, or stumbled across as a late-night urinal. Frances stood on the opposite side of the street, gazing up at the window, as if about to serenade her. From this vantage point she was able to watch Adrienne walking back and forth in the flat, sometimes coming to look out of the window as she talked on her phone, an activity she seemed to do an awful lot. She had removed her coat and was wearing a flouncy cream blouse, which would look matronly and ugly on anybody else but on her looked chic. Frances stared for several minutes, knowing she should move on—she could hardly stand there all night—but then suddenly the window slid open and Adrienne appeared in a dressing gown. She perched on the ledge and lit a cigarette as she looked out blankly across the evening street. Frances lingered in a doorway, aware she was as unremarkable as all the faces she had seen come and go in the café, yet hoping—willing—that should Adrienne look down and their eyes meet, maybe then some magic might occur. The dressing gown was pale green with a dusky pink fringe and looked silk or satin, shimmering slightly like her lush brown hair, which had a smooth, ancient quality, as if inspired by a painting. In fact, everything about her seemed in some way artistic and other-worldly. Cars sounded their horns and shopkeepers shouted and engines snarled, frustrated in the traffic, but she sat sweetly on the window ledge and Frances gazed up, longing for a lute, full of daydreams and fairy tales. A bluetit with a belly like a butterball landed beside her like a little woodland creature come calling for Snow White. Frances thought of the countless times she'd smoked from her own window, imagined them sitting there together, talking and smoking. It was the face she had given to her mother, yet, come to life, it was seductive and kissable, and she yearned to be both fondled and tucked in bed by her, loved in every way possible. A bus slouched in the road between them and churned out black smoke. Passengers spilled out in every direction. Above, Adrienne was looking back into the room; she flicked the cigarette out and shut the window.

Frances had at least some small, rational part of her mind; it had occasionally spoken before, and she was aware of it. And yet now, when it was surely needed the most, it remained silent, choosing instead to look on as Frances darted through the traffic to the opposite kerb, where she had seen the cigarette land. The sane, rational part of her mind was perhaps amused to witness Frances bend down and pick up the cigarette, still alight, and it was perhaps surprised when she smelled it, and then surely horrified when she put it to her lips and took a drag. This one action seemed to tip her from harmless observer to unhinged stalker. She walked away smoking, calm now, then arrived home and put the finished end into the wooden box.

After this, she couldn't stop thinking about Adrienne. Her previous relationships had been little more than flings, dim sex after dim conversations in dim restaurants with dim people, she made all the more dim by it. It had suited her, and she had been stunned when some of these lovers wanted more, wanted commitment and future plans and holidays in little cottages with fireplaces and cows in the field next door. She had always fled at this point, extracted herself from the budding relationship amidst a confusing row—"What do you mean, Frances? What do you mean this isn't what you want? We've been screwing for two months now; what are you talking about?"—and gone back to her isolated world with equal relief and befuddlement. But this felt different. Suddenly, she was going to the supermarket whenever she could, sitting on a bench at a bus stop and waiting for her, for a glimpse, for her voice. And she was pleasantly invisible within the everchanging queue and crowd; only the shopkeepers might have noticed the girl who sat there every day, but they didn't, because they were busy with things that mattered. So here she waited, and simultaneously convinced herself she was building a plan, a moment of introduction, because they were fated. But it never happened, because she was too intimidated and too afraid to give fate the necessary helping hand it is always in need of.

As time wore on, she began to feel like she actually knew this lovely woman, as if observing her had taught her all she needed to know. She could see the way Adrienne talked to people, the casual way she smiled—as if it were a hobby, as if she just enjoyed doing it—and how other people smiled in return. They couldn't help it, and Frances could understand why; sometimes she would smile from across the street as it happened, like a contagious yawn. She was amazed the shopkeeper and other passersby on the street got anything done, weren't standing on the spot, entranced by her. Perhaps most enigmatic of all was the eye-locking absolute focus Adrienne gave to anyone before her, no matter who they were. She was the sort of person who would stop a stranger on the street just to say she liked their hat and suddenly she had a new best friend for life. The noise of the world around her was of no distraction when she was listening to the owner of the supermarket talk about his problems with his damaged shutters. It did not interrupt her concentration as she spoke with her friend in the street before they parted ways, telling her to be brave, to call anytime, to be safe. She was deaf to it each time she returned with the man with the moustache who she shared cigarettes and cans of lemonade with. Frances increasingly longed, with a growing envy, to be one of these fortunates, to know what it felt like to be held in her gaze, with all her senses homed in on you. The friend, hugged quickly, pecked on the cheek: The bitch didn't know how lucky she was, how lucky they all were, these people Adrienne spontaneously blessed, like a celebrity in an open-topped car flinging money out at the adoring crowd. If only Frances knew how to approach her, what to say. The memories of humiliations from long ago resurfaced to taunt her: the rejections of friendship as a child (and, as she saw it, as an adult), the sense of existing on the periphery, forced into spectatorship through lack of access to contact and acceptance. At work, one of the chefs had jabbed her in the ribs and said, "I think someone's getting lucky. Look at her, she's in a world of her own these days," and Frances had replied, laughing gently, that no, she was still single, but yes, okay, she did have her eye on someone. These days the fear was not just of a new rejection, but the resultant confirmation that all the past ones were real: A new "no" would not hurt because of its isolated sound but, like a slammed door, because of its echo. As such, she dithered, and smoked, and watched, and waited.

And so their meeting by the bananas was, as she told it, a coincidence of sorts, because she was still in the process of simply observing. She thought Adrienne had gone out for the day; it was a Saturday, and Adrienne would normally be seeing friends, having lunch, going shopping. Frances had, once or twice, followed along on these weekend excursions, lying to herself that she fancied a wander, trying to stroll as casually as possible, as if she just happened to be going in the same direction, and just happened to be getting the same tube, and just happened to be browsing crystal decanters she neither wanted nor could afford. But it was exhausting—Adrienne was tall and moved swiftly, with the agility such people are afforded as a sea of bewitched faces parts for them—and Frances was compelled to scurry along behind, dashing through closing doors and along busy pavements, looking like a Russian dancer with her arms folded to appear aloof, legs darting about all over the place, desperately trying to keep up. In the end she realised she took greater pleasure from staying by the flat and awaiting her, not only for the sense of occasion and sudden thrill of seeing her, but for the reassurance that she had safely returned, as if she were her own private doorman. It was neither sinister nor perverted, at least not in Frances' mind: no binoculars, no photos, no journals of her comings and goings, but merely a dedicated observation. And she began to assume that this was how their relationship (as she now saw it) would continue *ad infinitum*, and it just might be enough. It had brought a new layer to her life, it was a pastime people become a bit obsessed with, like yoga or martial arts. It didn't harm anybody and it brought her if not joy, exactly, a sense of purpose. But then there came this certain Saturday, when she thought Adrienne was gone, and she remembered her fruit bowl was empty, so she crossed the road and went into the supermarket. Standing there holding a pink grapefruit in one hand, vaguely wondering if she should also get some limes, she heard the security bell chime on the door and looked up to see Adrienne come striding in.

"Allie, my friend, how are you today?" she loudly greeted the man behind the counter, high-fiving him as she hurried to the fridge. "What do you think of these boots, eh? I got them yesterday."

"You look like a cowboy," he replied, laughing gently. "Were they a bargain? They look like it."

"Shut up, you cheeky bastard. And yes, half-price, Allie—you know me."

"A steal, lucky lady. One day you must come shopping with me. I need something important and I don't want to pay full price for it."

"What is it?"

"A house."

They laughed. Adrienne gathered in her arms some samosas, a bottle of lemonade, and a cereal bar. She carried them over to the counter, where she dumped them down, saying, "Marlboros as well, please, Allie. I'll quit again tomorrow."

"I will if you will."

And they laughed again, enjoying this obviously familiar routine. Adrienne flung a bag of peanuts on the pile of items and dug around in her purse then said, "Shit, hang on—Mum wanted some bananas."

Frances was still holding her grapefruit, gormlessly now, like a ball she didn't know how to throw. Facing up the aisle, she watched with the sense that a movie was coming to life as Adrienne strode towards her, coat billowing open like a cape, like she should be walking in slow-motion with an explosion behind her. They stood face to face or, rather, eye to collarbone, and Frances kept her gaze straight ahead, hoping to appear relaxed but inadvertently staring directly at a rather exposed chest. Adrienne leant in past her, saying, "Excuse me," and her hair tumbled onto Frances' bare arm. She knew she should step aside, she was in the way, but it was impossible, so she remained there, staring ahead, as two breasts swung into view down a low-cut top and the warmth from Adrienne's head gave off a waft of peaches. The sleeve of her coat brushed by and, without thinking, Frances placed her hand ever so lightly on it. It would have seemed accidental to Adrienne, had she noticed, but it was a habit Frances had in moments of wonder around another human, as if anchoring herself. It happened rarely, and never this strongly. It stopped her feeling like she might be ripped out of reality, reduced to particles. She wanted to cling on there, paused in time, but ordered herself to let go.

Adrienne stood up with two bananas in her hand. "You look weirdly familiar," she said, looking squarely down at Frances. With all the courage she could muster, Frances looked back up at her.

"Really?" she said. She felt like she could cry.

Adrienne looked at her. Frances braced herself for a terrible question—"Have you been following me? Didn't I see you at Hyde Park? Or was it the florist's? Or the Central Line?"—and felt her heart pound so hard she thought she might cough it up. Then, a smile broke upon Adrienne's face—her sternness had only been a joke—and she chuckled and said, "Maybe not. But I think you could." Then she raised an eyebrow and winked. She tapped her card at the counter, fist-bumped Allie, picked up her carrier bags, and walked out, glancing in through the window as she passed it and smiling a blessing at Frances as she waved with the fingers of her right hand.

It was an awful pickup line—if that was what it was—but beautiful people can get away with such things. Frances took her single grapefruit to the counter and put it down, dazed. The man smirked at her, amused by the exchange, because he knew Adrienne, he knew what she was like, he had seen such things before. "She flirts with everyone," he might have said. "Don't flatter yourself into thinking you're special." In times to come, Frances would witness it first-hand. Adrienne liked to flirt. To her it was just another way of bringing some sparkle and joy into people's lives; it never occurred to her that it might hurt someone. "It doesn't mean anything," she would say, and she meant it, but it didn't stop Frances being crippled by jealousy whenever she saw it and it didn't stop her falling for it now. She ambled out into the street, grapefruit in hand, and was about to step into the road when a voice above her said, "Oi," and she looked up to see Adrienne smiling down from her window. "You little perv. Catch."

She dropped a banana. On it was written her name and number. When Frances looked back up, the window was sliding closed.

It took her two days to muster the courage to call. To some this could have looked like playing hard to get, but Frances simply didn't have the balls. She dried out the banana skin and put it in her box, and she lay awake at night planning what she might say. In the end, she drank a bottle of Shiraz and called at midnight, afraid of waking her or making her angry but unable to resist any longer. She needn't have worried, Adrienne was out with her friends. Amidst the beat and racket of a nightclub they shouted down the phone at each other and Adrienne said it was nice to hear from her, and what was her name, and where did she live?

Within half an hour she was at Frances' door. She was drunk, but not like Frances, who sat and stared and smoked and couldn't think what to say. No, Adrienne was drunk like a poet, talking tirelessly, explaining what her friends were like, where they'd been, which ones she liked best and why.

"I was relieved you called, to be honest. We were in this dreadful club, some typically sex-charged place where everyone is either trying to get laid or is in the process of getting laid, many times in the toilets, by all accounts. Why do people do that—it's literally the most intimate act and you're going at it in the filthiest of all filthy places, a club cubicle. I don't want to sound like a snob or anything, but I don't know how these people can touch the surfaces around where people shit, then take each other's genitals into their mouths. I suppose some think it's sexy. Like glory-holes. People think those are sexy too. I don't really get it but maybe that's just because it's not my thing."

Frances didn't have a clue what to say to any of this so she just said, "Sorry I interrupted your night with your friends."

"Did you hear what I was saying? About the glory-holes?"

"Yes."

"Do you like them?"

"No."

"You've experienced them, then?"

"No!"

"No need to get defensive," she laughed. "And you didn't interrupt my night. I was bored anyway."

"What about your friends?"

"I was bored of them too."

She picked at her teeth as she spoke and poured herself more wine, waving the glass around, breaking the stem when she slammed it down to emphasise what she was saying. She wiped wine from her lower lip with thumb and forefinger, pinching it into an isolated pout, then stood up and sauntered over to Frances. Plucking the cigarette from Frances' trembling hand, she dragged on it, raising an eyebrow, taking her time inhaling and exhaling, enveloping them both in smoke.

"I saw you staring at my tits the other day," she said.

Frances, too afraid to make eye contact, stared hopelessly ahead at the breasts in question. *There they are again.* She sighed. Adrienne was wearing a small, thin purple dress, the sort some might consider nightwear. Curves of hips and breasts pressed against the flimsy material as if yearning to be unleashed. Just as Frances was about to speak—to offer more wine, to compliment her name; anything would do—Adrienne bent down and kissed her, and all thoughts exploded, crackled, then vanished, like a firework which leaves no trace, only a blank black sky. It was not like any other kiss Frances had ever known. It was not intrusive, it was not rough, it did not feel like some sort of dental examination; Adrienne's kisses were slow and warm and soft, their tongues not colliding but rubbing like two stamens brushing together. Adrienne stayed the night, and the night after that. And Frances did not tell her the truth.

"We met by the bananas," Adrienne would coolly say, because Frances never corrected her, and because Adrienne did not remember ever having seen her before.

IT WAS A TEDIOUS, hot, horrible night. Elaine had groaned awake at midnight, saying, "I need to go to bed." Frances thought, *At last.* She did not want Elaine taking up space on the sofa for days: Bed was where Elaine should go, and bed was where Elaine would remain, then Frances could shut the door and get on with her days. She hauled her up off the sofa, shoulder buffering up beneath Elaine's sticky armpit, and half carried, half dragged her into the bedroom. Elaine spoke quietly, as if still asleep, fractured and random words and murmurs. She fell heavily onto the bed and rolled onto her side. "Bucket?" she said, flapping an arm in the air. Frances brought it through and put it beside the bed. Elaine's eyes remained closed as she mumbled, "Thank you."

The thought of sleeping beside her made Frances feel quite queasy herself. The sight of Elaine on the sofa, when she had thought she was dead, had left an unshakeable fear: What if she awoke to find a cold, stiff corpse beside her? "I think I'll sleep on the sofa," she said, mainly to herself, but Elaine whined in protest, semiconscious, and said, "Nooooo, whadifeye nee oo?" so Frances had reluctantly removed her clothes, except her T-shirt, and climbed under the bedsheets. She was sweating, but did not want to risk contact with that sickly, clammy body. Elaine was snoring within seconds. Frances spent most of the night listening with bated breath every time there was a pause. Elaine jolted in and out of sleep throughout the night, bursting awake at random before sinking heavily back into twitchy dreams. At three o'clock, Frances crept out of bed and moved to the sofa, satisfied that Elaine would last the night, and she watched the light change in the room, trying to sleep but also trying not to, just lying there, thinking. She heard every distant voice on the street, every thump from the flat above, every snore from the bedroom. At seven o'clock she made a pot of tea and smoked a joint, hoping to get some sleep, but completely unable to.

THE STREET DOWN BELOW was aglow in the full unhindered sun, and Friday traffic clogged the road as people tried to hurry, to get on, to get to the pub, to get home. It was lunchtime and the table and chairs outside the cafés were all busy, the pubs surrounded by patrons who spilled into the road and irritated the drivers. Elaine was still in bed. She had drifted in and out, and once shouted for help, to get to the bathroom. Frances was horrified to realise she needed assistance in there; it reminded her of care homes and frailty and weakness. Afterwards, Elaine had mumbled loving thanks, then crashed out again. Now, Frances sat smoking on the window ledge, wondering what would happen if Elaine awoke completely, if she should drop some more of the drug into her sleeping mouth, but then it might be too much—she might slip into a coma. It had not been simple up 'til now; it was not like stasis, and she knew the dosage must have been wrong, and it was very difficult to tell what were side effects and what were to be expected—it had all been bizarre and unexpected so far. But it was undeniably nice to now be in the quiet: untouched, undisturbed, alone. Then, gazing lazily down, she noticed the top of an enormous bright red sunhat whizzing its way down between the masses like a Frisbee. Frances watched, exhaling, absently wondering where such a hat could be going. She wondered more as it sidestepped the crowd and headed off, on a tangent, in the direction of the downstairs entrance. Peering over, ash dwindling down and away, she saw the man who lived upstairs hold the door open as he left, and the hat disappeared into the building. *Curious,* she thought. *We don't see hats like that around here much.* It looked better suited to Royal Ascot. Then, a few minutes later, she jumped as there came a knock at the door. A very loud *rat-a-tat-tat.*

Looking through the spyhole, she saw a pair of fiercely painted lips, perfectly matching the scarlet shield above. "Hello?" she said through the door. "Who is it?"

A voice replied: "Oh, hello. It's Mrs. Langthorn. Elaine's mother." Frances stepped back, as if the door were lying to her. "You must be Frances, I presume?" the voice enquired.

Just as Frances was about to lie—the wrong address, Elaine's not in, I've never even heard of her—another voice, from the bedroom this time, feebly called out, "Mummy?"

It was a difficult situation. If she let this woman in, who could tell what might happen, what she might say, what she might suspect. But if she turned her away, she'd have Elaine to deal with, she would have to explain. Besides, she doubted this lady in her bold colours and Head Mistress voice was going to be easily fobbed off. She seemed the type who might bang louder still, bellowing her daughter's name, demanding to be let in. Full of reluctance, Frances unlocked the door. The woman's mouth smiled. Her eyes did not.

"Hello," she said curtly. "I'm sorry we haven't met before but my daughter is frightfully protective of you." She looked Frances up and down. "My, my. Not at all what I expected!" And she feigned a laugh, then pressed her hand to her chest. "I'm Jennifer."

She was wearing glossy white gloves. Frances had never seen such gloves. Gloves were sensible things made of wool, surely. These were satin; it was like shaking hands with a doll. "Hope you don't mind me just dropping by," she continued, breezing in, "but I was in the neighbourhood doing some shopping and thought I might as well see if you were in, as my daughter clearly has no intention of arranging a formal introduction this side of Christmas," and she hhar-hhhar-hhharred again, in an imitation of laughter, as if she had heard laughter somewhere once and had been rehearsing it ever since.

Frances did not like the way this woman kept referring to Elaine as "my daughter"; it caused a sudden surge of ownership to rise in her and she silently swore to refer to Elaine as "my girlfriend." She closed the door. She also did not like the way the woman now stood in the hallway with elbows drawn tightly in as she clung to her handbag, as if danger lurked in every corner. And she especially didn't like the way she was dressed.

Jennifer Langthorn wore the sort of heels proper ladies wear. Too high or too thin and you were common, too low or too fat and you were unfeminine. Hers were the type that click-click-clicked in a sharp, immaculate way, as if every step were to scold the dirty pavement. Her legs, two squat stumps of eighty denier, were certainly shapely, but disproportionally so, as if some stuffing from her breasts had slid down inside her body and deposited itself around the calves and ankles. She wore a blue dress, stretched tight across the hips, suffocating a blue-and-red-striped blouse, tucked in at the waist, where a red leather belt was attempting to hold back a tide of spillage. She opened the handbag and produced a tiny mirror with which she proceeded to analyse her face as Frances watched on, her own face struggling to find and form the correct expression, whatever that might be.

"Nice to meet you," she eventually said, and Mrs. Langthorn snapped the little object closed and placed it carefully back in her bag.

"So, this is where my angel lives now, is it?" she said, looking around as if the hall were all that existed, like they curled up asleep at night on the doormat. "I can't say I'm surprised. She's always been a bit wild and rebellious, and I've been telling Lewis—Elaine's father—for years that one day she'd go roughing it. She was going help the Africans, you know. That's what she's been saying for years. Personally, I'd rather she stayed here, where she's safe. Well, when I say here . . ." and her words trailed off as her eyes looked fearfully at Frances' grubby shoes on newspaper by the front door. Clearly she was wondering if Elaine should have gone to help Africa after all. Then she turned on her heel and marched in the direction of the living room, visibly curling her nose up against the smell, wafting her gloved hand in front of her face and clutching her bag even tighter against the likelihood of thieves and ruffians. Frances wasn't blind—she knew the flat was a mess. Boxes were still piled up, some open, with their contents spilling out. She also knew it stank of sickness and stuffiness and sleep. She had grown used to it. She resisted the urge to explain, to say, "Most of this is thanks to your daughter." Had the woman been politer she might have fussed about, straightening the throws on the sofa, stacking the magazines, inviting her to sit down. Instead she hoped the woman would trip, stumble exaggeratedly and hilariously across the room, and land head-first in the wastepaper basket currently overflowing with her daughter's bile-encrusted tissues. But it seemed unlikely; the woman looked too affronted to move.

It always intrigued Frances that the wealthiest people, who had the most reason to be accustomed to dealing with those worse off than themselves (because, in almost every situation, they were better off than everyone), should be so ill at ease when amongst the common man. It was as if they lived a fantasy life straight from the pages of one of those haughty magazines, *The Lady*, or *Horse & Hound*. As if the only normal people they came into contact with were their staff. As if they didn't realise they made up but a small percentage of the population and the vast majority had significantly less than them, and they should perhaps adjust downwards when meeting them, rather than expecting people to adjust up. Frances didn't realise that Mrs. Langthorn had already, in fact, adjusted considerably downwards by even coming to this part of London. The problem was that, from those streets, to these flats, to this living room, with its offensive odour and empty beer bottles, Mrs. Langthorn wasn't sure how much more downwards there could possibly be left to go. The many thin and overlapping layers of social class completely passed her by because, in her world, there were simply the wealthy, and then everyone else. As far as she was concerned, the next step down from this flat must surely be homelessness. I mean, where else was there left? Had she known that Frances had built herself up from house shares and rented bedsits, and more house shares, eating noodles in hot water, adding penny by penny to her meagre inheritance until she could afford the down payment on this flat, she would have better understood, albeit only in a simple mathematical way, because she would have no comprehension of the emotions and efforts involved.

She removed her hat, and a mushroom of grey hair sprang up in its place. She held the hat in one hand and with the other stroked it lovingly, like it was a cat, reminding Frances of Elaine smoothing her cashmere cardigans. Perhaps it was a sign of class to stroke one's clothes. Deciding not to take Frances' proffered hand, Jennifer strode over to the kitchenette and placed the hat and handbag firstly on the counter, then changed her mind and put them neatly together on top of the microwave, noticing with a long look of undisguised disgust the thin layer of grime glued there. Her lip curled and her mouth turned down at the corners. She brushed her hands together. Frances wanted to say, "It's not normally like this," but resented the compulsion to explain herself to this overbearing snob.

"Shall I take your gloves for you?" she asked with a sigh and a great big smile.

"No, thank you. I think I'd rather keep them on." She interlaced her fingers. "Where is my daughter?"

"Mummy?" came a timid call from the bedroom. "Is that you?"

Mrs. Langthorn shot Frances a look of fire and rage, as if her daughter had been intentionally hidden away from her, and with a waft of perfume she brushed past, tottering loudly into the bedroom, crying, "Elaine? Oh, my angel! Oh! What has happened to you?"

Elaine had rolled onto her back and was looking over from her pillow, eyes barely open, forehead white and wet. The room was still in the chaos created by Elaine's hunt for running gear. Jennifer Langthorn proceeded carefully, clutching her skirt, placing her feet with exaggerated care as she stepped between piles of clothing, as if snakes might appear from amongst them. Elaine flung a hand out across the bed, reaching for her mother. Her mother reached back. It was like an enactment of *The Creation of Adam*. Frances stood in the doorway and watched.

"Food poisoning, Mummy."

"Oh, my goodness, you poor, poor thing. Come here, let me look at you—I had no idea." Another glance at Frances. "My poor darling, you look dreadful." She took Elaine's hand in hers and patted it.

Elaine's eyes dropped closed and she sighed, "I can't believe you're here."

"Well, I know you said we'd meet in a few weeks but I had a hunch, darling. I knew something was wrong, I could sense it. Mother's intuition, sweetheart. That's what it was."

"Really?" Frances chimed in. "But you said you were shopping in the neighbourhood and just decided to drop by."

Not a glance this time but a glare.

"Mummy and I have always had a special bond." Elaine smiled wanly.

Her mother nodded and patted her hand, as if to say, "It's true, it's true."

"I'll put the kettle on, shall I?" Frances turned and left them to it.

She empathised with the kettle as it fumed and boiled away. She could hear their conversation: The damn woman actually had the gall to come in here and blame her. As she was getting the teabags, she had heard her mutter, "The place is filthy, darling. No wonder you're ill, living in such squalor," and Frances clung on to a cook-book, wanting to slap her powder-puffed face with it, imagining a poof of make-up, like striking a dusty cushion. Frances knew she was to blame for Elaine's situation—she wasn't completely deluded, after all—but to suggest it was due to uncleanliness— an uncleanliness largely caused by Elaine—enraged Frances: She had always been, in her own way, rather house-proud and organ-ised. She put mugs, milk, and sugar together on a little wooden tray and stuck the teapot under the hot tap to warm it. She had some Victorian cups and saucers with pretty painted handles which she kept in the sideboard, but thought, *Fuck her;* it would be more fun to see how she handled a *Finding Nemo* mug. She leant back and overheard, "If I had come in the car I could have packed a bag and taken you back with me, my poor love. Why didn't you tell me you were ill? You look dreadful, darling. Had I known, I never would have come on the tube." She did not pro-nounce *tube* like everyone else. Frances smiled. Everyone else said "chube." This woman clipped the *t* and accentuated the *u.* "Te-uuuuube." For a moment Frances imagined her there, wedged between armpits, squirting perfume around her and putting on a nose-clip, the handbag strangled beneath ten white knuckles. As the kettle boiled and she made the tea, she realised she was doubly furious that Elaine had not defended her, not explained that it was her ton of junk that had filled the flat, it was her smell, her mess, all *her.* The way the mother spoke, as if Frances had been holding her precious daughter hostage, was almost amusing. Frances stirred the bags in the teapot. She just needed to get this woman out of her flat.

In the bedroom, she placed the tray on top of the dresser. Mrs. Langthorn did not acknowledge her entering the room. *Already relegated to staff,* Frances thought. She took the lid off the teapot and spun the bags around with a spoon, squeezing as much strength out of them as quickly as possible.

Mrs. Langthorn was perched on the bed now, patting her daughter's knee. Elaine had hunched herself into an almost upright position, rubbing her stomach in a circular motion as if she were pregnant. Mrs. Langthorn was right about one thing: Elaine did look awful. With the curtain closed, the dim light seemed to have faded her: Shadows crept into her diluted body, she peeped out from two small caves around her eyes, her face drawn and sallow. The dips behind her collarbones seemed more pronounced than ever, like the insides of two boats. She was practically black-and-white. Despite this, the resemblance to her mother was uncanny, especially as Frances looked over at them, both in profile: same nose, same chin, same brow. In a flash Frances had a glimpse— almost a threatening premonition—of a possible future: a proposal, a wedding, moving to a bigger house, Frances constantly working and bringing home the bacon, Elaine readjusting to the finer things in life until one day there's her wife in proper lady's heels and a matching sunhat, waving a gloved hand and saying, "Sweetheart, how was work? Do come and see how I've arranged the new garden furniture . . ."

"I said no sugar for me, dear."

Frances blinked. The woman was talking to her. She had clearly said this a number of times because she now turned back to her daughter with raised eyebrows as if to say, "You've picked a right one there." Frances poured the tea and handed Mrs. Langthorn the *Finding Nemo* mug. Elaine's mother turned it round in her hands several times, looking at it like it was a foreign object, then placed it on the windowsill. Elaine smiled wanly and shook her head no when Frances pointed to the teapot. This performance of Elaine's didn't seem real, somehow, like she was being ever so brave just to show her mother how ill and helpless she was. Frances poured herself a drink with lots of sugar, then sat on the opposite side of the bed.

"It was so strange, Mummy. I was fine one minute, then gone the next. Wasn't I, baby?"

Frances blew on her tea.

"I felt so ill."

"How are you feeling now, angel?"

"Like I don't know where I've been. I feel wiped out. Thank God I had Frances to look after me. I'm sorry you two had to meet like this. I'd rather hoped we'd go for a meal or something."

Frances was about to say, "Don't be silly—you're ill," when Mrs. Langthorn patted Elaine's knee again and said loudly, "Don't be silly, darling—you're ill! There's nothing to be sorry about. I only wish I had known, dear. I would have come sooner."

The passive-aggressive accusations were flying in full force around the flat today. Frances sighed deeply and looked away.

"We can always go out for a meal another time, when I'm better," Elaine said.

Frances drank her tea and Mrs. Langthorn said nothing. Then she cooed, "Don't you worry about that for now, dear. Let's just get you well again. Now, do you have everything you need? Is there anything I can get you? Do you have medicine, and vitamins, and rehydration sachets? Painkillers?"

Elaine smiled lovingly over at Frances and said, "Don't worry,

Mummy—she's taking good care of me," and Frances smiled an honest smile back, enjoying if not the sentiment, the victory. She knew that mothers like Mrs. Langthorn hated being usurped by anyone, especially another woman. She was also relieved to the point of gratitude that Elaine hadn't said anything that might make the woman want to stay any longer than absolutely necessary. To the contrary, she said, "I must go back to sleep soon. I'm so exhausted."

"Yes, yes, of course. But I do worry about you, darling," the woman suddenly said, reaching forwards and brushing Elaine's hair from her face. "And I don't mean just now. I worry about you all the time. We love you so much, you know, your father and I. He's going to be worried sick when he hears what a state you're in. He'll be furious with himself that he didn't come with me, in the Bentley. Not that it would have been easy. What on earth do you do for parking if you live in a flat?"

Frances coughed.

"I'll be fine," Elaine said, smiling her small, stoic smile. Then, as Frances watched on, Elaine tilted her head so that it rested in her mother's cupped hand, and they gazed lovingly at each other.

Perhaps it was having no mother of her own to gaze upon, perhaps it was just the disdain she held for these women, or perhaps it was simply that such lovey-dovey expressions always made her uncomfortable, but Frances felt a sort of horror as these two stared back at each other in a moment's mutual adoration. There was also another feeling. Envy? Ludicrous: She'd rather no mother at all than a mother like Mrs. Langthorn. But it was difficult to witness nevertheless, such parental, maternal love, and her standing yet again on the sidelines. She slurped her tea, hoping to disturb them, but all it seemed to do was encourage a gentle stroke of the cheek. This was too much. It looked intimate, almost inappropriate, indecent, practically incestuous, as if they were moments away from a kiss. Between them, she could see the *Finding Nemo* mug. "Don't let your tea go cold," she said loudly, and they parted, slowly, as if sad that the moment was over. The mother's hand returned to patting her daughter's knee.

Frances found it slightly unsettling how willing Elaine was to submit to being petted by her mother. How much of it was genuine, due to illness and weakness, and how much was a sort of affectation, she couldn't tell. Children, no matter how old, fall into the old roles when they are around their parents. She had witnessed it many times, especially with her ex-girlfriends. The person you know as a sharp, funny, intelligent adult suddenly becomes a sullen toddler whining about what's unfair, and old woes from ten years ago are randomly brought to the surface, as if these resentments are never gotten over. She imagined it was exactly like this when Elaine was seven years old, sat up in a frilly pink bed in a frilly pink bedroom, her mummy beside her, reading her a fairy tale and stroking her face. Any lingering respect she felt for Elaine was falling rapidly under threat as she watched the woman pull out a handkerchief and begin to dab Elaine's brow. Worse yet, Elaine closed her eyes and said, "Thank you, Mummy." It made Frances want to wrench open Elaine's box of horrors and start flinging out sex toys, waggle the wet-end of the LoveStud in her face and scream, "This! This is your daughter, you moron!" Edwin the Furby's two big white eyes stared out into the room as Elaine closed hers and allowed her forehead to be stroked.

Mercifully, Mrs. Langthorn didn't stay much longer. A few minutes later, after a whispered conversation Frances couldn't hear no matter how low she turned the television, Mrs. Langthorn reappeared, smoothing her dress down and fiddling with her blouse as if the flat itself had crumpled her. "She's asleep," she said to Frances, and walked over to her hat and handbag. Frances had been thumbing through the cookbook she'd previously considered as a weapon. It was hers, but Adrienne had used it often, flour and crumbs remaining on the page of her favourite bread recipe. Frances ran her finger idly about in them. The corner had been turned down for so long that the book fell open on it, as if expecting Adrienne, as if everything welcomed her and wanted her back, even inanimate objects. "Going to do some baking?" the woman asked, suddenly remembering some manners. Frances, however, was well past the point of polite conversation and just wanted the woman gone, hopefully forever. The awful thought occurred to her that, if this all went wrong, the next time she saw her might be at Elaine's funeral. She could see it now: the pearls, the hat, the same handkerchief dabbing beneath an eye, and the scowl she would throw at Frances then. "I shall never forgive myself," she would sob. "If only I hadn't taken the te-uuube."

"No. I'm just browsing," Frances said, and slammed the book closed. Mrs. Langthorn pulled on her hat and opened her handbag. She looked through the contents, as if checking it was all there. Then she pulled out a slip of a card, clicked the bag closed, and said, "Look. I'll be honest with you: I am very worried about her. She could barely keep her eyes open. I think the poor girl was even slurring as she dropped off. Could you do me the tiniest favour? Ring the doctor tomorrow. I didn't want to say in front of Elaine—it might have frightened her. Here's my card." She held it out. "Keep me informed, will you? I don't want the next phone call I get to be one telling me my only child has died."

Frances took the card and said, "Okay, no worries. It's only a touch of food poisoning, you know. I am taking care of her." This last sentence sounded fake, even to her own ears. Mrs. Langthorn smiled thinly.

"Promise me you'll call the doctor. We have a private one, an old family friend, let me give you his number." She produced a slim gold pen from the pocket of her handbag, wrote on the back of the card, and held it out to Frances. Frances read it, then said, "Thanks."

"Promise me."

"Yes, I promise I'll call the doctor," she huffed, and for a moment they looked at each other, as if refraining from squaring up for a fight. "Lovely to meet you. I'll see you to the door," Frances said.

She watched from the window, lighting a cigarette, as the enormous red hat appeared on the street outside. She saw the woman reach into her bag and hold a phone to her ear, then totter off in the direction of the tube station, hurriedly, as if being chased.

"I'm sorry if she gave you a hard time," Elaine mumbled, half-asleep and slightly delirious now, sweating huge blobs that slithered down her face and forehead. "She's not mean, really. Once you get to know her, you'll see. You'll love her. She'll love you. You'll love me. That's all that matters, really."

"Shhhh," Frances said. "Drink this—it'll help you sleep."

"What is it?"

"Sleepy time now."

"She's something else, though, isn't she," Elaine said between sips. "They don't make them like my mummy anymore, that's for sure."

"Shhhh," Frances said, setting the empty glass down.

"Why'd you give her that mug?"

It was still there, on the windowsill, full of tepid tea. Frances picked it up and ran her fingernail down a crack that sliced Dory's face in half.

"I don't like mothers," she said.

Elaine was asleep.

8

If only elaine had obeyed the rules that govern rebounds, none of this would have happened. If she had only acknowledged and accepted that this fling with Frances was not destined to be anything more than a brief sexual pastime—a hobby, of sorts—then she could have prevented it all from occurring. Frances might even have wanted her more, might have given chase, might have found Elaine tantalising and enigmatic, might even have grown to love her (impossible though it now seemed). But as it was, Elaine had buggered it all up by believing she was not just another rebound. You see, Elaine made the catastrophic error of believing she was different, believing she was special.

It had taken Frances some time to realise herself that the people she was with after Adrienne were rebounds. To begin with, and despite all evidence to the contrary, she assumed she was simply getting laid, scratching an itch, and thought nothing more of it. In the midst of the flatness there was some relief to be found in drunkenly staggering home with some new lovely and spending a night having very fast, rather clumsy sex. It was not genuine passion—it was scarcely even genuine attraction—but that didn't matter; to fashion a temporary lustfulness, to go through the motions of tugging off clothes and kissing cidered lips, was enough to help her cope, to feel awake again, and like there was an end in sight, even if it lasted only a few short hours. To feel another person's desire, to be sought and found in the dark, to hear the words *I want you*, and imagine it might be Adrienne. Even, for a short time in the mornings, having someone there to make coffee with, to have sex with again, perhaps, just once more. True, she hated the awkward talk on the sofa, nursing hangovers, looking at each other with clear eyes, bleary memories, and a beery taste in the mouth. True, she always swiftly felt the need to be alone again. And certainly, it did not take long to feel the guilt of having betrayed the person she loved, even if that person didn't want her. But it had temporarily brought the world back into colour again.

And most of these people could read the signs: The fact that Frances talked openly about Adrienne all the time, the fact that there was still a photograph of her on the sideboard in the hallway, the fact that Frances would sometimes grow exasperated during sex because they weren't "doing it right," all pointed to a broken person trying to feel less broken. These people would drink the coffee and endure the small talk, then obediently be on their way, and Frances would close the door behind them, and return to the silence of the flat. Deep within herself came a niggling sense that this was not working. It was either self-pity or self-destruction, she could not tell which, quite possibly both. All she knew was that she washed the sheets and cleaned up the coffee cups as swiftly as possible, and didn't try too hard to peer back into the fumblings of the night before.

She's being fucked by someone came the constant, taunting

thought, which propelled her and compelled this behaviour. As if in some sort of competition, she sought out the next person, and the next, and the next. She did as much as she could with each one, as much as they and their drunkenness would allow. She push, push, pushed those boundaries into and beyond what Adrienne would have consented to, as if saying to her, *You weren't so good, you weren't so desirable, compared to this you were a prude, even if now you act like a slut.* It was vengeful behaviour because, even if Adrienne never knew it, each passing lover was given Adrienne's face, her voice, her expression. Mutating through the slobbery wilderness of the bedsheets Frances would try to imagine it was Adrienne all the while. It made her feel both better and worse. She would sometimes fantasise, midway, that Adrienne knocked on the door, and Frances would have the victory of standing there, drunk and dishevelled, her hair a tangled cliché, looking at her defiantly as a voice from the bedroom called, "Come back to bed." She would imagine the look on Adrienne's face—hurt, angered, *jealous*—and then the fantasy took many different turns. Sometimes Frances slammed the door. Sometimes they cried and embraced. Sometimes Adrienne burst furiously into the bedroom and hauled the naked individual out, violently taking Frances back, kissing her, demanding her, claiming her. And, only once, she joined in. But Frances enjoyed that a lot less than she had imagined.

And this was how it had begun with Elaine. It was the end of a particularly bad day. Frances had discovered a T-shirt of Adrienne's at the back of a drawer. She had removed her clothes, pulled the T-shirt on, and spent a long and rather pathetic hour lying on the sofa, looking down at it, trying to remember where it had come from. She was still wearing it several hours later when she walked into The Swan and ordered a Jägerbomb.

She had only planned to get drunk enough to sleep. The pub was closing in half an hour, so she downed the first two before even paying. She propped herself up on a stool, cupped the glass with both hands, and stared in the mirror behind the bar.

It was a dive. She and Adrienne would never have come to a place like this. Adrienne liked wine bars, the sort of places that suggest what to drink with your meal and have cotton hand towels in the bathrooms. Adrienne liked to spoil her in these places, knowing Frances couldn't afford them, behaviour which Frances always saw as generosity because she was too smitten to see it as control. Frances watched in the mirror as a group of lads thwacked balls around a pool table, jostling one another, nudging, laughing, pints lined up along a nearby table. It was not the sort of place they would have visited, no, but it was perfect for her to drink in alone, undisturbed. Easily achieved: Frances was always undisturbed. Pleasant enough to look at—pretty, even, when she bothered to care—but her demeanour was defensive. Years of failure at talking to strangers had left her with a habit of hunching her shoulders away from crowds and staring at posters, TV screens, or menus with an intensity which screamed "Fuck off," to the world. Previous hook-ups had occurred only because she'd been drunk enough to interact with people, had managed to put on an act of bravado and humour, had even made jokes. Sober, Frances rarely spoke to strangers. It was as if the stranger-danger fear had never quite left her and, indeed, she felt small and childish most of the time.

But vulnerability is beautiful. All that we place value in is vulnerable, be it youth, nature, love, health, or wealth. Some people are drawn to vulnerability as protectors, others as destroyers, all depending on whether they seek to preserve or exploit. Frances, with her tiny, frigid eyes staring out defiantly—daringly—as if sticking a finger up to the world, blatantly concealed a fear which attracted these sorts. It was only through sheer luck and coincidence that she had mainly encountered nice people in life. And those who had not been nice had been clever at hiding it, so she did not realise she was being used or manipulated, such is the power of charm and beauty.

When Frances walked in, it was this vulnerability Elaine saw. She could not have said so, because she was not aware of it, but that was what it was.

She had been sat at a table with two friends, in such a dark and distant corner that Frances had not seen her, had not seemed to see anyone, just walked straight to the bar. But Elaine noticed Frances like she had walked in on fire.

Elaine had never believed in love at first sight but, like most people, she secretly longed to be proved wrong. Elaine's love life had been complicated in a rather repetitive and effortless way, always with the same sorts of people, always dwindling into friendship, no lasting passion for each other, no desire for commitment. She had begun to think this was how it was and always would be. What a shock it must have been then, to see the door swing open and in walk this fragile yet bolshy-looking creature, swaggering her tiny hips, hopping like a sparrow onto a seat at the bar.

"What are you looking at?" her friends asked, following her gaze.

Elaine had never felt like this about a woman before. Hell, Elaine had never felt like this about anyone. It shocked her, the sudden irresistible need to go up, to introduce herself, to hear her speak. It wasn't as if she were blinkered; she knew the girl looked sullen, she knew the body language said "Fuck off," and she knew her friends were laughing at her because this was sudden and strange and very unlike Elaine, who always chose nice, safe, sensible men. Her most recent ex was Harry. He was a paramedic, for heaven's sake. But they were her friends, and they were a bit drunk, so they not only humoured her but encouraged her when she said, "I'm going to get a drink."

"Oooh, go on, then!" they goaded loudly.

Frances was on her fourth Jägerbomb and was beginning to feel it. She barely noticed the woman standing beside her. Nor did she immediately realise the woman's proximity, that she was practically sliding onto her lap. Frances looked down along the bar. It was empty.

"Excuse me," she said, nudging with her elbow. "Would you mind moving the fuck down a bit?"

And so they met. Elaine apologised in mock surprise; she hadn't noticed, "Do let me buy you a drink," and so whether Frances liked it or not, Elaine took the seat beside her. She introduced herself, and pointed out her friends, who waved over wildly as if Frances were a celebrity, then began prattling on about her work, her family, her friends, the usual. Frances wasn't sure at what point she realised this woman was hitting on her, but it took a while. When Elaine touched Frances' shoulder, leaning in to whisper some secret or other, Frances wasn't listening. She was by now drunk and aware enough of what was happening, and it suddenly became acceptable to leer at Elaine's breasts. She was braless beneath her white shirt and Frances stared at the hazy shadows of two new and mysterious nipples. She reached out and touched Elaine's sleeve to steady herself, physically more than emotionally this time; there was no sense of being wrenched from reality other than the feeling of drunkenness. Seated as they were, she did not even notice the gargantuan size of this person. It was, in fact, only as they stood to leave together, that Frances looked up and observed, "Jesus, you're enormous," and Elaine laughed, stroked Frances' hair, and said, "That depends what angle you're looking from," and, bam, first kiss, then off they stumbled together, as Frances had stumbled many times before.

It was the most sex she had ever had in one night, so much sex that, at several points, her heart seemed to spasm and she genuinely feared a heart attack. She awoke the following morning sore in some places, slick in others, with a head that felt like she'd befallen some terrible accident. She sat on the edge of the bed for some time, clinging on as if it were a rocking boat, trying not to throw up. Behind her the naked woman slept, snoring in the way that would become so familiar. Frances followed a trail of clothes, as if she were Hansel or Gretel, picking them up one by one until she reached the front door. There, she found shoes and a bag that were not her own. She pulled out the wallet and read the driver's licence. At least now she knew her name. She made coffee, drank water, and turned on the television, but Elaine slept on and Frances felt it would be rude to wake her; it would be like saying, "Come on, time to get out." She looked at the photo of Adrienne. In a sudden moment of panic she rushed about looking for the T-shirt she'd worn the night before, eventually finding it at the foot of the bed, slightly torn down one side. A vague memory returned: "Hey, be careful—this shirt is important," followed by a sharp ripping sound. Now here it was, and Elaine had ruined it.

Depression was so much worse when you regretted drinking and regretted what you'd done whilst drunk. As she sat on the sofa she began to realise there was some small comfort, for the time being, knowing this woman was in her bed, as if it would be enough just to have her there, unconscious, so she wasn't completely alone. Wobbly, half-remembered images came back to her from the night before. Not so much the physical responses and activities, but Elaine's voice, her wide eyes, her mouth as she asked for more, what she wanted to do, how good it felt, how she'd never experienced anything like it. Her giggles, her dirty words, her delight in this sudden newness, exploring Frances not just as herself, individually, but as Woman, the first female body Elaine had slept with. And the hunger that emanated from her, as if Frances were a meal laid out for her enjoyment; Frances had never felt so utterly devoured. It was both disturbing and intensely arousing.

At midday Elaine was still asleep and Frances grew tired of waiting, so she took a shower. Soaped and rinsed, she was standing, as she always did, with the jets on her face, her eyes closed, trying to keep her mind blank, just feeling the water, when the shower door opened behind her and a voice whispered, "Good morning, beautiful." Hands slid under her arms, around her waist, hugging her tightly. Fragile Frances, captured by a giant: She hung there, limbs dangling forwards like a cat held out at arm's-length. Elaine nibbled her earlobe and said, "Last night was magic. You are magic," and it would have been rude to disagree, so Frances said nothing at all. The hands ran over her belly, down her thighs, over her buttocks, and as one arm clasped her tightly the other reached down, fingers sliding into the drenched parting. Frances clung on to the huge forearm. She saw the vast shadow of Elaine looming over her on the shower wall and she felt small, captured, held; safe. Afterwards, as their breathing calmed, Elaine said, "Come here," and turned Frances round to face her, drawing her head into her chest, kissing the soggy, matted crown. "Shall we spend the day together?" she said. And without knowing why, Frances said, "Yes."

After this, Frances had never quite managed to shake her off. Before she knew it, they were dating. It was purely logistical to begin with: Sex made them hungry, so they went out for meals.

Sex made them thirsty, so they went out for drinks. Then the little gifts began arriving—a bottle of wine, a plant, a cookbook—and before she knew it, they were in a relationship. It was during the trip to the seaside, when they had gotten high and gone on the Waltzer, that Elaine had kissed her with ice-creamy lips and said, "I love you." High, Frances had smiled back, and that was that.

The main problem was, there was nothing really wrong with Elaine. She was not a bad person, she was smart (in her way), and witty (in her way), and loving (in her way). She found joy in childish things: a kite in the sky, a yapping pup, a strawberry milkshake. She was gleeful most of the time. Had Frances been more self-aware, she might have noticed the dynamic was flawed because she too wanted to be a child and she felt an intense irritation at Elaine's easy joy because it reminded her of all that she had missed out on, the kites and pups and milkshakes, all that had never been present when she was young. Much of her resentment and confused tetchiness stemmed from emotions similar to those she'd had in the playground watching the children at play. She thought she disliked them, but in fact she wanted to be them.

"Come on!" Elaine had yelled as they stumbled, stoned and spun about, from the Waltzer. She ran up the beach, high and happy, full of weed and sugar, jumping with both feet into the wash, bending over to splash up the waves. But Frances did not want to run after her, or join in, or appear with a towel: She wanted to be the one to shout, "Come on!" and be chased, she wanted to be the kid in the waves, she wanted to be towel-dried by gentle hands. Elaine ran up the pier in her Wellington boots, stomping on the rickety wooden boards, and Frances sullenly followed. Fishermen rested their elbows on the rails and stared expressionlessly at the water, Elaine ran off with her arms wide and her steps thudding back through the floorboards, and Frances felt a sick urge to topple them all—the fishermen, Elaine, every passerby—into the sea, a compulsion not so much murderous as pathetic, like she might stand there afterwards, head back, eyes wetted, and wail up at the sky. As if her mother might hear and make it alright.

SATURDAY.

The bank opened at nine o'clock. She would get the money, then message Dom, arrange to meet him, and be done with it: The whole situation was beginning to feel a tad uncontrollable and frightening. Elaine was deeply unconscious, not even snoring now, just immoveable, motionless, a lump in the bed. During the night, whenever Frances had stood in the doorway and looked at her—which she had frequently; in fact, she'd never looked at her so much in her life—she looked like one of those stone statues of dead royalty in crypts beneath churches, as if she should be clutching a sword. Frances had checked she was breathing several times in the night and spent the rest of the hours falling in and out of heavy, story-filled sleeps on the sofa, more like hallucinations than dreams, until her alarm went off. Now she dragged herself to the bathroom, kicking her way through bottles and boxes as she went, picking up jeans and a shirt from the floor, numbly deciding she should shower before she dressed because the smell of the flat seemed to have seeped into her, seemed to have made her part of the collage of mess.

The strain was taking its toll—that was for sure. It was not meant to be like this. True, she was untouched and free, in many ways, from Elaine. But all that seemed to really have happened was a change in the type of annoyance. Now, instead of singing and joking and grabbing, she was snoring and whimpering and unpredictable. Frances had barely slept in two days because of it, contrary to her plans for lazing around, cooking, watching TV, doing what she pleased. She felt like a nurse on call-out, constantly on edge, not trusting the quiet, sensing that at any moment her name might be yelled. She stared at the walls, at the ceiling, and out the window. She smoked and drank, and tried not to think of her comatose girlfriend, tried not to think of anything. She pretended that the scene in the bedroom was totally separate from her, as if the door opened to another universe. Out from the gloom she could still see Dory's smile on the mug, grinning across the room at her in a way which made her feel silly and afraid. She was relieved it was all nearly over.

She turned on the bathroom light and put her hands either side of the wash basin, then slowly looked up at herself in the mirror. She laughed, once, sardonically. She saw a scrawny, undernourished half-human. The bones of her chest rippled outwards and her hands looked like two dead crabs. She had scarcely eaten in days, spooning a few mouthfuls of cold soup as she passed the pan, existing mainly on booze, which was in worryingly low supply. She knew she would look tired but did not expect to look so unlike herself, so weirdly sinister, as if her face and body denounced her as a monster, a murderer, insisting on revealing it to the world.

She showered, using every loofah, sponge, and soap to scrub and scour herself until her skin was sore, fingernails sliding through her soapy hair twice, three times, scratching her scalp. Then she dried herself, dressed, and went back to the mirror. Wiping steam away revealed at least a normal human being; it was the best she could do.

She paused in the quiet hallway. It felt strange leaving Elaine without writing a note or yelling a goodbye, just shoes on feet, bag on shoulder, keys in pocket. She lingered at the front door and eventually shouted, "Won't be long," to the silent flat. Paused, listened, then left.

She ran down the stairs, bursting onto the street as if gasping for air. Wonderful normality greeted her: the people, the sounds, the postman coming, his red van parked across the street. The car horns were blaring, the cafés were opening, shutters all along the pavement were being lifted and doors unlocked. The morning sun was warm and threatened a scorcher, but not yet, not for a few hours; right now, a gentle breeze tousled the garbage on the street and swept coolly through her wet hair. She passed her café with its usual queue and the shop selling orange and mango smoothies and the bus stop where the early elderly shoppers sat looking up the road in mute expectation. She walked quickly, light on her feet, tottering along. The bank was not far, just around the corner—hopefully there would not be a queue. Dom might even be awake and able to meet her soon. A man on a skateboard rolled past her as she turned, then she hurried through the glass doors into the bank.

Banks always made her nervous. To the unwealthy they have a similar atmosphere to police stations, as if everyone who works there is superior and poor people are guilty, simply because they are poor. And those staff, who do not know you, have access to an inconceivable amount of personal information. Not a problem if you are rich and your bank account reflects a lavish lifestyle. Not a problem if you are humble and careful and save. But deeply humiliating if you are poor, and they know it, and see your feeble bank balance as you beg them for help or time or just a statement. It's as if they go home each night and say to their families, "The most pathetic one I've ever seen came in today, nothing but five pounds in there, yet there she was, bold as brass, asking for a bigger overdraft. When will these people learn?" Frances always hated it. She hated the primary colours of the walls, the little stacks of leaflets everywhere, the beaming smile that approached the second she arrived, asking how they might help. She felt they could somehow tell just by the look of her that she didn't have any money, despite her shower and clean hair. "It's not true," Elaine had once said to her. "Banks love skint folk—that's how they make most of their money. People who get in debt and they can wring dry whilst pretending to help."

"Sounds like exploitation," Frances had said.

"Just don't get in debt."

Easier said than done. Elaine had probably never felt nervous in a bank in her life. To the contrary, she probably liked that the bank staff would see her balance and be impressed. "How the other half live," they'd say at the dinner table. "It's alright for some."

She navigated the maze created for queuing and found herself behind two people. Only one desk was open, and a short woman with a wizened face was handing over several cards, cash, and envelopes, each with individual instructions. The cashier was a young man, chewing gum and looking like he'd been summoned to work in the middle of a night out. He handled each request moodily, repeatedly asking, "Anything else?" Frances looked at the clock on the wall. It was nine-fifteen. She sent Dom a message—JUST GETTING IT NOW—and shifted forwards as the woman walked away, tucking handfuls of cash into her bag and looking ready to bite anyone who dared approach her.

Frances had her bank card in her hand. She rehearsed the words in her head. *I'd like to withdraw two thousand pounds, please.* She had never seen that much money in real life before. She was about to know how mobsters feel when passed a briefcase full of cash.

She would, for a short time, be spectacularly rich. She smiled at the thought and reminded herself, it was not hers. Then the customer in front of her left and the gum chewer yawned. "Next."

She held her card out and smiled, saying, "Good morning." He rolled his eyes—clearly there was nothing good about it—and pointed at the card machine with the chewed end of his pen. She inserted her card. Then he looked up and said, "How can I help you?"

"I'd like to withdraw two thousand pounds, please," she said as confidently as she could muster, and felt quite proud of herself. She hadn't stumbled on the words, and it felt good to say them, like she was temporarily part of an elite club. She wished she'd said them louder so people could overhear. Then the cashier frowned, looked at the screen and back at her several times, and said, "Um, I'm afraid you have insufficient funds."

"I'm sorry?"

He leant over and said louder, slower, through breath of burger and spearmint, "You have insufficient funds," and he turned the screen so she could see it. He pointed at the balance with his pen.

Seventy-seven pounds.

It wasn't there. The money wasn't there.

"That can't be right," Frances said. "Two grand should have gone in today. Maybe it will be in later?"

"Nothing pending," he said, and stared dumbly at her.

"But that can't be right."

He typed and clicked and printed her off a statement. It showed her salary, the rent, her other outgoings. Nothing pending for today. She held it in her hands and looked at it as if it didn't make sense, because it didn't. Anger and humiliation washed over her. The cashier showed no pity; they saw this sort of thing all the time.

"I need it today. I need the money today."

He shrugged. "Do you want to see an advisor?"

"Could they give me two grand today?"

"Unlikely."

"Then I don't think I'll bother."

She looked at the paper in her hands. Nothing pending. Her phone pinged. A message from Dom. It just said GOOD.

"Fuck."

"Can I help you with anything else?"

She wanted to throw something at him. She wanted to shout, "Anything else? You haven't helped me at all." She wanted to beg for some money, some mercy. She wanted to sit down, where she was, and refuse to move. She folded the paper neatly like it contained the last remnants of her dignity, and said, "No, thank you. I guess there's been a misunderstanding."

"Have a good one, then," he said.

"Thanks. You too."

She tried to leave with her head held high but had the suspicion that every staff member and every customer and every person in the world had witnessed her shame. She should have laughed and asked for fifty pounds—at least that would have shown she had something. Like when her card was declined in the supermarket and she'd go through the charade of pretending it was out of date and she'd forgotten her new one, she should have played the part and saved herself from this exposure. However, the horror did not last long because it was swiftly overshadowed by a new one: Dom, and Betty, and her straightening irons. The moment Frances was outside the bank, she ran home.

She wished now that Elaine would be awake and normal, sitting up in bed, maybe tidying the living room. She prayed, as she opened the front door, that she would hear her call out, "Babes? Is that you? Where have you been?" She hoped more than anything that Elaine would tell her she'd forgotten the transfer, but not to worry, she'd sort it out right now. She slammed the door closed behind her and ran to the bedroom, shouting, "Elaine. Elaine. Elaine . . ."

Elaine was just as she'd left her. A spider scurried across her sleeping chest and vanished into the gloom. Frances rushed around the bed and tugged at her limp arm.

"Elaine. Elaine, wake up."

She shoved her, gently at first, then in a growing frenzy.

"Elaine!"

She grabbed both shoulders and shook her like a snow globe. She bellowed into her ear. Nothing. In desperation she mounted her like a jockey on a filly, bouncing around from gallop to canter, repeatedly shouting, "Elaine!" She grabbed the *Finding Nemo* mug from the windowsill and threw the cold tea over her. Elaine slept on.

"Wake up, for fuck's sake. Please, wake up."

The mug fell to the floor. Dory's face broke in half. Frances fell limply forwards as if for a hug, and wailed noisily. Gradually, she sat up and took her phone from her pocket. Blowing her nose on Elaine's pillow, she dialled Dom's number. Best to call him whilst crying. He might take pity on her.

"Yeah?"

"Dom. It's Frances."

"Yeah?"

"I've got a problem."

There was a slight pause, then he said, "If you don't have my money you've got more than one problem."

"I do. I mean, I should. I don't know what's happened," she cried noisily. "She was meant to send it to me today, I went to get it for you, but it's not in there, and I can't wake her up—I've tried everything."

"That's who you gave the stuff to? The girl who was going to send you money?"

"Yes."

"Well that was a dumb-ass thing to do."

"Regardless, I can't wake her up to ask her or to get her to give it to me."

"Of course not. I already told you, it knocks you clean out for several days."

"It wasn't clean out—it's been a fucking nightmare."

"Give a shit. Where's my money?"

"I'll get it. As soon as she wakes up. I promise."

"Tomorrow."

"What if she's not awake by then?"

"What if that ain't my problem?"

"Don't be like this, please."

"I told you how it was. You already knew it."

"Monday, please. Please Dom. Monday, I promise, one hundred percent."

He sighed. Then he hung up.

FRANCES HAD PROMISED Jennifer Langthorn she'd call a doctor and, true to her word, she did. Admittedly, it was her own doctor, and the appointment was for herself, but she felt a promise had been kept nonetheless.

She simply had to get out of the flat, sit down with someone who would listen and provide some temporary respite away from the real world. The doctor had remained in her mind as someone kind and understanding. Useless, yes, but kind and under-standing. And right now that was all she felt she needed—a bit of sympathy, a gentle word—and there was nowhere else she could think to get it. Who else was there? King? Not likely. Besides, you never know, he might actually be able to help her in some way, give advice and check she wasn't completely unstable. You know, behave like a doctor. Stranger things have happened.

And so, because it was a walk-in appointment, she found her-self sitting in the waiting room of the surgery for over an hour, watching a toddler in dungarees playing with building bricks. Every seat was taken by every common variable: the anxious mothers, the elderly couples, the teens flicking through back issues of *Cosmo*. Behind reception, two harassed-looking women bore the faces of people who used to be normal but are now so continually stressed, angered, and inquisitioned, they looked like they probably kept machine guns under their desks. Time stood still in here. Every now and then the electronic screen on the wall would beep and summon an individual—a Chosen One—whom everyone would watch enviously, wondering if they'd perhaps been forgotten and were doomed to die here, most likely from starvation. After seventy-five minutes sitting in this atmosphere of stifled rebellion, an elderly man—with all the bravery of an old soldier—limped over to the terrors at reception, and the whole room watched this leader of the uprising in awe and admiration.

"Excuse me, how long—"

"I don't know." Instant, snappish fury. The poor man wobbled on his bad leg. "Sit down and be patient and you'll be called when the doctor is ready,"

"Oh, fine, fine, thank you."

Rebellion quashed. He shuffled back, shakier now, as the whole room returned to staring at their hands or floor or magazine, joined together in his humiliation. By the time Frances' name finally beeped onto the screen, she practically ran to the door.

He looked very different from the last time she'd seen him but, distracted by her own thoughts and problems, she couldn't say exactly why. He greeted her with a friendly hello, and she sat opposite him as he typed, then he leant back in his chair and looked at her. "How can I help you today?" he said. He clearly didn't remember her.

She wanted to ask if he could cast his mind back to last time, many months ago, if he could recall what she had said about her broken heart and the flatness. She wanted to say she had felt sorry for him then, because of his problems, and she hoped he was feeling better, but if he wasn't, could he please talk like that again? The stuff about being a participant in a game you didn't know you were playing? Could he at least consider the hit or hug option? And she wanted to apologise for not having used the medication or gone to the meetings, but surely he understood that too. She tried to think of the right words as he sat there with a tiny smile, waiting for her patiently. In the end he opened his hands and said, "What's troubling you? Maybe begin there." His eyes twinkled.

"Do you remember when I came here before? You said I was depressed. You prescribed me pills and therapy."

He said, "Aaaahhh," knowingly, then turned to his computer screen for assistance.

"I asked you to hug or hit me."

"Oh, yes." He looked back to her. "I remember. Of course. So, how have you been feeling?"

She felt she needed a friend, and this was the best she could do. She felt she needed a priest and maybe he could be that too. Doctors have a code of confidentiality: She should be able to tell him anything, she should feel free to confess, to ease the burdens in her mind. Instead she simply said, "Well, I don't feel flat anymore."

"Excellent!"

"Yes. Although I think I might have gotten worse."

His eyes flickered back to the computer screen. It was like they were drawn there in moments of difficulty.

"Worse? How so?" he said.

"Well, I think I might have become a bit, sort of, unhinged. I'm worried, about myself. I'm hurting my girlfriend, you see—"

"Ah, I understand." He nodded slowly, wisely.

"Do you?" Frances was willing to believe anyone could understand. She was completely open to the idea of empathy, to telepathy, even.

"Yes, you're feeling bad because you've hurt your girlfriend?"

"Yes."

"You've upset her? Had a row?"

"No, not exactly—"

"You're feeling anxious? Depressed?"

"No. Yes. Kind of. I don't know, to be honest. I feel like I need some sort of assessment."

"For what?"

"I don't know. Mental health? Mental disorders?"

"Because you've upset your girlfriend?"

"*Upset* is the wrong word."

"What is the right word?"

"I don't know." She pondered for a moment, then shrugged. "I can't say."

"You can't say because you don't know?"

"No. I know. But I can't say because I can't face what I know, you know?"

He rubbed his forehead beneath an impossible curl of hair and she realised with sudden and unnecessary embarrassment what it was about him that was so very different: He was wearing a toupee. The obviousness of it—like a cutting of faux fur that had been Hoopla'd onto his head—made her wonder how she hadn't noticed it the moment she walked in; she certainly couldn't mistake it now. Quite the opposite: She couldn't take her eyes off it. It was a worrying example of how wrapped up in herself she'd become. In fact, as if this weren't absurd enough, a hundred tweaks and changes appeared at once: his withdrawn waistline, his neatly ironed shirt, the smell of cigars replaced with an eye-watering eau de cologne. A waistcoat. Elbow patches. He looked like an actor playing the part of landed gentry just returned from hunting. A wedding band still choked his ring finger. There was but one obvious conclusion: His wife had returned.

Did he look happier? She couldn't quite tell. But certainly, within the tightened, neatened, weird bewigged look of him there came some other result, the buttoning up and pinning down that is so suggestive of an animal tamed. Willingly so, perhaps, but tamed, nevertheless. As Frances sat there staring and staring, the doctor became aware of it, coughed a little, and shifted around in his seat. Caught out, figured out, revealed, as it were. He began to nervously run his hand down his tie in his usual habit, but was halted by its disappearance beneath the waistcoat, so he resorted to gently stroking his belly a little instead, then cleared his throat, smiled, and said, "Let's approach this differently, shall we?" He settled his face into an expression of calmness and openness, and said, "Start again."

A tiny, repetitive sound caught her attention: Beneath the table, his foot tap-tap-tapped.

"Okay," Frances said. She took a deep breath. "I have drugged my girlfriend, and that's not an exaggeration or a metaphor, but a fact. I have spiked her drinks and she's currently unconscious in my flat. When she has occasionally woken up, sometimes she slurs, sometimes she talks nonsense. I had to do it, though. I needed the money, and I haven't even got that now. I just wanted a break, really, you understand, a bit of goddamned peace. I didn't know what else to do. It all made sense at the time."

This was what she wanted to say. In the event, however, she just mumbled, "I think I'm mad."

The doctor shook his head side to side and said, "You're not mad. It's part of life to argue with each other, to have stress; it's unpleasant but perfectly normal. People bicker, quarrel, fall out, make up. It's just how it goes sometimes," and he smiled softly again with an air of would-be smugness diminished only by the absurdity of his appearance.

"For fuck's sake," she snapped. "It's not a bicker. Will you stop being so dismissive? Something is seriously wrong."

"With your girlfriend?"

"No! With me!"

"But you said you'd upset her. I thought you meant—"

"Okay, both of us, then."

He rocked back in his chair and pursed his lips apologetically. "I'm not a relationship counsellor," he said.

Frances groaned.

"But," he continued, "I can help you if you tell me what is actually wrong with you. You are anxious, yes?"

"Well, yes, obviously."

"Right!" He looked pleased. "I can give you something for that." He began to type.

"That wasn't really why I came here."

"Hmm?" He wasn't listening. He was concentrating on his typing.

"I wanted to tell you something. A secret. I just wanted to tell someone, to get it off my chest. It's building up in there like a huge pressure and I need to get it out."

"Anything you say is confidential in here," he said, merrily tippy-tapping away.

She waited. Eventually he stopped and looked at her. She opened and closed her mouth several times, then pushed her fingers through her hair. "I can't" was all that she said. "Fuck. I can't."

He smiled and smiled and typed. He looked ever so cheery. "Baby steps," he said to Frances. "Just take baby steps. Talk to your girlfriend. Be kind to yourself and maybe practice meditation, some breathing exercises." He didn't personally believe in any of that mumbo-jumbo but they were encouraged to suggest it these days. When all else fails, there's always spiritual hippie stuff to give a little false hope.

Frances felt this had been a waste of time. She'd hoped to get the miserable, sympathetic doctor; instead she'd gotten some usurper who was two steps away from suggesting she light candles and start chanting, a man who—if his clothing was anything to go by—was a total lunatic himself. She wondered why she'd bothered to come here. But then she suddenly noticed a slight twitch in his movements: Beneath the desk his leg was bouncing away like it was part of an Irish jig.

She felt sorry for him, differently this time. Reunited with his wife, clearly, but look at the result. What on earth do they do to us, these people that we love? He was not himself; he was a crash test dummy strapped into his life, unable to change direction or apply the brakes, all because he loved someone, which meant they had control of the car, the speed, the end result. One day he might wake up, drag himself out of the wreckage for good, but as Frances knew all too well, he'd be so mangled and damaged by then, he might well wish he'd waited 'til it went up in flames. He was still beaming away and Frances began to see it as an expression not of happiness, but the fixed grin of blind optimism hoping to God everything would be okay. She realised, sadly, that the similarity and empathy which had existed between them before was gone, and there was very little he could do or say to help her now, trapped as he was in this new persona. Still a doctor, of course, and just about able to function as one, but his ability to reach her as another human being was locked away beneath the pocket of his suit jacket. As if to prove the point he said, "Shall we try you on some antianxiety tablets, and the therapy again?"

She sighed. "Group therapy isn't for me, Doctor."

"The medication?"

Frances huffed and stood up to leave. She thought he was the one who needed medication.

"Are you sure you want to leave? I might be able to recommend some charities to call." He faffed about beneath the papers on his desk. Frances paused with her hand on the door and looked back so as not to be rude. Eventually he produced a pamphlet for the Samaritans, which he held out. Frances looked down at it, then him, then opened the door. "Would you like to book another appointment, for a couple of weeks' time? We can catch up and see how you're doing," he said, and she stopped in the doorway.

"No," she said. "I'll be alright."

"Goodbye, then. And take it easy."

"Yes. Thanks. Bye, then."

And he continued to smile an almost demented smile, as if something might be about to erupt out of him, as if he might tear the toupee from his head and rip all his clothes off and roar. He began to type randomly, just punching furiously into the keyboard. From the doorway, Frances could see both legs now, dancing away. He looked like a mallard, plump and proud above the surface of the desk, feet flapping about beneath it. Strange to think he was one complete person, as if he had been given someone else's legs.

"Goodbye!" he said again and waved, a gesture both of them knew was ridiculous.

In the car park, lighting up, she almost didn't recognise his car; it too had undergone a transformation. Gleaming and glimmering, as shiny as all the others, an air freshener dangling from the rearview mirror, the seats spotless and smart. But, like him, it was vaguely unsettling: the urgency in the skewed parking, the duster balled up on the dashboard, the slight dent in the door, which, when put together, suggested some small but permanent sense of panic. And, on reflection, as she considered his appearance, his words, his demeanour, she recognised the one person she knew most of all, knew better than anyone, knew as herself and most other people as well: a liar. A liar trapped in lies, living lies, enacting lies, trying to convince themselves it is all reality. Shut away in the box of his office, playing the parts of his life. He had a way to go before it could be considered convincing. Frances could have taught him a thing or two. Walking away, she was passed by a woman she recognised from the waiting room. She snatched at the hand of the little boy in dungarees, dragging him away, running late for something, as the boy looked back over his shoulder at her, smiling.

9

Lies. Let us talk about lies. Let us talk about these words, thoughts, and actions which are the deceptive contradictions—but sometimes the greatest truths—of ourselves.

When Frances was a little girl, she told lies, like any little girl does. And, like those other little girls, her lies were usually of the trivial kind. A stolen satsuma at lunch time, a denial amongst the broken remnants of a teapot, feigned ignorance at muddy shoes and torn clothes. She knew she needn't lie, and that lying was bad, but she lied nonetheless, and did so regularly enough that she didn't notice it. Lying was, to her, no different to playing make-believe, just another layer to the game of Families, where she'd boss around her invisible children and scold her invisible husband, playing the role of her unavailable, unreachable mother. The only difference between her and the other little girls was that throughout the day, the game vividly continued.

From too much time spent alone, her imagination bled into her reality until she could co-exist quite comfortably in both places simultaneously. At school, teachers grew exasperated with her lack of focus and attention; only reading and drawing interested her, her other workbooks filled with sketches and doodles or snippets of stories. More often than not she was to be seen with her cheek slumped against her fist, chewing on the end of a pencil or a tatter of hair. She was not naughty, just vacant. And as she caused no real bother—and Lord knows the teachers had their hands full enough with the ones who did—they all resigned to giving up on her. They'd drag her through the curriculum, ensure she'd pass tests, shrug their shoulders at average effort and average grades, teach, in other words, just enough to prove she wasn't an idiot and they were doing the best they could with her. There was enough to cope with, between the bickering and hair-pulling and raucous energy of the other children; to have one sit quietly daydreaming was, in many respects, a godsend. And if, perhaps, some time had been taken to talk softly with her and ask about her thoughts, her feelings, her problems, they might have discovered some potential there. But they didn't.

It would be difficult, as an adult, for her to recall what she dreamt about then; her childhood seemed like a poorly-remembered and patchy dream heightened at intervals with moments of emotion. The relief when her father came home, the sadness and resentment and jealousy of other girls hand-in-hand with their mothers, and the anger which reared up from nowhere, and just as swiftly went. She knew from insinuations at school and the books she read that there was a boyish quality to her actions and reactions—not only the rough and tumble but the swiftness of her temper, which frightened other children. This was why teachers said to "leave her alone," because when she was alone she was calm and thoughtful and not scary. Her fantasyland was difficult to recall because it was not exuberant or memorable in any way; it was not pirates or castles or magic dragons. Hers were the daydreams of other people's normalities, and this was why fact and fiction so neatly overlapped.

She had a make-believe mother. She walked home from school beside her, a mother of her own imagining, who always asked about her day, always wanted to know what she'd done, always listened. Her make-believe mother was strict, like the other mothers, and sometimes scolded her if her hair was grotty or if she dawdled, but she also told her she loved her, she was proud, she was a clever little girl. She didn't realise it but her make-believe mother was in fact the actress Sharon Maughan, from the Gold Blend advert; she was the prettiest and most enviable of all the mothers. Frances looked up at her devotedly as they walked along home. At the ice cream van she would always ask if she could have a Popeye, but her mother said no, it was bad for you, and they'd be having tea soon anyway. At this point Frances would start to skip ahead, and her mother would call for her to be careful and wait for her at the corner of the road.

Her father was a lorry driver—that was all that she knew. More often than not, as she swung in through the back door and shouted, "Hello," he wouldn't be there, but she always shouted it nevertheless. Coins and bread would be left on the sideboard, and she'd look into the under-stairs cupboard to check for his coat and hat; if they were gone, then so was he. On occasion she'd find them there, then stand at the foot of the stairs to listen for the sound of him wheezing in his sleep. She was always quiet, regardless; if he was home she did not want to wake him, and if he wasn't she did not want to feel the silence come back at her. In the kitchen, she put on an apron. The daydream shifted here to her being the mother. Her imaginary daughter would sit in the chair, swinging her feet, as Frances buttered bread and wrenched the lid from the jam jar, licking the knife clean afterwards, placing the sandwich on her round brown plate. When she ate it, she was the daughter again. And so this pattern continued throughout the day, this habit of switching from mother to daughter, filling the bathtub as mother, climbing in as daughter, pulling the bedsheets back as mother, settling in as daughter, hearing her mother's voice in her head, telling a story, "You saved my life the other night." She fell asleep with the sheets wrapped round her as tight as a mother's arms.

Loneliness was never an issue because they were inseparable. And nobody could have known it, but her sense of right and wrong came not from teachers or her father, but the voice and expressions of Sharon Maughan, praising her when she was good and frowning when she was bad. It was this make-believe mother who stopped her hand reaching for loose change when the ice cream van warbled demandingly into the street. It was she who turned Frances' head away from another girl's test sheet at school. It was she who patted her wrist at petty playground acts of revenge.

"Don't be mean to them just because they are mean to you," she said.

In a very true and literal sense she feared displeasing her make-believe mother more than anything.

Each day she left the classroom last, slowly packing away her books and pencils, listening to the cheery rabble being gathered up and led away, before she hoisted her heavy bag up and took a mental picture of the scene. The teachers would see her and exchange silent, pitying looks, wishing a mother would miraculously appear. They did not realise this was her happiest time of day, nor that their pity would have been better spent during the friendless lunches. She looked forward to leaving. When the crowd cleared and all other children had been ushered away, Frances ran out to meet her make-believe mother beneath the tree. In a white blouse and beige skirt, her mother would raise her hand high and wave a big side-to-side arc as if painting a rainbow in the sky, then crouch down slightly and open her arms wide. Off they went, alone, together. There had to be somewhere to put the love, you see. Just because her mother wasn't there didn't mean Frances didn't have the love to give. Children are experts at coping and making do.

Their house was a mid terrace down a sloping cul-de-sac street, filled with sounds of neighbouring children throwing balls and riding bikes. To the rear of the house was a long, thin garden, lined on either side with hedges and trees, which slid off to a narrow ditch. This ditch cut across the lawn like a gash in the earth, slashing either side through the neighbouring land, to some unfathomable source several miles away. The width and depth of a tallish man, it filled with water in the winter and nettles in the summer, huge, unstoppable things which grew dark and dangerous to the flat of the land, so that from the house the ditch seemed to have disappeared altogether, just a black shadow replacing it. Beyond was a small patch of grass, a short extension of the garden, just big enough for a few trees and a shed. Two wobbly planks of wood, laid by Frances when she was big enough to drag them, acted as a bridge, from one side to the other.

Down the rabbit hole, through the wardrobe, up the beanstalk, over the bridge. Here was the passageway to wonder, to Frances' secret, special land. Nothing more than the shabby grass and old sloping shed, unused by her father or a gardener, yet here the improvisations and imaginations of childhood occurred in all their wildness, undisturbed and unhindered by teachers and grown-ups and the demands of the world. A doll strapped to a lawnmower as a makeshift pram, rows of nails standing on their heads acting as a circus, trowels and pitchforks played with as weapons ready to defend the realm. She was a princess, her mother a queen, the shed was a castle, the ditch was their moat. Fairy-tale happenings could occur here away from the necessary business of cleaning and washing and working. Here, she was alone, yet had more company than anywhere else in the entire world. Beyond the shed and grass, over a thin wire fence, stretched a vast golden cornfield that spilled away like a lake of honey. Frances would sometimes climb a ladder, carefully propped against the shed wall, and sit on the roof, watching it, spotting kestrels and deer, gazing across to the blue crust of horizon, which was in fact the sea. Once or twice as she perched there she felt the imagined wriggling of fingers up her spine and looked over her shoulder to see her father in the upstairs window of the house. They observed each other across this chasm like two strangers in separate houses, then each flicked a hand in the air and turned away. This was how it was between them. Tokens of attention slipped from him, generally as money on the kitchen counter, or a pat on the head, or a nod from afar. These unspoken acts of communication were less satisfying than those with her make-believe mother because, as a real human being, she couldn't help expecting more from him, like actual words. But at school they had learnt to be grateful so she kept such selfish whimsies to herself and accepted that, when it came to paternal love, this was as good as it was going to get: not completely absent, just painfully awkward and unmentionable, living around rather than with each other, a cohabitation of upstairs thuds, scattered coins, and distant glances. Had he only tried—only crossed the ditch once—he might have gained better understanding of his daughter and bridged a gap between them. He might also have noticed that the ditch was dangerous, the bridge unsteady, a disaster possible, even likely. But he didn't, and so by the time he learnt all this it would be too late, and his daughter would carry a burden he had no idea about, believing it to be his instead.

Every year there is one day that is the hottest, and this was that day. Crickets cried out from the parched earth, pigeons squatted in the green goo that lurked in the bottom of the bird baths. The grass had grown tall during the virile rains of previous months, but the recent drought had withered it back to a flat, matted straw. The winding weeds and wild flowers which co-existed ecstatically in the borders had flung themselves about in an orgasmic tangle of nubile limbs and pouting buds during all the damp and delicious spring; now, they collapsed, exhausted, upon one another, gasping in remorse. All nature—the hushed trees and silent birds and static puffs of cloud—seemed stuck in an expectant pause, awaiting the one blessed gift of mercy: rain. The only movement at all was the shuddering haze of heat rising from the earth, as if all the souls beneath the surface—the worms, the bugs, the moles—were jointly trembling in fear and fury for a bit of fucking respite.

One plant alone was thriving. In the ditch, the nettles stood robust and green. Hand-sized leaves open, a dense and threatening crowd, like the poisonous palms of prisoners reaching up out of a pit, ready to snatch whatever they could.

Frances was ten. She skipped down the garden with a jug of water and two glasses, still wearing her blue-and-white-chequered school dress, planning to lie in the shade of the shed and chat to her mother awhile. She came to a halt when she looked up and saw a little boy of three or four standing on the lawn, as if he had shot up from the earth. For a moment the two just looked at each other. "Who are you?" Frances eventually said, and the little boy didn't answer. "How did you get in here?" she asked, and he pointed to a gap in the hedge, through which she could see a woman hanging clothes on a washing line. It was Ben, the boy from next door. She hadn't seen him in a while. She was surprised he wasn't a baby anymore. His mother used to push him in a pram with a red hood and she'd always stop to say hello to Frances. She'd let Frances hold him once, when he was small and jellyish. He wasn't a baby anymore, though. He stood very still, chewed on his thumb, and stared at her.

"There's your mummy, hanging out the clothes," she said. "Where's your daddy?"

"Work," the little boy said wetly.

"So is my daddy. He works a lot. He works very hard. He's always at work."

"Where's your mummy?" the little boy asked.

Frances shifted the glasses from one hand to the other and said, "Gone."

"Gone where?"

"Just gone."

The little boy blinked back.

She shrugged. "I don't know where. I don't remember her. We don't talk about her. One day she was here, then she was gone."

Ben looked over at his mother as if to check she was still there. She was. Other people's mothers never left. Frances looked down at the two glasses in her hand.

"You're lucky to have your mummy," she said.

Ben scratched his nose and blinked at her again.

"Do you want to play a game?" she asked him, and he nodded eagerly.

He had a line of sweat on his upper lip, like a translucent moustache. His bare feet stood fat upon the prickly grass and his belly poked out in perfect roundness as he sucked his thumb. He wore blue shorts with a yellow boat sewn on a pocket. Even from several feet away, Frances could smell sun cream. She suddenly felt responsible for him. After all, she knew about mothering; she had been mothering herself for years.

"Wanna play," he garbled sloppily through his thumb.

She had a ball in her bedroom, stolen from the school playground. She kicked it against the wall of the house sometimes, or lay in bed and threw it in the air, counting. She looked at the jug of water and glasses in her hand and said, "Wait here. I just need to put these down, then I'll go and get a ball for us to play with," and hurried down the garden to the bridge.

She couldn't have known he had run after her; barefoot, barechested, in only a pair of cotton shorts, he didn't make a sound. Enticed by a new friend, he had waddled behind her, bright-eyed and curious, thinking the game had begun. Frances crossed the ditch slowly, one foot in front of the other as she had done hundreds of times before, and she put the jug and glasses down on the grass. Nothing felt abnormal, no sense of trepidation, but by the time she turned around it was too late: He was already halfway across the bridge, arms out either side as the wood wobbled.

"No, no," she shouted impulsively, sticking a hand out. "Get back. Go on," and she shooed him like he was a dog, not wanting him on her special side. A mischievous grin spread across his face, drool dribbling down his wrist. His blond hair wafted slightly: a shudder in the atmosphere, more a tremble than a breeze. But he didn't budge.

"Go on." She urged him with her hands. "Get back. We can play in the garden but not in here."

He giggled at her and still didn't move. He was having fun. Frances did not like it.

"Get back or I won't play with you at all," she said haughtily, putting her hands on her hips, but this only made him laugh louder. Dribble ran off his chin. Infuriated, she stepped forwards with her hands out, repeating through gritted teeth, "I said, get *back*," and the boy squealed, turned, too close to the edge, much too close.

He wobbled on one foot for a fraction of a second, arms still straight out either side, as if on a tightrope. The waiting palms in the ditch reached greedily, each tiny hair erect with its sting. His arms flapped briefly, and for a moment he was steady. Then, without a sound, he tumbled from the bridge into grappling grasps of green below.

Frances stood, frozen.

There came a pause, so long that she thought he might have disappeared, lost to the stingers, consumed by them. But then one long, solid, piercing scream came bursting out, so sudden and so shrill it sent the pigeons into the air. From nowhere specific, just deep within the ditch, the dreadful noise rang out, seeming to go on forever, as Frances clasped her hands over her mouth, then over her ears. She could just about see his white skin, flashes of blond hair, the jerky movement of the nettles as he struggled, flinched, fell in pain. And this was how she was, with her hands over her ears, as the woman from next door burst through the hedge shouting, "Ben! Ben! Oh my God," ran over to the ditch, and without hesitation plunged her arms in, raising up her screaming son. His white skin was turning scarlet, his face a tightened knot. "What happened?" she yelled at Frances, but before she could respond, before she could explain, the woman was gone, bellowing, "Michael! Call an ambulance. Call an ambulance," and they vanished back through the hedge.

Frances stood on the bridge and looked down at the dark hollow where he had fallen, barely discernible now. The nettles had come up and over his head. From the house next door she could hear a mix of screams and voices. She ran back indoors, up the stairs, and into her bedroom. She drew the curtains and climbed into bed, where she waited, waited, waited. An ambulance wailed into the street, followed a short time later by doors slamming, then it tore off, bellowing up the road, blue lights flashing on her bedroom wall until they grew distant, faded, and vanished.

She stayed in bed and watched the daylight dwindle, dim, and eventually disappear. In the middle of the night her father came. She did not remember this part clearly, just the presence of him in the room and the movement of the bed as he sat down beside her. He stroked her cheek once and explained quietly: Ben had allergies and asthma—the poor boy had had a seizure in the ambulance and had gone into shock, then died in hospital. It wasn't her fault, her father said. It was an accident; she mustn't blame herself. He had kissed her forehead and told her not to be upset. *You have not done anything wrong.* He stayed with her awhile, even though she did not speak, just lay there with her eyes closed. Then, when perhaps he thought she was falling asleep, he whispered, "I'm sorry," and she was too traumatised to wonder what he had apologised for. He left her alone and went to bed.

It had just been an accident, she hadn't pushed him, he had lost his balance. *You have not done anything wrong.* And yet she felt she must be to blame; she had asked him to play, she had walked over the bridge, she had urged him back across it. She had failed to jump in to rescue him. The guilt of it sank inside her in a most heavy and physical way, a solid lump, like a block of ice, that rushed through her veins when she saw the tiny coffin leave the house, a shadowy pair return two hours later, childless, bereft. Returning from school some time later, she found the shed and bridge fuelling a fire at the bottom of the garden as her father stood upright, for hours, watching over it. A few days later, a four-foot fence was erected along the ditch and she was cut off from her land and view altogether. Action taken to protect her by the father who felt it was all his fault, but interpreted as punishment for grievous wrongdoing, confirmation of blame and guilt. And it signalled the end of her childhood and any sense of who she was in the world; there was no more make-believe after that, she could not conjure her mother up, could not find her anywhere. No more talks, no more stories, no more walks home together, no more comfort, no more discipline, and she knew that she'd never see her again. Her father grew even more remote. She and her mind were left unchecked, to their own devices. She was guideless.

"You are not a murderer," a therapist had once said. "You know that, don't you? It was not your fault," and she felt she had fooled them all, was continuing to get away with it, had somehow escaped trial and judgement and walked around, free, like any other person. She thought herself capable of great evil because of one accident a long time ago, an accident guilt had proportioned blame to. Not the deed itself, nor the facts of it, but the unshakeable sense of culpability.

10

THE RISE AND FALL of Elaine's chest was so slight Frances could barely see it, especially as she was peering through her fingers.

She had hurried—in a most ambivalent way—home from the doctor's office and now stood at the foot of the bed, taking in the scene before her. Any hope of an awakening had been dashed within two seconds of entering the flat: Here was Elaine, just as before. She did not look like Evelyn McHale. She looked, unsurprisingly, like a poor woman who had been drugged and doused in tea.

Frances floated around the quiet flat, enveloped and shut away from the world, looking at the mess and absurdity. The remnants of implausible previous days—champagne flutes, cactus flower, discarded underwear—felt staged now, as if someone had placed it all there to taunt her. From some other planet came a minute vibration, barely even a sound—a bus in the road below—and as a galaxy imploded so came the sound of car horns and shouting women far, far away. Here, in the flat, nothing happened. Four rooms in an isolated universe all of their own, untouched by time until a big bang occurred. Elaine slept on.

JUST A LONDON CAFÉ, like any other.

Frances took an espresso to her usual seat at the back. The cleaner was new—she didn't recognise him—and someone had mended the tear in the cushion with gaffer tape. The sounds were the same: the slam of the till, the hiss of the machine. The posters were the same, the beaming Kenyan, the beetle-like coffee bean. The drink was the same, with its sugary kick. But, like the doctor, it all seemed different now.

She considered her options. She could take the seventy-seven pounds from her account to a casino, but luck didn't seem to be on her side at the moment. She could run away, but go where? And what about her home, and Elaine? Busking, prostitution, theft, and false moustaches all raced through her mind. At one point she imagined climbing in through an open window at Elaine's parents' house, wearing a balaclava and carrying a kitchen knife (Elaine had brought a nice set of santokus into the house), and holding them hostage whilst she stripped the place of fine art and sped away in the Bentley, but it seemed a bit far-fetched, and she knew nothing about fine art. "What about calling an ambulance and the police and confessing all?" a little voice said, but nowhere near loudly enough to be taken seriously—in fact, the burglary stood a better chance. She realised she was beginning to feel like both the villain and the victim, the hunter and the hunted, which left her very few options—few appealing ones, anyway. She remembered a poem she had read at school. It often went round and round in her mind, drumming along in a continuous pattern, rearing up at random moments like these, like it had a point, like it was trying to be heard.

> Trying to be good
> has become the mission of my life, but
> I'm moving mainly map-less, and
> I can barely drive.
> No. Fucking. Sightseeing.
> Just show me the way;
> I'm sure if I could find the gear I'd get there in a day.
> But the damn car keeps stalling, and
> I find that I am driving
> into some place uninvited, saying,
> "Oooh, this looks exciting . . ."

Yes, just show me the way, she thought. It sounded like a plea to God. She'd never had much time for religion but it suddenly came to her, with offerings of comfort and safety, like she'd heard it did on death row. A place she might escape to, even if only temporarily, and get a break from herself, her thoughts. Churches were always open, weren't they, full of comfort and warmth and hope. And one thing was for sure: Betty wouldn't be there. She finished her coffee and left.

The nearest church was only half a mile down the road, an ugly 1970s build, all square edges and teak furniture and plastic collection pots. Frances stood on the path, which ribboned between flat sheets of green, buttoned up with rows of grey headstones. She dithered in the doorway like the sinner she was until an aged gardener passed by with some decapitated rose heads in his hand and said hello, and she fled inside.

It smelled of tea, books, furniture polish, and the sort of dust continually being troubled into the air. Frances was surprised to find it felt strangely hollow, a cold lung waiting for the resuscitation of prayers. She slid along the nearest pew and sat down, already wondering what she was doing here: She knew nothing about God, or the Bible, and had no idea how to pray, nor where to begin if she did. *Have you got all day, God? Pull up a pew—we've got some talking to do.* Knowing her luck, He'd be in a meeting. Beneath the vaulted ceiling of curved wood, in the joyless gaze of several stained-glass saints, she felt even smaller and insignificant than usual. Like at the bank, she was out of place, unwelcome, nervous. A board outside had said GOD IS LOVE. She wondered how a place could feel so chilly on such a stifling day, did they polystyrene the building for insulation, or did God not function above twelve degrees? She shivered. Movement caught her eye: a perfectly permed parishioner puttered about amongst the flowers by the pulpit. Other than that, she was alone.

God, do you receive me? Testing, testing, one, two, three . . .

She had heard of those in need receiving signs from the Lord and wondered what to look out for. Did one have to ask for them, or did they just appear? If only there were instructions, perhaps pasted into the front of the prayer books, one of which she now opened and flicked through, a quick fan of the pages, releasing a waft, a smell of sleepy words. The permed lady disappeared through a side door. Frances put the book back on the little ledge before her, then didn't know what to do with her hands, so she sat on them, and bowed her head. She squeezed her eyes closed as tightly as she could and tried with all her might to do it, to pray.

Just show me the way. It doesn't have to be huge, God—anything will do. I will listen, I promise. I will try. I want to be good. Would a sign be possible, if you're not too busy? Slap a sunbeam across my

face, stick a dove on the doorstep, a car radio playing "Bohemian
Rhapsody": "Beelzebub has a devil put aside for meee, for meeee,
for meeeeeee..."

It was as good as she could do. She opened her eyes and looked
round, as if she might find herself on the shores of Babylon. As
it was, nothing happened, nothing at all. Except, of course, the
main door swinging slowly closed on the breeze that wasn't there,
followed by a thousand-decibel thud and echo as it shut, trapping
her in the dim vacancy of her half-assed prayer. She sat a moment
in this so-obvious sign, decided she didn't want it, apologised to
the universe in general, and got up and ran to the door.

BY THE TIME she arrived home, a miracle had actually occurred:
Elaine was awake. Of sorts. Deliriously, she responded to the
sound of footsteps in the flat and the recognisable thud of Frances'
bag hitting the floor. She did not speak, or open her eyes, but
made a noise like a dog in distress. Frances ran to the bedroom.
Elaine's head rolled towards her in a horrific lurching movement
and she flopped a hand out in a gesture for Frances to take it. She
did. It was the weight and texture of a slab of salmon.

"Frances," she muttered.

"Elaine. I'm here."

It was a relief, in so many ways, to find she was talking. Frances
almost wanted to hug her. Unspoken confession hung from her
lips like the kisses she couldn't bring herself to give. She tried to
look in Elaine's eyes but they did not stay open long enough, just
rolled back and forth, slits revealing moist whites, then closing
again; she would not be awake for long. "Elaine," she said, "what
happened to the money, baby? I didn't get the money."

"Is it Friday?" Elaine mumbled.

"No, Elaine. It's Saturday. And I really need the money, sweetie. It didn't come through. What happened? Did you not do it? Did you forget?" She took Elaine's head in her hands. She shook it a little side to side. "Elaine. Stay with me. When's the money coming, baby?"

Elaine flopped her head back and breathed deeply. "You have to do something," she said. "I'm late. So late. I had it all planned."

"What? What is it?"

"Go to the second drawer." She pointed a limp finger in the direction of the dresser. "At the back."

Frances did as she said. Rummaging past underwear and a few jewellery boxes, she found a small bag. It was black, with a red heart on it, tied up with scarlet ribbon. "Have you found it?" Elaine said.

"I think so."

"Bring it here," she patted the bed.

Frances carried it to her, knowing, in a dawning and unavoidable way, what was about to happen. "It shouldn't be like this," Elaine said, "but it is what it is . . ."

Her words trailed off as her head rolled to the side and she snored, once, loudly, jolting awake again, eyes looking like they were filled with glue. "Open it," she said.

Frances didn't want to. In fact she wanted to throw the bag on the floor and run from the room, the flat, the city. She wanted to get on a train, run into the sea, swim out and just keep on going. This room seemed smaller every time she entered it, as if the walls were inching in.

"Go on." Elaine patted the bed encouragingly.

Frances undid the bow and opened the bag, then removed the little box from inside. The heart motif was repeated on its lid. "Don't be nervous," Elaine said. Frances opened it.

It was the sort of ring she had imagined proposing to Adrienne with; she had, in fact, looked at a similar one several times in a nearby jeweller's but was too afraid, too wary of scaring her off. A sapphire with two small diamonds either side. Elegant, grown up—not suited to her at all. She held the box in her hand and looked at it, not daring to touch it, as if she would decrease its value. In the stuffy shadows of the room, it shone.

"I love you," Elaine whispered. "I'm sorry it's this way. I had a plan, and now it's late. I'm not sure what I'm saying or if this is even real. But I want you to know I love you. I do. I do. The one thing I know is that I love you."

Frances stared down at the ring and said nothing.

"You look after me. I love you."

The ring stared back like a single, expectant blue eye.

"Marry me?"

Perhaps she was too accustomed to lying, or perhaps she didn't know what she was saying, perhaps she was so reminded of Adrienne that she heard her voice; whatever the reason, Frances stared at the ring as a voice very quietly said, "Yes."

Elaine smiled. "I knew you would. I knew you were good. I love you."

Then she stopped speaking. Frances put the box on the floor, and leant closer to Elaine, saying, "But, Elaine, what about the money? I need to know—it's very important," but no answer came.

She stood up and drifted out of the room, unaware that she was wearing a ring Elaine had paid several thousands of pounds for.

"YO, PUPPY."

The Saturday night rush was on at Gabe's and Frances worked

amongst the chaos, feeling chaotic, feeling it made no difference anymore where she was, here or at home or anywhere, rather slowly and grimly returning the words *You're fucked, you're fucked, you're fucked.* Before she'd left for work, she had removed the sheets from around Elaine and gagged at the sight—and smell—revealed. Whimpering apologies, she had shoved, pulled, hauled, and tugged Elaine and the sheets around so she could strip and clean both before remaking and reassembling them, then, unsure what to do with the evidence, she'd thrown the soiled items in the industrial bins outside the flats as she left. It was a scene she knew she'd never forget, and she was forced to acknowledge that her greater concern was now not that Elaine might awaken too soon or alone or stumble semiconscious out of an open window, but that she might fall deeper and deeper asleep until she couldn't wake up at all. A situation once laughed at as impossible was nudging nightmarishly into view. She had arrived at pot-wash glad to get her hands deep into steaming water, tempted to stick her whole head in too.

"Yo, Puppy," King shouted again from the kitchen doorway. "How's your family?"

"What?"

"The sickness. The emergency."

"Oh. Yeah. They're okay, thanks."

"Nothing catching, right? We don't need no sickness round here."

Nothing catching, yet she felt sick to her core.

She kept her head down and worked so fast even the chefs noticed, cheering her, clapping her on the back. An hour into service and her mind—wherever it was—was jolted back into the kitchen as a string of bellowed obscenities burst above the slamming, shouting, chopping sounds. Frances stopped and looked over but couldn't see through the white coats, all suddenly swarming in the far corner, where the word "motherfucker!" was being yelled in increasing pain, almost to a scream. King was on the phone, demanding an ambulance, and amidst the confusion and noise and shouting, she saw a chef being led out, swiftly followed by barked orders to change stations, reorganise, come back together, get back to work. King came up to her and said, "Puppy, over here," and dragged her away by the elbow, hands still dripping, to a surface covered in onions.

"What happened?" she said.

"Dude knocked a pan of boiling caramel over his hand. You never seen that before? It's like lava. Nothing worse than a caramel burn. Nothing."

"Why? Is he okay?"

"Stuff gets hotter than hell and it sticks to you like glue. But it's burning you, right, so you try to wipe it off and what happens? It rips your fucking skin off. Just tears it clean off. We all gotta pull together tonight, okay? You can do it. Just chop. Nothing complicated. Chop, chop, chop. When you're done, go to him." He pointed to a chef. "He'll tell you what to do. Now go, go, go," and he left before she could say another word.

All around her people moved, yelled, snatched. They flung handfuls of garlic into pots, they stirred and sipped, and scraped chilli from chopping boards into frying pans. The ticket machine spluttered orders repeatedly into the room, accompanied by demands and shouts and "Yes, Chef." Frances looked at the pile of onions with shaking hands, a sense that this was it, this was the edge. Years of being unable to cope had come to an end and it was here, now. She could just drag the knife across her wrist and join the chef in hospital. At least there she'd be looked after, at least she could get some rest.

"Oi," the chef nearby shouted. "Chop, chop, my little friend."

So she did. And she was surprised to discover she was quick at it and, despite everything else, she was almost enjoying it. Soon she was slicing peppers, mushrooms, tomatoes. Within an hour she had learnt to make two starters, and she was one of the voices in the chorus of "Yes, Chef." Tea towel over her shoulder, spatula in hand, she was halfway through a dish when King came to her and said, "Outside. Quickly. Someone to see you. Little shit won't go away."

She froze. "Who is it?"

"How the hell should I know?" he snatched the knife out of her hand. "Just don't be long, okay? I got my own work to do."

She walked to the back door, which was propped open with a fire extinguisher and led to an alley. She stood, wiping her hands on the tea towel whilst also wringing them in panic as she saw Dom standing a few feet away. He exhaled cigarette smoke, pointed at her and grinned. "There you are."

Frances stepped outside, just past the extinguisher, still in the light from the doorway. Dom approached her, flicking his cigarette aside.

"What are you doing here?" she asked. "We said Monday. We agreed Monday."

"No, *you* said Monday."

"So did you. I'm sure you did."

"Why the fuck would I agree to Monday? Because you promised it? Promises don't mean shit."

"So why are you here?" she asked again, more reluctantly, beginning to understand.

"Betty said you weren't at home."

Frances looked up at him. "She went there? To my flat?"

He nodded. "You're lucky. She normally kicks the door in and ransacks the place. As it happens, she called me first, and I said I'd pop down and have a little word with you. Saturday night, I figured you'd be here."

"She didn't break in, then?" she said.

"No."

"Did she hear anything?"

"Hear anything?"

"It doesn't matter."

"No," he said. "But what does matter is the money. My money. And here you are, hiding."

"I'm not hiding, I'm working."

He held his hands out. "All the same to me."

"I told you, I couldn't get it. I'm sorry. I don't know what happened. I'll sort it out. I will. I promise. Just, give me 'til Monday, okay? What difference does it really make, two more days? Everything's gone a bit crazy."

He sighed and dropped his head, shaking it from side to side. Frances was about to apologise again when she found herself hurtling backwards between two huge waste bins. She fell to the floor, and looked up, shocked, to see Dom standing over her. "What are you doing?" She coughed.

Dom squatted down before her, elbows on knees, and looked straight into her eyes. He wiped his nose with the back of his hand and said, "It's no fucking joke, you know? This is serious shit now. You know I don't deal with the women, but Betty will fuck you up. No kidding, you little shit, she will fucking maim you. Her repertoire is quite advanced these days. I wonder if you know what it's like to have a hot curling tong shoved up your ass like a poker? Just imagine that. What do you think it feels like? And she ain't quick about it, you know. She takes her time."

"I'm sorry—" Frances began, but Dom held up a finger to silence her.

"I don't want to hear it. I'm not your problem now. She is. Know what I'm saying? Now, I don't care if you rob, steal, kill, whatever. I don't care if you sell your whole fucking family. All I am interested in is my money. Understand?"

Frances nodded. "I can get it. Soon. I promise," she said.

Dom's head tilted to the side and he held her stare as he took a cigarette from his top pocket. He lit it, and exhaled with a sigh. "I hate all this," he said. "I truly do. It's not me, y'know? It's unfortunate. But it's part of the business, and if you buy from me you're part of the business, and if you're part of the business you need to help keep profits flowing. Capiche?"

Frances nodded, too terrified to speak. Dom looked like a different person, a total stranger. The fire behind his eyes, which she had always thought enigmatic, the hunched way he walked, the intensity of his face, all shifted into a person filled with darkness. Like a wolf, he snarled over her.

"Puppy," King's voice called out. "What you doing?" He appeared as a shadow in the doorway, and in two paces was towering above them.

Frances and Dom looked at each other, then Dom stood and backed away. Frances got shakily to her feet and brushed herself down. King looked from one to the other. "You okay?" he said to her, scowling at Dom.

"Yeah," she replied.

"Can I help you?" he said to Dom, stepping out into the alleyway, fists by his sides.

Dom continued to smoke slowly, then turned and walked away. Frances rushed back indoors and leant against the wall, catching her breath.

"Who was that?" King said. "Are you alright? What did he want?"

She put her hands on her knees and tried to catch her breath. "I didn't know he was like that," she said. "I knew he was pissed off, but not like that. He looked like he wanted to kill me."

"Some boyfriend of yours? He needs sorting out?"

"No, no. It's okay. It's okay."

"People always show their true colours, remember that. Never trust people. You only think you know them. Get a dog—you count on them to save your life and train them to bite the bollocks off scum like that. You want some water?"

She shook her head no. He looked out into the alleyway, checking no one was there, then closed the door and said, "Come on. Work to do. You're doing well, Puppy, they've all been saying so—you're a natural in there. Don't worry about that streak of piss. He comes back here and I'll sling that caramel in his fucking face."

11

Five o'clock the next morning and Frances was watching out the window. She had been awake all night, expecting Betty to turn up with her curling tongs. Even alcohol did not seem to help her now. No matter how much she drank, she couldn't get drunk; reality kept barging its way back in. Elaine had not moved and Frances began to fret about malnutrition and bedsores and brain damage. She wondered at what point she should ring an ambulance but had palpitations at the very thought. Three days in stasis—Dom had said so. She should wake up soon. Surely she would wake up soon. The whole plan had gone so horribly wrong.

For several hours she paced by the window, not knowing if she should stand guard or run away. She barely factored Elaine into the equation anymore; there seemed nothing she could do about her, so she could plan only for herself. Stay, and if Elaine awoke, she might be able to get the money, but if she didn't stay and Betty came knocking, she was terrified to think what might happen. If she ran they might break in, find Elaine in bed unconscious, or perhaps she would awake to find two strangers there.

That said, she could hardly protect Elaine and herself from Dom and Betty. Perhaps she could hide in amongst the jumble of boxes and mess, clutch a santoku, wait and see what happened. She had asked King to lend her some money—he said he wished he could but he was skint himself. She'd called several loan companies in the night, twenty-four-hour hotlines promising to magic you money instantly, but none could send her any until Monday. She had rifled through Elaine's possessions, further obliterating the place, hunting for bank details or cash, anything that might help. At five o'clock she gave up and took up guard post at the living room window, wondering how it would end.

At eight o'clock her heart jumped at a knock at the door, until she recognised it, and then her pounding heart sank. *Rat-a-tat-tat* of a gloved knuckle. *Rat-a-tat-tat.* Then it came again—*rat-a-tat-tat*—followed by a warble: "Elaine, sweetie, let Mummy in. Your father is here as well. Elaine? Darling? We're not leaving 'til you let us in, I mean it." *Rat-a-tat-tat.*

Frances ran to the bedroom to see if Elaine had miraculously awoken. She hadn't. She tucked the sheets in around her and frantically attempted to tidy the room, stuffing paperwork and clothing into drawers, as if a neater appearance might detract from the unconscious body in the bed. She shoved plates and books under the bed and opened the window. She had kept it closed in case Elaine awoke in a daze and fell out of it, but the result had been a stifling, airless, sweaty room which was beginning to smell distinctly rancid. The knocking persisted, getting louder now, as were the warbles: *Rat-a-tat-tat! "Elaine!"* Frances sprayed some antiperspirant around the room and then over herself. Then, smoothing her hair, she went to the door.

Despite her preparations, she did not intend to let this woman in the flat, let alone anywhere near her bedroom, but she remembered the assertiveness of Mrs. Langthorn, so Mr. Langthorn was probably a force to be reckoned with. Most importantly, she must try to act completely normal, whatever that was. She opened the door with a huge grin.

"Jennifer, hello again! How lovely to see you."

The woman had clearly been expecting her daughter; a sickly, simpering smile vanished from her face. It was as if she'd forgotten that Frances lived there.

"Oh," she said. "Lewis, this is the person I was telling you about," and she held her hand out as if to say "Exhibit A." "I've come to speak to my daughter. Our daughter. Is she alright? I've been ringing her phone but there's no answer, which is most unlike her. We've been ever so worried. I would have telephoned ahead to say we were coming, of course, but, well, how could I?"

"She lost her phone," Frances said. "We're going to get her a new one once she's better."

"You mean she's not better?" Warble and eyebrows raised simultaneously.

"She's getting there, but she's still very tired. She's asleep now, in fact, and it's probably best not to disturb—"

"Elaine!" she screeched over Frances' shoulder. Frances kept her arm across the doorway, barring entrance. Mrs. Langthorn looked at the arm, then up at Frances. "Excuse me," she said through gritted teeth. "I wish to see my daughter."

"And I just told you, she is asleep."

"I don't believe this," she said. "Who the hell do you think you are?"

"Interesting you should ask. I'm your daughter's fiancée." She held out her hand, presenting the ring as evidence.

Jennifer Langthorn looked down at it, then slowly up at Frances, like a baddie in a Spaghetti Western, and said, "I don't think so," and pushed her way, with surprising force, into the flat. Frances stumbled backwards and tripped over Elaine's Wellington boots. Lewis entered, wiping his feet, and held out his hand to help Frances back up from an entanglement with the hatstand. "She's been ever so worried," he explained. Frances smiled at him and shut the door. As it turned out, he was not a force to be reckoned with. In fact, he looked—as Frances now imagined he always looked—like he didn't know what to do: hurry off after his wife or wait to be formally invited in. He sighed—as Frances imagined he often sighed—by way of apology, and also hopelessness, as if to say, "What can you do?" He was a tall man but he had the posture of one who has spent a lifetime being backed into corners. Because of this crookedness he seemed thin, when in fact he was muscular, and fragile, when in fact he was strong. His Adam's apple poked out like an item he'd choked on but had gotten used to. His suit was smart but a touch too small. She imagined his shoes pinched his feet. His whole demeanour was of a person who is used to closing his eyes and putting up with things.

"Elaine? Elaine?" Mrs. Langthorn tottered into the living room, where she dramatically gasped and put her hand to her chest. "My goodness, it's worse. Lewis. Lewis, it's worse. I didn't think it was possible." She looked around, aghast, the hand patting away at her chest in a demure flutter of self-comfort. Frances had grown used to the mess but it was amusing to see Mrs. Langthorn back amongst it in her patent leather shoes. "You see what I mean, Lewis? This is exactly what I was talking about. Now, do you still think I'm exaggerating? Look at me now and tell me I'm panicking unnecessarily. Just look at the state of it. Is it any wonder she's unwell? Are you happy now? Do you believe me? See—

I told you, didn't I? It looks like they've been burgled, for heaven's sake. The place is probably riddled with germs and all sorts. They should bulldoze the whole place down."

"That seems a bit unfair on my neighbours."

Mrs. Langthorn was not wearing a hat today and Frances suspected she had just had her hair styled; it certainly looked smoothed, dyed, rollered, and lacquered into obedience. Even as Elaine's mother turned her head in jerky, horrified movements, taking in the scale of the nightmare before her, not a single hair moved out of place. It probably daren't. She was again in sensible heels, but this time wore a flowy dress that wrapped itself round and round her body, up to the neck, where it appeared to be trying to strangle her. "I was actually just in the middle of cleaning up," Frances said, and Mrs. Langthorn made a "Hmph!" noise. Lewis said he was sorry for their intrusion, they just wanted to make sure Elaine was alright, but as they could see, she was in safe hands . . .

"Safe hands?" erupted Mrs. Langthorn. "I wouldn't store a bike in here!"

The three of them looked at Elaine's bike leant against the wall. Mrs. Langthorn went, "Hmph!" again. Frances had a brief mental image of Mr. and Mrs. Langthorn on a tandem, him sweating and pedalling as hard as he could whilst she reclined and whipped him. He had the permanent half-smile of a person who exists under the mantra "Anything for a quiet life." Not feeble, exactly, but as if he were forever humouring her, which he probably was. There was even old, accustomed affection in the way he looked at her. When her back was turned he rolled his eyes cheekily at Frances. "You know what she's like," he seemed to say. Mrs. Langthorn had disappeared into the bedroom, but not before pausing at the bathroom, leaning in, then closing the door swiftly and muttering, "Good Lord." Frances followed her. She could see Elaine, thankfully, had not moved. It seemed the situation would be far worse now if she were to awake. And yet she felt oddly comforted by Mrs. Langthorn's presence, as if, were Dom to appear, he would be so shocked he might just think he had the wrong flat. Besides, Mrs. Langthorn wasn't the sort of woman you would want to fight with; she had the type of incredulous confidence that can make an average person formidable. The sort of person who would be furious with the rude young man and put him over her knee. Frances almost wanted to see it happen.

Mrs. Langthorn crept into the room and sniffed the air, then looked at her husband over her shoulder. She moved carefully forwards.

"Elaine, are you awake, dear? We've brought the car, my angel. To take you home with us. You don't want to stay here."

Frances was livid. How dare this upper-class tart with her fat calves and Parker Bowles hair come traipsing into her house and suggest Frances wasn't taking proper care of her daughter? She said, "Excuse me, but I don't think she should be going anywhere. The doctor said for her to rest, which she was doing up until a moment ago."

The woman scoffed. "Lewis, bring the car round, park it out the front."

"But the sign said 'No Parking,'" Lewis said, stepping into the room as if this were his moment in a play.

"I don't care, Lewis. We'll only be a moment. I'm not leaving her here."

"You're over-reacting," Frances said.

"Over-reacting?" the woman yodelled.

"Yes. You'll make her feel worse if you stick her in a car. She's fine, really."

"Fine?" She was going operatic. "Darling, it's Mummy. Are you awake? Wake up, dear, there's a good angel."

"For God's sake, just leave her be."

"Lewis, get the car."

"No, Lewis. Don't."

Lewis looked back and forth between both women. Frances stared stoically at him. "Jennifer," he said softly, but his wife had turned away again and was tugging at Elaine's shoulder. "Jennifer, we've checked on her, we know she's alright now, maybe we should leave them in peace."

"For heaven's sake, Lewis. Look at this place. You really want to leave your daughter here? In this filth?"

"Come on now, Jenny. Don't be like that. I'm sure this young woman is trying her best."

"Don't try to placate me, Lewis. I'm not being like anything. And don't tell me what to do. You know I can't stand being bossed about. Now do as you're told and go and get the car and park it out the front."

Lewis dallied in the doorway, a sidestepping dance of uncertainty. He and Frances exchanged desperate looks. Neither of them wanted Elaine stuffed into a car, least of all Frances, who feared the hospital, blood tests, and subsequent exposure. A level of panic seemed to be rising in the room. Mrs. Langthorn was growing angry at being disobeyed and Frances was worrying that the sheets were about to be pulled back and Elaine would be exposed in a moment of pale, bony revelation. She imagined her sitting up, arms out, groaning like a Frankenstein. As it was, Mrs. Langthorn was getting closer and closer to Elaine's face, scrutinising it, with a growing look of suspicion. Frances played the only hand she had: "I'm sorry, but this is my house, and I'm going to have to ask you both to leave. You must stop coming round here and bursting in like this. If you do it again I'll call the police."

"The police," the woman scoffed, as if the very notion were preposterous.

"Yes," Lewis stepped forwards again. "Come on now, Jen. Please. Let's leave them be. Elaine will be alright."

"I'm not going without my angel. She should be at home with her mummy to look after her. I should have known to inspect this place before she moved. Now look." She sounded like she was going to cry.

"I have asked you to leave."

"This is my daughter, young lady."

"I know that."

"So I know what's best for her."

"For fuck's sake, she's not a child, she's a grown woman!"

"I do not appreciate that language, and her age is neither here nor there. She is my daughter, I have responsibility for her. Lewis, get the car."

"She isn't a piece of furniture—you can't just come in and seize her."

"I think you'll find I can."

"You can't and you won't."

"Lewis, get the car."

"No, Lewis. Don't."

There was an awful silence as they glared at each other. Lewis looked like he wanted to run out the door. Just as he cleared his throat and stood up a little taller—presumably in preparation to say something authoritative and manly—Mrs. Langthorn sneered, "You've never had any bloody spine, Lewis. It's always been the same."

"Come on, Jennifer," he said, deflated. "Let's go. Let Elaine sleep. She's out of it, and we're bothering this young woman. We should go."

Mrs. Langthorn took Elaine's hand in her own and patted it. Whether by reflex or semiconscious reaction, the hand was suddenly snatched back, accompanied by a flicker of a frown on the sweaty brow. Mrs. Langthorn sighed—defeated at last—then turned and stared at the ring on Frances' finger. She stuck her nose in the air and said, "Fine. But if you think you're marrying my daughter you've got another think coming. She must not have known what she was saying. That's all I've got to say on the matter." Then, despite having nothing more to say on the matter, she turned in the doorway, and said, "You're just a passing thrill, a novelty. Nothing more. You'll see." Then she flounced out of the room. Lewis followed. Frances stood looking at Elaine in the bed, feeling thankful, like she'd just narrowly escaped exposure, and turned the ring round and round on her finger in the new habit she had already formed.

Mrs. Langthorn and her husband were by the sofa, having words. She was talking quickly and he was nodding and making a motion with his hands like pressing down on a lid. She was whispering and gesturing in the direction of the bedroom, and he was trying to calm her. Whatever he was saying, it didn't appear to be working.

As Frances approached he suddenly said, "Right. We'll be off, then." Mrs. Langthorn turned around.

"I shall expect to hear from her in the next day or two. I'll talk to her then, in private, and we shall sort out this fiasco amongst ourselves." And after one parting look around the living room, she tore into the hallway and out of the door.

"Congratulations," Lewis said quietly as he passed, and hurried after her.

On the stairwell Frances overheard Mrs. Langthorn ranting, "I don't care if she wants to be a lesbian but I am not having her marry that monstrosity." If Mr. Langthorn responded, she did not hear it.

STEAM HUNG AND BILLOWED with the mystery of fog across a moor, and memories rose with it from the water like the ghosts of sunken seamen. Frances stuck her big toe into the tap and felt a cold drip run with a thrill down the sole of her foot and land—*plink*—into the bathwater. Her limbs felt weary and lifeless, one arm bobbing by her thighs, the other dangling over the side, where a spliff very nearly fell from two fingers almost too inert to hold it. Her mind fuggy, drugged, exhausted.

Early evening. She had smoked and drunk the day away, not even bothering to sit by the window. There seemed to be little point; she could not stop whatever was about to happen. The Langthorns, Dom, Betty, the police—it didn't matter who got there first, all she could do was hope Elaine awoke before the end arrived, or her death would be the ending in itself. She had been in the bath for over an hour, no longer even anxious about knocks on the door, just tired. Completely, deeply tired.

Of course, it was here that her tired mind succeeded in summoning Adrienne as if with some accidental witchcraft; she had not been trying, not yearning like usual, just wandering through her memories like pages in a book. In the heady other-worldliness of steam and visions, Frances could lie back and rest her chin beneath the surface so she had a crocodile-view of the grey glimmering water. Holding her breath, half closing her eyes, submerging her ears to hear the burbles and gurgles of distant pipes, remembering the times they shared together, here, in the bathtub. Then, as formed by the steam, she appeared. It was not a shock or surprise; it suddenly seemed obvious that, were this ever to happen, it would be now. Frances smiled at her. Real or not, it did not matter.

Adrienne. Adrienne, who seemed born from the water like a relic the past had yielded. Adrienne, who seemed to not have come from a womb but as if she had always existed, as if the earth itself had created her, out of its beauty, out of its magic. Adrienne, with a grace beyond human or animalistic limitations, a pure grace, like that of the clouds or sands, an elegance of limbs like thin spring branches. The voice of an aria at rest, the laugh of ancient chimes, the smile of pure offerings: Here, take joy, I have plenty to give. She sometimes longed to forget her, wished she had never met her, hoped she would never see her again, but it all was pointless, and never true, merely a reaction to the pain, like a wince, wanting more than anything for some temporary relief. Temporary, because the pain contained a pleasure for her masochistic blood-muscle. To remember was both a suffering and a pleasure, and she couldn't help but indulge in it.

Between Frances' legs, facing her, Adrienne appeared, giggling. Frances felt the legs slide between her own, felt her toes wriggle and poke about for a resting place, saw her breasts bob up like buoys on the surface, her elbows fan out on either side. They spoke without words, telepathically, as Frances had convinced herself they occasionally did in real life. "Hello, Adrienne," she said. "How are you, my love? I have missed you."

Adrienne grinned back and said, "And here I was, thinking you were trying to forget me."

"Never. I can't. It's impossible, you know that."

And Adrienne rested her head back against the tiled wall, closing her eyes and saying, "I know."

Frances slid her hands up the outside of Adrienne's legs, up and down, up and down, leaning forwards to kiss the crown of each knee.

"I love you," she said, and rested her forehead where her lips had kissed. "I love you so much. So much. So much."

"How much?" Adrienne whispered. "Tell me."

"With all of me. You know that. This is the problem now, you see—there's nothing left but that. And without you to give it to, it waits and waits and torments me. It has changed everything. All my goodness is tied up in it. All kindness and generosity and forgiveness, they all wait with it. All that is left to me now, to live with, are the counterparts. The bad bits."

"You aren't bad."

"That's because you got all the good, so you don't see it."

"Do you remember when we stayed at that cottage?"

"The one with the paintings of otters everywhere?"

"Yes. Do you remember what we said in the garden, on the iron bench, by the bird feeders?"

"We said, 'Until never-end.' "

"Until never-end. And I meant it. I meant that."

"Then why did you leave me?"

"You know why, darling. I don't want to talk about it."

She did know why, and she rested her head on Adrienne's knee and rocked side to side. "I'm sorry," she said.

"It wasn't your fault, as such—it's just the way you are, it's your personality. I couldn't handle it, so intense. It's one of your best qualities, really, and what I loved best in the beginning, but you had no control over it—it swamped me, it swamped us. I needed to be freer than that. You were my first monogamous relationship, I wasn't used to it, and I thought I'd adapt but I couldn't. It's just not me. Loving one person. I can't do it. Maybe I just have too much love to give." She opened her eyes. "But I never stopped loving you. I still do. You just . . . wanted me completely, and I was losing myself to you. You demanded a loyalty that was not in my nature; you were so terrified, as always, that you'd be abandoned."

"And then you left me anyway."

"You knew I would have been happy to share. An open relationship. But you didn't want that."

"I couldn't have handled it. It would have killed me."

"Your love is selfish. It's greedy. It all had to be on your terms."

"Because I didn't want anyone else. I just wanted you."

"All or nothing, isn't it? Always, all or nothing."

"Except I didn't think nothing was an option. You sprang that on me in the restaurant. I'd have done anything for you."

"Except let me breathe."

They'd had this conversation and others like it many times in real life. One typically drunken night shortly after it ended Frances had called her and they'd argued. Frances had promised to change, to be better, to relax, but Adrienne said she'd heard it before, and she needed space. "I need to get back to myself," she had said.

"Did you get back to yourself?" Frances asked now as Adrienne closed her eyes again.

"Eventually. It wasn't easy."

"What does it mean, getting back to yourself?"

"The fact that you have to ask that says a lot about you."

"What do you mean?"

"You have no idea of your own self. You shy away from it and hide from it and try to fill the void with other people. You're beyond an identity crisis. I'm not sure you've ever really known who you are."

"It hasn't been easy for me. Because, well, you know——"

"I know, I know. Your mother. All the loss. The pain. I know," Adrienne inspected her fingernails. "Honestly, you have to stop clinging on to that stuff—it's not good for you, it messes you up."

Frances felt very small. She felt like she had shrivelled up at the end of the tub. They sat in silence for a while.

"I saw a kingfisher once," Frances said. "It flew up along a river on a horrible grey day. A streak of bright colour. I stood between the barges and barren hedges and the scene was so still and colourless, I could respond to it. I try to keep life grey, because too much makes me feel like I'm in sensory overload, and I can't cope. That's why I'm like I am. Loving you was the only sensory overload I could bear. Love, the only thing I could bear."

Adrienne sighed impatiently. "Yes, but you know this is simply because you can't handle feelings. Call it being grey or flat or whatever you like, it's wanting to be numb, darling. And that's what I'm saying. That's why it isn't easy for you. All this feeling-abandoned nonsense. It doesn't take a genius to figure it out."

Frances remembered feeling like this on several occasions, when she was unhappy or confused by Adrienne's actions, and Adrienne had exasperatedly explained them, but somehow left her more confused. She knew what she meant at the beginning, when she was talking, but always by the end she'd be trying to quickly figure out what Adrienne meant before she turned away and said, "I don't want to talk about it anymore."

"She proposed to me," Frances eventually said.

"I know."

"With the sort of ring I would have given you, but I was too afraid you'd reject me. You would have, wouldn't you?"

"What's it like?"

"What?"

"The ring."

She held out her hand. Adrienne grinned. "You said yes, you minx."

"No idea why. It doesn't mean anything. Nothing seems to at the moment. It's just another prop in the movie."

"It's beautiful."

"It is. Would you have married me? If I'd asked before? Before it all went wrong?"

Adrienne tilted her head to one side, as she always did when she thought Frances was being awkward and lovely.

"My funny little Frances and her funny little mind."

"Please, Adrienne. Don't."

In the next room, Elaine groaned in her sleep. Frances and Adrienne looked at the wall beside them, listening. "What are you going to do about her? Your little situation?" Adrienne said, cocking her head.

"I'm sort of figuring that out as I go along."

"I always said you smoked too much weed."

"So did you."

"I know, but it's different with me. Anyway, you should have a plan of sorts. You know what you're like, darling, poodling along without thinking until you hit a mountainside, then suddenly you're surprised to find yourself there. You need to think it through."

Frances scrunched her eyes closed, not wanting to think about it. "I'll figure it out, okay?"

"I just worry about you."

"You do?"

"Where would we get married, then?"

"Outdoors. In Scotland. By a loch. With thunderous clouds overhead and no other sounds than nature. The wind and trees and an eagle."

"The clouds reflected in the water, I bet."

"Lightning bolts in the distance, striking the earth as we say 'I do.'"

"Thunderbolts and lightning—so very, very frightening."

"And a deer on the hill in the distance."

"You and your imagination."

"Why not? You never know."

"Then back to some tiny cabin, I suppose, with a view across the water and mountains all around, a log fire, red wine, no bed, just a huge pile of quilts and blankets and enormous pillows laid on the floor in the glow of the flames."

"It sounds perfect."

"Of course it does."

"I didn't first see you by the bananas, Adrienne. I first saw you in the café. I bumped into you outside, when you were on your phone."

"I don't remember that."

"No. I know you don't."

Adrienne vanished.

Frances sat up in the bathtub and steam peeled away from her body like smoke.

12

WHETHER BY A GUST of wind or the hand of God
or an honest glance in a mirror, the toupee was gone. There was
some reassurance in it, as if it affirmed a return to normality, or
at least an attempt to. Frances managed to refrain from the temptation of mentioning it and sat down in the familiar chair. She
thought he looked tired, and she could tell he thought the same
of her. His eyes were puffy, as if he had suddenly awoken at his
desk, or been crying. Hers looked like she'd spent the night drinking gin through her tear ducts. For several seconds they stared at
each other, then he opened and closed his hands and said, "So,
how are we today?"

"I literally have no one else to talk to."

"Right."

"And I'm afraid and lost and just need some help, even if it's
just sitting here a few minutes."

"I see. Well, anything you say in here is confidential—"

"Please, don't talk to me like that—talk to me like a human

being. Don't try to pretend to be a doctor. Do something you're good at."

He looked hurt.

"I'm sorry," she said. "I didn't mean it like that. I meant, you helped me once. When I came here that first time and you talked like a real person. I know you shouldn't have done but that helps more than anything else—can't you see that? More than fucking pills and prescriptions."

The doctor leant back in his chair and looked at her. For several moments he said nothing, and Frances began to wonder if she'd overstepped the mark, if she should just get up, kick the desk, and leave. What was the use of coming back here anyway? Then he suddenly announced: "My wife left me last night, for the second time in a year, to go back to the vet she'd been fucking when she decided our marriage was dull and I was too pointless to be with."

Frances looked at him. He continued:

"The first time she left, I fell apart. I felt humiliated, crushed, finished with. Then she came back and I told myself now everything would be fine and I almost believed it. But I always knew, deep down, that she would leave again. Then, as I sat there last night with the dog beside me, I realised something. I realised I had always been unhappy. During the marriage I was unhappy because she was. Then she left and I was unhappy because she wasn't. Then she came back and I was unhappy because I knew she didn't want to be with me. Then when she left again, last night, I felt doomed to it, to this unhappiness. And why? Because it was all caught up in a constant state of wanting, which did nothing but leave me miserable and reaching for her, changing myself, trying to be who I thought she'd like me to be. You see, my unhappiness was not caused by my wife, but by me wanting to change her, change us, change myself, wanting things to be different. I realised I could spend a lifetime blaming myself and being miserable, or I could work on forgiveness, and something in me changed. Perspective, I suppose. It was a sudden and huge and brilliant shift. Would I take her back now? No. But I can try to understand that every person is flawed, and we all have choices: You can let the past continue to dictate your future, or you can change it for yourself. Old patterns of behaviour are only that: old patterns. This is why it's called 'mental health' despite the fact that we're mainly talking about emotions—because thoughts determine feelings. Change how you think in order to change how you feel. Is it easy? No. But I can promise you something: if you don't learn to forgive whoever and whatever must be forgiven, and get over the past, you pave the way for a painful future. If you can't face it and cope with real life, you are going to be forced to shut away, or shut down, and suffer. Only you know who or what needs forgiving, but I'm telling you now, that's where you need to begin."

She had sat up in her seat, head tilted slightly, listening. Then she said, "What if it's me? What if I've done wrong?"

"Then that's the first person you have to forgive. Life is all about learning. If we don't, we go round and round in circles. I have learnt that I can't trust my wife with my feelings. I can't trust her at all. But I have also learnt that, although I'm not perfect, I am enough. I don't need to chase or wait for her, or try to be someone else—it's pointless, and all it will do is hurt me more. So it is done, and in time I'll move on."

His expression settled into one of openness. There was a blob of jam on his tie. He said, "You aren't who you think you are, remember that. None of us are. You aren't the labels and terms and ideas you have about yourself. Ditch those—they only hold you back. If I think I'm only a husband and father and doctor, where does that leave me when my wife goes, my daughter leaves, I retire? Labels only hold us further back from the truth."

"Which is?"

"The more you cling to pain, anger, resentment, the more you tell yourself who you think you are, the harder it is to be yourself, a loving and compassionate human."

He closed his eyes and inhaled. The jam glistened, his head gleamed, his round cheeks shone.

As she regarded him across the desk, Frances felt a sad old feeling, of a man near yet far, present but unreachable, reminiscent of the rare occasions she sat across the dinner table from her father, eating soup. The inner voice of the unheard child wailed inside her, pummelling its fists on her heart. Suddenly, for the first time in years, she thought of her father's funeral, the final parting, down, down, down, forever it seemed, as if he were being lowered ten feet instead of six, just to make a point of how hopeless their relationship had been.

She leant forwards and put her arms on the desk and rested her head on them, hiding her face, willing the doctor to say a kindly word more or, better yet, pat her on the head. In a moment's break from correct conduct and rules, his hand arrived not on her head, but her arm, and he softly said, "It's okay."

Sometimes that is all it takes. Sometimes we are so deeply fractured—not on the surface, perhaps, but like the veined scars of an earthquake splintered through us, down, down, down—all it takes is the gentleness of touch and voice to make us temporarily feel cemented again; a close approximation to affection and we can absorb all the solace as if it were love. She stayed there a moment, allowing the feeling, the warmth of his hand on her arm, feeling grounded and seen and temporarily held. Then the hand was removed, and she looked up and was met with his roundish, plumpish face smiling serenely at her in a way she would previously have seen as condescending but now recognised as the genuine tenderness that exists in the empathy one fucked-up human has for another. With the light coming in through a gap in the blinds bouncing off his brilliantly bald head, he looked more saintly and wonderful than any person she'd seen before.

"It's okay to say you can't cope," he said. "A strength that is too stubborn is a weakness in the end. But remember, you can cope better than you think you can. That's why you are here. It's why you keep coming back. You are coping. It doesn't feel like it, but that's what it is. If you weren't, you'd be dead. So be brave. Find what needs forgiving, what needs fixing, then forgive and fix."

It made sense. She sat up in her chair, thinking. Not about Elaine, or Adrienne, or Dom, or even her mother; in this place of sudden contemplation an understanding occurred, a recognition of a startling truth: that the chasm she had always felt between herself and her father was not a chasm at all, but a sign of their incredible likenesses and similarities she had misconstrued throughout the years. Their mutual quietness, their thoughtfulness, their introspection, their introversion. All the time she had thought him to be far away but she could see, now, he'd been right there all along, being exactly the same as her. Waving across the garden—separate, yes, but mirrored. Across the dinner table, eating soup, it had not been awkwardness that caused the silence but the simple lack of a need to talk. And, in realising that this was so, another truth came along and struck her a blow; if she carried the guilt of a child's death, then he would have carried it tenfold. A gap which had resided in her narrowed. "I have to go," she said.

"Can I do anything to help?" he said.

"You already have." She stood up, pulling her bag onto her shoulder. "Thank you."

"It will be alright, whatever it is. Just, keep going. And face whatever needs to be faced. And remember, forgiveness is key.""

SHE RUSHED OUTSIDE and collided into Monday morning chaos; streets and pavements heaved, the temperature had risen. The impetus of unavoidable facts, of the past rearranging itself into some new image, plus the panic that it was Monday—*the* day— rushed through her body as she passed through the throngs of people. In the thick crowd of shuffling bodies she walked close to the curb, stepping into the road now and then to avoid an on-comer. Thoughts flashing through her mind as a confused rabble, she hurried with the understanding that she was heading in the right direction, wherever that may be, feet leading the way. Faces, bodies, people blurred. The traffic beside her slowed to a crawl, caught up in rush-hour congestion, then slowly rolled along no faster than the pedestrians walking. Beside her, Frances became aware of a bus, only a few inches away. It moved along like a friend of hers, like a companion, keeping pace. And because it was there, Frances looked to her right. And there was the tiny, terrifying face of Betty staring back at her.

Very briefly, Frances hoped Betty did not remember or recog-nise her. But then, getting to her feet, separated only by a pane of glass, Betty rose up like a cobra in a vivarium, eyes fixated and ready to attack. She slammed her fist on the glass. For whatever reason—shock or disbelief or British decorum—Frances just con-tinued walking forwards, facing ahead, as the bus moved along beside her and Betty proceeded to bang, bang, bang on the glass, bellowing muffled yet recognisable words at Frances as she walked along, whilst several fellow travellers sat frozen in their seats, pretending nothing was happening. The bus began to indicate it was pulling over to stop. Betty, in a lull to catch her breath or perhaps search her vocabulary for further insults, also noticed that the bus was stopping, slammed her fist once more on the glass, and yelled something even Frances could make out: "Wait there."

Not likely.

Frances ran. She shoved and barged her way through the crowd with Betty's voice screeching out above the voices and traffic, "Come back, bitch!" One brief glance behind her and Betty's eyes and hair—both huge on such a small person—were all Frances could see weaving and sliding her way through the people. Frances reached the train station; she turned in, ran to the pile-up shoving its way through the barrier, pushed her way in, and dashed to an escalator. This was a chase but not in a random direction; she knew where she was going, if only she could get there. With luck finally on her side, the train was in and due to depart; she jumped on board and passed through several carriages before sitting down, her bag on her lap, hunkered behind it. Out of the window, she could see Betty, looking back and forth between this train and the other on the neighbouring platform, unsure which one the mark had got on. Finally, the whistle blew, the door beeped shut, and the train began to move. Just as it did, Frances lowered the bag and stared hard over at Betty. She caught her eye. Betty pointed at her with the fingers of both hands like guns, and then she laughed ferociously. Frances was terrified, but at least now Betty would have no reason to go to the flat. As Betty became smaller and smaller, watching the train depart and still laughing her head off, Frances sank back in the chair and wiped the sweat from her face, looking around at the faces on the carriage as if

Dom and the rest of the Ladies might be there. They weren't. Very gradually, her heart began to calm.

This train journey was so synonymous with one destination, it seemed impossible that the tracks might go anywhere else. She rested her head against the window and watched the changing scenery, from city to suburbs to endless fields until, an hour later, the train slowed and she saw the familiar view. Nothing special or unusual at first—just a car park and a jumble of buildings—but then, there, a sudden stencil of silver: the sea, and with it the excitement and nostalgia synonymous with hope and home.

She disembarked onto the platform behind the backpacks of happy day-trippers and holiday makers, all following the signs: TO THE SEAFRONT. She pushed through the crowds and hurried along the tired streets she loved so much, rows of front gardens filled with wind-stripped faceless gnomes and tinkling wind chimes, twee lace curtains billowing out through bungalow windows, the uncanny sense of having stepped back in time. She jogged along, past the decaying gift shops propped up by beach balls and body boards, the street market flogging brown mushrooms and boxes of batteries, voices calling, "Best strawbs, two pound a punnet!" then suddenly the scene opened up before her, as if exhaling, and there it was: the sea. Not a pretty nor dainty sea, but strong, healthy, muscular, up for a fight; it wrestled and rolled off to a cold gold horizon. Half a mile to the right was the pier, two miles to the left was the lighthouse, and everything in between was gay and vibrant. A long, endless line of towering Victorian townhouses in varying states of disrepair trailed off to the sunny, multicoloured beach huts, going on forever, or so it appeared. Barefoot pedestrians with windbreakers under their arms walked noisily along with their families, bickering, shouting, laughing, mothers herding them all together, fathers bare-chested and beery-eyed. Kids, shiny and slippery out of the water, pattered like seals to go and buy ice cream. Hordes of people sat in rows along the seawall, ripping into cod with their fingers and stabbing chips with little wooden forks, and outside the arcades and in the pub gardens people talked and drank and smoked. And there it was, the smell she loved. Seaweed and sun cream and cigarettes, blending with varying foods as she jogged past: doughnuts, vinegar, candyfloss. The intermingling sound of squealing kids and screaming seagulls, all ecstatic and right where they wanted to be.

She didn't know how many times she'd been here. Hundreds, possibly. Heart, eyes, mind, all knew it and darted off in the direction of the lighthouse. She ran. Parents pulled their children aside and dogs were yanked out of the way, determination and purpose paving the path ahead. Over the seawall beside her, the tide was out; inflatables of all colours dappled the shallows as bathers dangled their warm bodies in the cold water. She ran. The sound of people lessened; soon they were behind her, their voices carrying on the breeze like a record played through a distant window. The path divided at a fork in the road and she followed it away from the seafront; up, up, up it went along a now people-less path, the only sounds coming from her feet below and the gulls above. She ran, and she ran. As the lighthouse came into view so did the row of big red roses that preceded the gate to the church. An old, beautiful building made of many stones, many colours, many centuries. The gate creaked as she burst through it. No dallying this time, no dawdling on the path; she knew why she was here and paused only a moment to remember where to go. There, by the far wall, beside three wind-stripped silver birches, she saw it, the headstone, the name: her family name, her father's name.

She had not been here for many years, in fact, only once since the burial. The perceived distance that she had thought existed in his lifetime had left her feeling it would be an affectation to suddenly feign closeness by visiting him more after death than when he was alive. Even in his final moments he had been a man of few words, just handed her a piece of paper with an address on it and said, "For whenever you're ready, if you do want to see her," then he had slipped away as quietly and unremarkably as he had lived. She had thought it was shock, or perhaps just years of stunted emotions, but she hadn't cried when he died, just sat there silently with him until it seemed like time to leave.

She knelt down beside the wild, weedy grave, sitting on her heels, wiping her wet brow, her hot, exhausted face. Everything else seemed very far away; she could only just hear the sea, a tiny sound that floated around the graveyard like the hush of sleeping souls saying "Shhh" to mortal visitors. She had no flowers, but idly plucked some daisies, which she toyed with until they formed a chain. A robin bounced along beside her. With her heart and breathing and mind finally slowed, she allowed herself a few minutes' rest, just thinking, and keeping these thoughts separate, for once. Within this blip in time came a feeling of purpose and reason. She brushed her hair back from her face, then swept some dirt from the headstone. The sea air had gnawed at its edges. The words, however, were as vivid as they had been on the day they were chiselled there, as if it had happened yesterday. Frances ran her finger through them, as if writing out his name. She looked up through the branches of the birches and wondered if they had grown at all—they seemed the same height as she remembered them. Seven years had passed. Seven long yet little years.

"I thought you were a pretty crap father," she suddenly said aloud. "I don't know why. I don't know what I was expecting. Trips to the cinema, maybe. Holidays, that sort of thing. Not that I particularly wanted them—I just thought we should do them, be a father and daughter, you know? I used to see all the other kids kicking balls around or riding bikes with their dads and I'd wonder why we weren't like that. I thought perhaps there was something wrong with us, with me, maybe that I wasn't a boy. Nothing you ever said or did—I just wondered. Thought maybe you didn't know what to do with me, because I was a girl, albeit never a very girly one. But it wasn't anything to do with that. We weren't like that because we weren't like that, neither of us. Given all the flights and cruises in the world, we'd both still be holed up reading a book somewhere, eating soup.

"You weren't crap at all, Dad. You didn't tuck me in or do the motherly stuff, but you gave me space and freedom and trust. I just couldn't see it; all I saw was absence. It was always tomato soup, wasn't it, because that was what we both liked. I came back home to visit once, when I was eighteen, and there was no answer at the front door so I let myself in round the back. You were standing on a bucket, looking over the fence at the fields and the sea, and I felt like an intruder, so I left. Imagine if, just once, one of us had had the guts to mention the one big obvious thing which kept us from one another. But it was an unwritten rule, wasn't it? Don't mention it. Don't mention her. You kept that pain all to yourself, hoping it wouldn't hurt me, unaware that it was already, and always, there. The fences you built up around yourself to protect me from her, from pain. Like with Ben. That wasn't your fault, Dad. You didn't do anything wrong. I wish you had known that."

She pulled up some weeds and placed the daisy chain on the headstone. No tears, but a fullness in the throat as she said, "Well, I just wanted to tell you I understand. I mean, I do now. I get it. I'll come by more often. I promise." She stood up and for a moment stood there, looking down at it, at him. She nudged the headstone with her foot and said, "Bye, Dad." Then paused, kissed her fingers, and placed them swiftly on his name. *I'm sorry*, she wanted to say. *I wish I'd been good, endlessly and permanently good. It would have been easier on you, I think. You bought the house and garden but I built the bridge. What idiots we are, the two of us. Absolute fucking idiots.* It was suddenly almost too much to bear. She scrunched her eyes closed and thought—and mouthed— *Love you.* Then she left.

Days of stress and sleeplessness descended on her, combined with the heat, and made her feel giddy. Almost stumbling, she took a shortcut through a narrow lane on her way back down to the seafront and stood outside the house she knew. The house with the pink door. It always looked the same, whenever she visited. Very neat, very quaint, in keeping with the area, sheer curtains and flowers on the windowsills. She stood across the road from it and imagined walking up to the front door, knocking, footsteps on the other side approaching nearer and nearer, the click of a lock turning. Maybe one day but not today. *Whenever you are ready*. She slumped heavily back down to the seafront.

Down the stone steps, onto the beach—cliffs to her left, sea to the right—a stretch ahead of her like the yellow brick road. *Just a few minutes*, she thought, *just a few minutes before going back*. The sand was still wet and cool from its time beneath the tide, and it felt nice, sponging up between her bare toes and around her feet, shoes in hand. It was different here, away from the sunbathers and ice cream stalls, more peaceful and dreamlike. Several individuals strolled along this stretch, indenting the sand with the feet of dog walkers, fossil hunters, and metal detectorists. She turned and looked out to sea. To the right, the pier looked ever so far away, like a rulered pencil line above the waves. Behind her were the clay cliffs where the lighthouse shot up to the sky. Serious, solitary people examined the base where it met the beach, peering intently, searching for ancient shark teeth and the imprints of curled bodies long since squashed into history. Smooth, flat black rocks blanketed where the shore met the sea, permanently laced with glowing green seaweed like the floor of an enchanted forest. She strolled further along, pocketing the odd shell as she went, until she felt she must rest, must sit down for a minute. She flopped in front of the cliffs where the sand was smooth and quilted, glanced side to side at the people, the water a thin far-away mirror, the staircase on her right, protruding forwards in the corner of her eye, then she lay down flat on her back. Here, she could hardly hear anything, as if all sounds were absorbed by the sand. Distantly came the rocking sea, lunge and crash, lunge and crash, reverberating from the wash through the sand to her body. She squinted up at the sky. It was empty apart from the tortuous sunlight, not so much beaming as flinging itself about fluorescently. She put her hands across her eyes. She suddenly felt she could sleep for days. *I must not sleep,* she told herself, *I must not sleep,* but each blink dragged her eyelids down as if weighted with all the weariness of the past week.

Then she began to imagine a woman approaching her from the sea, not swimming but wading, the waves rolling up and over her shoulders, dropping down to her waist. It was not her make-believe mother, and it was not an hallucination or a conjuring; it was a dream. She was wearing a turquoise dress that, despite being wet, still shone brightly, and looked as soft as feathers. She moved her hands through the water to help her walk and looked all around her, at the pier and the lighthouse, the beaches, the beach huts, the cliffs. Then, finally, when all else had been looked at, she turned her eyes to Frances. She raised a hand and smiled, beamed, laughed. Then, she stuck her hands into the water and pulled out a swaddled baby. She held it out, as if offering it, inviting Frances to look. Then, just as she started to wade through the breakers, a huge wave grew behind her, much higher than all the others. Frances tried to shout but couldn't; her mouth was suddenly clogged with sand, and she gagged and coughed and retched. The wave grew and grew like a demon, foaming at the mouth, curled claws and flashing eyes, standing over mother and child, and they did not know it. And just as she stepped foot onshore, it crashed down upon her, and both of them disappeared.

Frances awoke suddenly, and for a brief time was confused; all around her she heard shouting. It was a strange noise, made no sense at all. The sunlight hurt her eyes, and she rolled onto her side, sitting up on one elbow. She dug out her phone; she'd been there for over an hour. As she blinked, an unusual sight came into view.

Water.

All around her, water.

On the steps, now semi-submerged, several people stood. They seemed to be shouting at her.

"Get the hell off the beach!"

The tide had crept up on her as she slept and now it almost touched her ankles. She stood up and looked around bewilderedly, scooping up her shoes and bag. On the cliff behind her several people had gathered. They looked at her in unison from very far away, just their concerned faces peering down from on top of their bodies. They were all yelling and gesticulating, pointing to the impossible, impassable steps, becoming further engulfed as the waves reached to tag the cliffs. The people on the steps were yelling back for her to clamber up, to climb, quickly. Neither option was easy or appealing. The cliffs were neither very high nor steep but they crumbled like shortbread; oftentimes when she'd been walking along, a portion of them had slid onto the beach, much to the delight of the fossil hunters. She turned to the water. It lapped away near the top step. She stuffed her shoes inside her bag and checked her phone and keys were in there, then put the bag on top of her head with one hand, and waded in. Spectators yelled in encouragement and waved their hands. By the steps, a policeman had appeared and seemed to be watching with the crowd, arms folded. She wondered if she was going to be comforted or scolded. She quickly wished she had taken her jeans off; submerged, they seemed to have become her enemy, trying to drag her down. She walked in further and further, the beach suddenly sloping off to a murky depth, her feet just about touching the slimy rocks beneath her as the water came up to her chest.

"Keep going," people yelled. "Nearly there."

She had no choice but to paddle. Kicking her feet, she used her free hand to help her swim as the other held her bag on her head, and she was rocked back and forth like the seaweed on the surface, one minute to the coast then drawn further out, battling and flapping her way over to the steps. Finally, she reached them; her foot touched down and she was able to haul herself up. Two men waded down and grabbed her under the arms. She gasped thanks. She seemed to weigh a ton.

Already most of the spectators had walked off. As she sat on a bench in her drenched clothes, she felt the transformation from damsel in distress to village idiot. "I'm so sorry," she said. "I'm so stupid."

"You'd be surprised how often it happens," the police officer said. "We put the tide times up and warning signs—nobody takes a blind bit of notice." He sighed and shook his head at her. "Are you alright?"

She nodded. Someone handed her a bottle of water, someone

else their damp towel. She kept saying, "Thank you. I'm so stupid. I'm so stupid."

"Shall I get you a beach dress from a gift shop?" a young woman said. She was sucking on an ice lolly and had cute freckles. She was about twenty-five. Frances said, "God. Yes. Thanks. Let me give you some money," and she rummaged in the bag and handed over a few notes. "Anything will do," she said. "Thank you so much."

"New here, are you?" the police officer said.

"No, but I come here often. I fell asleep. I feel such a fool."

He laughed. "No bother. If I had a quid every time someone got pissed and passed out on that beach . . ." He didn't finish this statement. He didn't need to.

People who hadn't witnessed it but were just passing by stared at her and her wet clothes. She suddenly felt something in her jeans pocket and stuck her hand inside. It was Elaine's phone. "That's a goner," the police officer said cheerfully. "Looks like you'll be needing a new one of those. Anyone you need me to call?" and she said no, no one, thank you, then threw it in the bin beside her.

Wearing a shapeless pink beach dress with a huge sequinned palm tree on the back, she trudged back along the promenade in her heavy black boots, to the pier entrance. THE HAPPIEST SOUND IN ALL THE WORLD IS THAT OF CHILDREN'S LAUGHTER. Standing there, as people rushed in and out and passed her, she watched a little girl in a yellow sunhat waddle over to a huge blue elephant. It was one of those rides you put a coin in and it blasts out a deafening melody whilst shunting back and forth. The girl's mother helped her in, then set the thing in motion. As it slowly moved, the girl smiled and smiled whilst her mother clung to her hand for dear life. Frances stayed there a moment, leaning on a metal barrier, then suddenly her phone rang.

"Where the hell are you, Puppy?" King shouted. "Your shift started half an hour ago."

"Shit."

"Get your ass down here. Three guys off sick and Ant's been arrested. Wherever the fuck you are, get a move on—we need you."

Her mind raced, as if waking up, then she said, "Okay. Okay, I'm coming. Um, I need to just pop home quickly. Fuck, I'll be a couple of hours."

"What the fuck, Puppy? You get here now!"

"You don't understand—I have to go home, I need to check on something, I need to change—"

"I don't want to hear that shit! What the fuck is this? This ain't like you. Get your ass down here!"

"I'll be as quick as I can."

"Move!"

BY THE TIME she arrived in the kitchen she was nearly three hours late. She did not go home; she reasoned, in her bewildered and irrational way, fuelled mainly by a mixture of panic and ill-founded hope, that if Dom went to the flat and there was no answer, then he would come here, in which case she would hide. She would lock herself in the walk-in freezer if needs be. It sounded rather appealing. King would protect her. He might not be much of a friend but he was king of the kitchen and there was no way he'd let Dom enter the place. She was still weaving her way through the chefs to pot-wash when she heard him: "Oi! Puppy!"

She turned and he was striding towards her, a whole wheel of cheese in his hands. He stopped, looked her up and down, and said, "What the fuck happened to you?"

Sweat and saltwater were wet in her hair, beach dress and walking boots topped off the crazed look. She held her hands up and said, "You told me to come straight here."

"You can't work in a kitchen like that!"

Several of the chefs were laughing.

"Well, what am I supposed to do?" she said, and King's face turned into a twisted little grin. "No problem, Puppy," he said. "They need help upstairs too. You go up there for this evening."

"What? King, no, please. I can't go up there like this."

"Well, you sure as shit can't work down here. I guess this'll be the last time you're three hours late, huh?"

"Look at me! King, come on. Don't do this to me, don't send me upstairs looking like this."

He laughed gently and put an arm around her. "Puppy, Puppy, Puppy, as if I would. You think I'm so mean?"

She sighed with relief. Then he slung an apron over her shoulder. "Not without one of these. Now, go!"

She turned, dazed-looking, and he called after her, "Oh, and Puppy. Smile, for fuck's sake."

She had seldom been to the restaurant upstairs, but she was petrified of the place. As she walked in through the door, a server came barging past, carrying trays and glasses and shouting, "Out of the way!" Behind the bar, two girls shook cocktail shakers and cracked open beer bottles and popped bottles of wine. Speeding through and around the tables wove servers keeping smiles glued to their faces whilst they forced a fake laugh at the patrons' jokes and hurried away with orders. It looked and sounded like every table was full. On the wall, beside the specials board, was the new

Monday Menu, a cheap set dinner of soup and pasta and tiramisu. This was why they were so busy. Frances walked over to the only girl she recognised, who greeted her with "Thank God, finally. Right, it's dead easy: Write down what they order and bring it over here, then I'll show you how to put it through. Don't drop anything, don't swear at anyone, and put your tips in the jar by the till. The table by the door has just arrived so start with them. That whole side is yours. I'll explain more in a minute. I've just got to take these drinks over. Pads and pens are over there." She paused just long enough to look her up and down and raise an eyebrow, then vanished.

Frances stood, dumbstruck, for several moments, with her back to the restaurant, feeling like she might pass out. She remembered this feeling when she was at school, like she wanted to make herself as small as possible, then people might not see her, and she might be left alone. She could stay there being small and invisible all night, if needs be. Beside her, a telephone rang. She stared at it, then looked around, silently pleading for help. The girl who had just taken drinks dashed over to it and began a very fast, half-shouted conversation about a wrong booking, then slammed it down, turned to Frances, and said sarcastically, "I'm sorry, do you have a reservation? Or are you waiting for a fucking invite?"

Frances picked up a pad and a pen, feeling like she'd just been handed a rifle and told to go and shoot someone. Then, she heard it.

The laugh. It stood out not because it was louder than any other, but because she knew it so well. It immediately reawakened a hundred memories, a hundred occasions, a hundred emotions. Frances' eyes followed it and found her there, across the restaurant.

Her hair was different—cut into a harsh bob—but it was the

sameness, the lack of change, that surprised Frances, as if time should have changed her more. Same red lipstick, same Celtic earrings, same military boots, same composure, resting her chin on her fist as the woman opposite her talked. Same supple face, same engaging smile. She picked up a menu and began to fan herself with it, laughing again, wafting it back and forth casually, carelessly, chattering away. The restaurant did not stop for her, the scene did not pause, but she might as well have been the only woman in there, such was the precision of focus from Frances' eyes. It created a mixture of repulsion and desire, horror and self-preservation, the urge to sprint from her and yet also run into her arms. Their time apart had left no visible negative signs, had not aged her at all, had not hardened her expression or hollowed her eyes. Frances suddenly thought of each time she had stepped on the scales, each pound lost through grief, each sleepless night, each crease on her skin. Each drink, each tear, each nightmare. They had not suffered together, it seemed. If anything, sitting there, sipping her wine and flicking her hair, she looked more beautiful than ever. Frances looked at herself in the mirror behind the bar, saw her sallow face, her scraggly hair, her extreme visible weariness, and the ludicrous dress, all beyond help. She looked over at the others round the table. Beside her sat a dapper, moustachioed man of about thirty, wearing a waistcoat and cravat, his sleeves rolled up and his hair swept aside as he examined himself in the back of a spoon. The woman opposite her was roughly the same age and seemed to be out to impress, talking uncontrollably, running her hand up the back of her neck as she spoke, occasionally twizzling a curl of hair. Next to her was a much older man, grey hair and grey suit, who looked around uncomfortably, as if he'd sat at the wrong table. It occurred to her that she could refuse to do it; all she needed to do was walk back downstairs. This was a restaurant, not the army. But then she discovered she was moving forwards as if on a conveyor belt; all the other servers seemed to twist and dart around her in a blur. She arrived by the table and they all looked up—all except her, because she was by now scrolling through her phone, bored. Frances recognised the behaviour and expression; she had seen it many times before. She did not notice Frances until Frances said, "Hello, Adrienne."

Frances had often imagined this moment. In the fantasy, she approached Adrienne as a model of smooth, chic sophistication: immaculate hair, businesslike yet subtly sexual clothing, creating such a picture of success and carefree happiness it took Adrienne a moment to recognise her and, when she did, she stumbled back a little, gasping, saying something like "Frances? Is that you? Wow, you look incredible." Much flirtation followed. It was painfully apparent, even to Frances, that reality was unlikely to meet expectation, but still she couldn't help hoping—just a tiny bit—that something wonderful might be about to happen. As it was, Adrienne just slowly looked up, frowned, and laughed. "Holy fuck, is that Frances?" Frances' arms instantly twitched forwards as if to offer an embrace but Adrienne did not stand up, she barely even moved, just looked as if she had bumped into a person she'd almost forgotten about. The little hope was extinguished like thumb and forefinger to a flame, and Frances felt the coldness of shame sink inside her again, compounded now by Adrienne's wandering eyes taking in boots, dress, apron, hair. She wanted to be smashed to pieces like a dropped bottle and sink into the floorboards.

"Hello, Adrienne," she repeated quietly. She didn't know what to do with her face, how to look, to smile or snarl or frown. She wished more than anything that she might appear light-hearted, even dismissive, but she was too overwhelmed and far too daft-looking. The coldness had almost filled her entire body; one tear-drop and she'd turn into an ice sculpture. The other three at the table looked back and forth between them, trying to understand, waiting for the necessary introductions or, for this person, if she wasn't a waitress—and they weren't entirely sure—to leave.

"Wow!" Adrienne said. "What are you doing here?"

"I work here. I've worked here for ten years."

There was a pause between them and the looks kept darting back and forth, up and down. Frances tugged at the tassels around the hem of her dress.

"Yes." Adrienne tossed her head. "But only ever downstairs, doing the dirty dishes, never upstairs. You always said you wouldn't. Well, I think you actually said you couldn't. But I see you've been promoted because here you are!"

"Here I am."

Then she sighed, that easy breezy sigh. "Oh, my goodness, what a world," and leant back in her chair, chuckling. Frances felt so exposed and stupid. She could not tell if Adrienne was happy to see her or not. That laugh of hers could be joy, shock, or sarcasm. It was always difficult to know, especially when you were the target. Adrienne tucked her hair behind her ear and stared at Frances for several seconds, then wafted her hand and said, "Everyone, this is my old friend Frances."

It was the sort of casual cutting comment Frances would previously have defended, saying, "She didn't want to make it awkward for everyone," or, "Well, everyone is Adrienne's friend, after all," but now she found it angered her. Adrienne introduced the table: "This is Ralph, Freddie, and Amy." Freddie—the moustache—grinned up at her and poured himself some more wine, as if the entertainment had arrived.

"More friends?" Frances said.

Adrienne put her elbow over the back of her chair and paused there a moment before smirking. "Yes, darling. More friends."

Frances pulled her pad and pen out. Her hands were trembling, and Adrienne looked at them.

"How have you been?" she said.

"Fine." Frances scribbled on the pad.

"Are you still living at the same place, your adorable little flat?"

Frances wanted to say it wasn't any of her business. For some reason, the thought that Adrienne knew where she lived made her suddenly feel uncomfortable, not because she might turn up there, but because it struck her as unfair; she hadn't a clue where Adrienne was living. And she wanted to ask why, out of all the restaurants in London, she had to come here, tonight. Was it for a meal, or for sport? She could imagine Adrienne saying to her friends later, "I mean, can it really be coincidence that I arrive and suddenly she appears? She must have seen me. There's no other explanation for it—she was always terrified of being a server. She's too awkward for it, in an adorable way, of course."

"What have you been up to? You must fill me in—it's been ages," Adrienne said, and leant in on her elbows as if to listen to a story. Then, when there came no reply, she said, "We should meet for a drink, darling. It would be lovely to catch up properly."

Frances stood still for several moments, barely realising she was holding in an urgent panicked reaction, an outburst or scream. The feeling of being reeled in, of being toyed with, of being teased, of feeling foolish, and not knowing which parts were serious and which were not, was all too much, and too familiar. She realised, standing there, pen in hand, that she could not trust Adrienne. It seemed obvious now. She could never trust her, not even in the beginning. Her feelings were not safe with her, so nothing was. The doctor's words tried to barge in: perspective, forgiveness, want, want, want. She saw him sitting there like a fat Buddha with jam on his tie and tried to hear his voice. *Just show me the way.* All four of them looked at her. "Are you ready to order?" she said as flatly as possible. Adrienne turned back to her menu and sipped her wine, leaning her body towards the moustache.

"I'll have the carbonara," Amy said.

"Lasagne," said first the moustache and then the grey suit.

"And I'll have fillet steak. Rare," Adrienne said without looking up.

"That isn't on the set menu," said Frances.

"I don't care. Let's be crazy." Her friends laughed. Adrienne finished her glass and swung around boldly to face her. "Wow, it is so nice to see you," she said.

Frances juddered internally. *How can you say that?* she wanted to scream. *You've always known where I am, you've always known you could come to me, at any time, I loved you. Seeing you here is like seeing every dream of every time we were together, every time I looked at you and wanted you and gave myself up to you. You have blasted back into my vision, internally, externally, and drained me of every other feeling, other than reminding me how much I loved and wanted you, and how much pain you left me in. Not just by leaving me, but the days and months together when you made me feel small and unworthy of you, and I accepted it because I thought it was true. I longed for you. I adored you. You were every missing part of me come to life, my mother, my friend, my lover. You encouraged me to create a nest in you and made me feel at home, but it was all a lie, all untrue, just to love me and leave me to die. And now you sit there and say it's nice to see me, just like you'd say to anyone else, a placatory statement, an emotionless fact. It is not nice to see you. Wonderful, awful, and a thousand other feelings, but nice? Never a word I could associate with you.*

"Why are you doing this to me?" she said.

Adrienne's face dropped to an expression not unlike sorrow. "Doing what to you?" she said. "I'm sorry—it's been a long time. I assumed we could be friends. If you want to. I mean, I don't mind."

"You don't have friends," Frances said.

"Excuse me?"

This, on top of everything else—it was all too much. She did the only thing she could: She turned and hurried away.

Just gotta get out.

She hadn't written anything down and immediately forgot their orders. By the bar, she stood with her hands flat out before her and tried to breathe. In the reflection of the glassware and the mirror behind it she could see her there, pouring wine into their glasses and laughing as if nothing unusual had happened. They all seemed to be having a party. Wound up in the pain of seeing her was the old uncomforted six-year-old who never got invited and tried to act like she didn't care whilst the kids had a fabulous time without her. She wrapped her arms around herself and bowed her head. The servers whizzed, customers rushed to the bar or outside to smoke, a man with a bottle of Barolo barged past her, and no one seemed to see her there. She had succeeded: She was so small, she was invisible. If she could just hide there like that until the end of service, perhaps she could slip out under the door.

"Nice dress."

She looked up, and in the reflection of the mirror saw the grey suit standing there, behind her. She turned around.

He was very nearly smiling, very nearly offering gentle sympathy, but his face could not resist the opportunity to sneer, as many people do when they've finally found someone slightly less fortunate than themselves. He had a podgy neck which blobbed out above his shirt collar, and his eyes sat in hammocks of fat that hung down his face. His suit was typically dull, but obviously expensive. A big fat gold ring glittered on his little finger, like a slug wearing a diamond collar. Frances said, "Can I help you?"

"So, you're Funny Frances," he said, and he stuck his hand out.

"What?"

"Oh"—he waved the ignored hand nonchalantly—"that's just what she called you sometimes. I'm sure she meant it as a term of endearment."

"Sure. Everyone does. Can I get you something?"

"I just wanted to say hi. We've a lot in common, you and I."

Frances looked him up and down.

"Maybe not outwardly," he laughed, "but believe me, we do. That little social butterfly over there, we both know her, don't we? Both know her well. Both know the sting in her tail. And I'd bet good money that you'd still give anything for another night with her, wouldn't you?" He bore a Chelsea smile of red wine either side of his mouth.

"It wasn't like that between us," Frances said, "and I don't want to talk about it with you. I don't know you, and there is nothing between me and her now. Now, can I get you any more drinks?"

"Do you know what she describes you as? Oliver Twist with tits. When I heard that I was impressed, of course, a Dickens reference, a bit of humour—that's how she grabs us, isn't it, so smart and bold and unique and quick. None of us want to be on the wrong side of her, but it's not our choice, is it. She decides when she wants us and when she doesn't, she decides when we're fun, when we amuse her. That's all it is. She's been fucking the dude with the moustache for seven years. No, no, don't look like that— I hate that prick, do you know that? I hate him, let me just say that, right now, he's no friend of mine, so calm down, missy. I'm just telling you the facts. She used to let him know when the two of you would be in the shops late at night and he'd come in, pretending to buy milk or something, watching you grope each other. The night she ditched you, he was at the next table. They're as bad as each other, really. Tonight's a double whammy, though. I thought it would be just me and her—I didn't know that cunt was coming and I didn't know you worked here, I swear I didn't know. But here I am and here we are, because it's better to have a piece of her than have nothing at all, isn't it? Because she's . . . well . . . she's special. You know what I mean. The other woman is new. I haven't seen her before, but I think she's here to stay for a while because they keep laughing and joking and, well, two minutes alone together and I think we both know what would be happening. Unlike me. I think she's bored of me. But seeing us talk here for a few minutes might have bought me some renewed interest." He looked over his shoulder hopefully.

"She said she loved me," Frances whispered.

"That's the problem with words, isn't it—absolutely anyone can say absolutely anything. You never know, she might have even meant it at the time." He held his hands up in a shrug.

And then she recognised him, the man at the table with the moustache. Back when she used to wait across the street and stare up at the flat, this was the man Adrienne shared cigarettes and lemonade with. She didn't remember him anywhere else, though, but she never noticed anything when Adrienne was around; he might have been there the whole time, he might have been everywhere.

"This is the problem when a person makes everyone feel special; it means none of them are special. She has a free heart, but we all want to be the one to pin her down. I've never flattered

myself that it might be me. I see exactly how it is, almost a trans-
action between us. I love her, and she loves my money. I could be
fine with it if it weren't for all the others. But like I said, it's not
our choice, is it. And I know she's tiring of me because you can't
buy someone's interest, not if what they're interested in is new
people and different personalities."

And she remembered the night she had called, when Adrienne had been clubbing with her friends, saying how she'd grown
bored of them. She was forever growing bored. It wasn't enough
to be with Adrienne; you had to entertain her. It was an unspoken
part of the deal. Don't be dull or she'll be gone.

"I thought I was different," Frances said.

The man smirked. "Don't kid yourself. I mean, from what
I've heard, yeah, she liked you. She thought you were, y'know,
cute. Quirky. Odd. She liked that you were all over her, until it got
annoying. It's a fine balance with her, isn't it? Doting just enough
to keep her happy but not so much she wants to punch you. Anyway, I'd better be getting back. I think she's looking over."

This was said with such a pathetic tone of hope Frances almost
felt sorry for him. He checked himself in the bar mirror, then
said, "Chin up. You're free again. She can't hurt you anymore,"
and stumbled back to the table. As he sat down, Adrienne held her
hand out for him to take, then asked him some questions, looking
concerned and inquisitive. She glanced at Frances several times,
refilled his glass, and blew him a succession of kisses, then talked
as they all listened like kittens sucking dreamily at her delectable
teats.

Frances watched her in the mirror and could not stop trembling. She looked at the woman she had cried for and longed for
and missed and got sick and shrunken away for. She thought of
all the efforts to forget her. All the time spent in the café, wonder-

ing if she might appear. All the time imagining her, and how it used to be, how it could be again. All the guilt and self-hatred at having smothered her, pushed her away, made her lose herself. And she watched now as she leant over to the man beside her and tongued his mouth open until he grabbed her face and kissed her. Maybe she didn't know Frances was watching, but the point was, she didn't care. *Is she fucking someone?* What a stupid question it seemed now. *Just gotta get right out of here.* Frances turned, and fled down the stairs.

13

Sʜᴇ ʀᴀɴ. She ran and ran and ran. The sky had darkened now; it seemed like she had been away from home for days. She ran and ran and ran. She knew if she stopped running she would cry and there would be no stopping it. It would all come out, all that she had reined in for so long, all she thought she had tucked away. Numbness, flatness, nothingness, impossible now; feelings burst in upon her and fought to be felt, understood. Only running prevented it; she sprinted as hard as she could, tearing through the miles, thoughts charging round in circles.

I hate her. I hate her. I hate her. I hate her.

How could she? How could she? How could she? How could she?

Who is she? Who is she? Who is she? Who is she?

What were we? What were we? What were we? What were we?

Questions, unanswerable questions. Questions she, until an hour ago, could have made sense of. Now the questions rolled in one after the other, no space for answers, just questions and more questions and all these slaughtered feelings.

She arrived at the duck pond, gasping, exhausted, and stood

with her hands on her knees. They buckled, and she sank slowly to the ground as the tears burst their restraints and came charging forth. A very small sound spilled out from her and she gasped it back in again, then sat back on her haunches, her face in her hands. *I don't understand any of it,* she said to herself, but in fact she did understand, she saw it all very clearly now—it was just too much to accept.

Truth. Truths. And each truth a stitch in the tapestry, forming a picture, a complete truth. The lies, the booze, the women, the house with the pink door, the items in the wooden box with a heart on the lid. The stifling, the numbing, the searching. Unravel it all and sew back truths and what you had was a life—her life—as one single scene leading to all of these consequences. It all began at one point: a man—her father—weeping as a door closed and a car sped away. He, watching from the window, then turning and picking her up, holding her as he cried. "You'll see her again," he said, but she never did. And through the years a deception had formed to cope with the hurt, telling herself that gone meant dead and dead meant gone, and she'd been so young she almost believed it.

Eventually, drained, she went and sat on the bench and looked up at the blank black window of the flat. The metal mallard, poised over the water, stretched its wings and shone darkly in the cooling of the day. The two litter bins were overflowing, the opposite bench had a crumpled beer can wedged into it, and the smell of damp decay was riper than ever before. Her eyes felt gritty and sore, her head hurt, her face felt strained and uncomfortable. She looked at the water and wondered how deep it was, the perfect ending, a perfect hiding place, a final escape.

"Are you okay?"

She looked to her left; a man in shorts and a T-shirt sat there, two benches away, new moonlight shimmering across the undulations of his arm muscles. He was looking at her.

"Yes," she said.

"You sure? You don't look okay."

"I'm fine."

"I hate to see a woman crying—it's like seeing a baby cry, but worse. You can't just feed or rock a woman okay again. There's always real pain underneath. I hate it."

"I'll be fine."

"It's okay. We don't have to talk. Sorry if I disturbed you. I just wanted to check."

She rested her elbows on her knees and said, "I feel sick."

"It's the heat," he replied.

"I have to get away."

"From the heat? I hear you. You know what they say: A change is as good as a rest."

"I have to get away from myself."

"Ah. Destination impossible." He laughed softly. It was a smooth, deep laugh, the purr of a big cat. "One thing I know, if you run away, your problems follow you."

"Depends how far you go."

He came and sat on the bench beside her. She didn't slide away or move. She didn't feel capable of reacting. She didn't mind or care that he was there; he meant nothing. She looked at him and he wasn't smiling or frowning, he was staring at her lips, her mouth. It was such a stare—so intense—she couldn't help but stare back at his lips, his mouth. Not a pout, but as if they were plumped, swollen from lots of fighting or kissing. She reached out to touch his arm, then stopped, preferring to believe he perhaps wasn't real, none of it was real. His neck looked hard, almost solid. The top of a tattoo disappeared beneath his T-shirt. He was reclining with one arm along the back of the bench, behind her; if she sat back, she would fall into an embrace. The impulse was suddenly appealing, just ease back into the arms of a stranger and be held for a while, talked to about nothing as if nothing mattered, held safe in strong arms that would protect her from herself, stay there forever. She needed comfort. She needed comforting. She needed love.

She needed love.

She was about to turn to him and explain it, about to sink back and feel his warmth, rest her head on his chest, but the moment passed. The moment passed, because suddenly he was pressing his cushioned lips against hers, and a tongue as soft as beaten leather was softly caressing hers.

To hell with all of it. To hell with all of them.

A hand came to the back of her head, pressing it slightly, then it clutched her hair as the other took a hold of her jaw and he pulled away, holding her face there, before him, eyes a few inches away as if sizing up a repeat attack. "You're beautiful," he said. "Do you know that?"

"No."

"Well, you are."

To hell with the past, to hell with lies that hurt and truths that burnt and all the want want want for change, for difference. To hell with fighting and resisting and thinking too much or trying not to think. To hell with plans and worries and outcomes and threats. To hell with debts and strangers and the whole lot of it. She stood by the pond in the moonlight and streetlight and half-light, lifted her dress, then climbed on top of him, her back to the pond, the birds, the flat, the world. He unzipped, unleashed, and stared into her eyes. She wrapped her arms around his head and slid down in one direct movement onto him: a rush, a shock, a wrench from the earth, from existence, into a momentum like waves, again and again, and with each rise she felt blank and dark, and with each crash she felt full of need, she felt held, she felt wanted, she felt protected; she felt loved. He was speaking, holding her breasts, trying to kiss her lips, to lick her neck, but she stayed upright, her back arched away from him, and took every moment she could, every feeling, every bit of him, as if she were owed—owed relief, owed forgetfulness, owed a change, a reinvention. To feel. To feel again. Any feeling. Anything.

To hell with all of them.

To hell with Elaine, and Adrienne, and Dom. To hell with teachers and schoolgirls and fat men in grey suits. To hell with her father, the doctor, the self-satisfied parents, to hell with white satin gloves and neat little heels. And to hell with her mother, never there, never there, never there.

"Bite me," she said.

He gently sucked her neck, her jaw.

"No," she said. "Bite me." And she sank her teeth into the hard curve of his ear. He flinched and pulled away. "What are you doing?"

"Bite me, I said. Hit me. Do something."

"I'm not going to hit you."

"Then grab me, hold on to me, anything."

He wrapped his arms around her waist and squeezed. She felt every part of him harden, and felt his hands dig into her back. She bent down and kissed him, wanting his tongue, his lips, all of him, now. For this brief moment, nothing mattered; there were only actions, never consequences.

But then, one sound. One word: "Frances?"

There in the entrance to the duck pond, between the two high hedges, stood Elaine.

Her head shaking slightly, saying, "No, no, no," a hand in her hair, the other to her mouth. Shorts, shirt, barefoot. But she was not mad, and she was not hallucinating: She looked, clear-eyed, and saw. She saw everything.

Then she turned and ran.

"Shit!" Frances tried to clamber off. The man half helped her, half tucked himself in, looking over at the gap in the hedge, saying, "What the hell? Who was that?"

"Shit," Frances said again. She tripped, fell over, clambered up again, then shouted, "Elaine!" and sprinted after her.

There was no sight of her in the street, no sign of anyone. Frances ran to the entrance of the flats, then tore up the steps, two at a time, the sound of her feet echoing up the building. The front door was open to blackness. She stepped quietly into the eeriness. Only shapes were visible, the outlines of boxes and objects and the back of the sofa. The stench, like some sort of horror, crept inside her. Then she heard a loud thudding sound coming from the living room.

"Elaine?" she said. "Elaine?"

She turned the light on.

Over by the window, Elaine was in a low squat, striking something against the floor, rising it up over her head and hitting again and again. Frances slowly approached around the sofa but Elaine did not stop, even as she looked up, shark-eyed, at Frances. She kept on striking and smashing.

The wooden box, and all its contents, ripped or broken or shredded. Elaine picked up a handful of it, and tossed it out the open window.

"No!" Frances leapt forwards.

Elaine picked up the cactus on the windowsill, spun, and hurled it at Frances as hard as she could. It smacked into her temple before colliding with the toaster. Elaine rushed at her, fists pummelling, as Frances clutched her head and tried to grab the beating arms. "Elaine, stop, please, calm down."

"You fucking lying bitch!"

She paused a moment and sobbed. "You're a lying bitch," she said, quieter, then went back to the shattered box and broken items on the floor and continued throwing them out the window. "You think I didn't know? You think I didn't know about all this, didn't know what it was? Your little box of souvenirs—do you think I'm stupid?"

Frances bent over and reached out into a tangle of arms— Elaine's smashing, hers grabbing—as she snatched at a piece of paper on the floor. "Please, not that," Frances begged. "Please, Elaine. Please."

Elaine swiped up the paper and read it. "Who the fuck is Anne?"

"Please give it to me."

"Some other girlfriend you're not over? Someone else you're stalking? Some other fuck-buddy? How could I have ever trusted you?"

"No, you don't understand. Please. Please give it to me."

There came a banging on the door but neither heard it.

"You're damn right I don't understand. What the fuck has been going on? Who was that guy and what's happened here and who the hell are you? Who the hell *are* you?"

"Please, Elaine, it's not what you think." She reached for the paper but Elaine held it away. "My father gave that to me. Please. Please."

"What about that out there? Is that what I think? Because I think that was you riding some dude's prick round the corner from our house whilst I was sick in bed and didn't know where the fuck you were or what the fuck has happened here. I woke up to find the house looking like we've been robbed and you nowhere in sight. I can't find my phone, the place is dark—look at it. I don't even know what fucking day it is. Then I look outside and see you. And him." Her face dropped. Her hands dropped. The paper fell to the floor.

The pounding at the door came again, persistent, a rhythmic *bang, bang, bang*.

"I'm sorry. I'm sorry. It wasn't about you."

"It never fucking is, is it. It never has been. Nothing is ever about me. I love you, but that doesn't matter, because you don't love me. You love her. It's always her. When we have sex and you don't look at me, it's her. When you say 'I love you,' it's her. When you kiss me, it's her. All this stuff, here, in this box, this bunch of rotten, faded souvenirs, did you think I didn't know? Do you think I'm stupid? I know you don't want me. I get it, okay," then she screamed, "I always have! But why him, out there? Will anyone do? Anyone who isn't her—it doesn't make a difference to you, does it? If you can't have her, then we're all the same."

"No, that isn't it, I promise you."

"You promise! Do you even fucking hear yourself? Promise?"

"I'm sorry. I'm sorry. Elaine, I can explain—"

But she didn't get the chance to. Suddenly, the door to the flat burst open and Dom, Betty, and three other women stormed into the flat, rushing upon them. Dom saw Frances immediately, and before she could move, he strode straight up to her, grabbed her by the neck, and pushed her up against the wall by the window. Frances, too stunned to move, dangled there, her hands grappling at his arms, looking at the face she once knew, the person she thought she knew, transformed into two frozen eyes, a hand crushing her windpipe, and a voice muttering, "I fucking warned you."

The women had grabbed hold of Elaine, who grappled and kicked and yelled, "What the hell is this?"

"Tell her," Dom said to Frances, his breath full of smoke. "Tell her what this is."

"I don't have it," Frances gasped. "Please. Please don't."

"I know you haven't got it, you idiot—we haven't exactly popped round for tea."

"Please, don't hurt her—she's nothing to do with it, she doesn't know anything about it."

"I can see that."

"Got what?" Elaine shouted. The women had wrangled her into the armchair, where she now sat, unrestrained, as one of the Ladies held a knife out before her and said, "Oi. Keep it down."

"Your lady friend owes me money," Dom said. His nose was so close Frances could see each pore. She tried to swallow, but couldn't. A pressure behind her eyes and ears was building, and as she choked she said again, "Please."

"She's owed me it for a while now," he continued, "and I'm sick of waiting. But she knows I don't do the dirty work where women are involved, which is why I've brought my own lady friends with me." Frances blinked pleadingly. Then she watched as Betty stood up and opened her bag.

Shorter than Frances, slimmer than Frances, it made no difference; she reached in her bag and pulled out her curling tongs, then pointed beside the television and said, "I see a socket. That's handy."

"No, please."

"Or"—Betty walked up beside Dom and stared into Frances'

watering eyes—"maybe I'll have some fun with her girlfriend and she can watch. What do you think, Dom?"

Dom examined the whole of Frances' face, then said, "Yeah. Go on."

Frances could barely breathe, could hardly see. She managed to squeak one desperate word, barely audible in the room: "No." She watched as Betty plugged in her tongs and the two other women tackled Elaine to the ground, face down.

"How much money?" Elaine yelled.

"Shut it," Betty snarled.

"Please! How much money? I have money. I have money. I do."

"Two thousand and fifty" said Dom.

"I have that. I have it. I have it. I have it."

Betty waved her tongs around and said, "She's bullshitting you."

"I'm not. I promise. I have it. I can get it."

"Where is it?" Dom said.

"In there. In my room. I can get it."

He motioned for the Ladies to move. They all watched as Elaine stood up and ran into the bedroom. Through blurred vision Frances saw Elaine return with Edwin the Furby in her hands. She stood there before them and popped his head off, then pulled out two rolls of cash and a few extra notes.

"There." She held it out to him.

He looked at it, released Frances, and flicked through it. "You've been lucky," he said to Frances. Then, grinning, he winked at her and said, "No hard feelings."

The front door swung off its hinges. Betty could be heard cackling and squealing up the street. Frances fell onto the floor, and Elaine slumped on the arm of the sofa. They both looked, dazed, before them. Elaine didn't move as Frances gasped and coughed and clutched her neck.

"Why didn't you tell me?" Elaine said. "It's only money. You only had to ask. You only ever had to ask."

THEY SAT amongst the debris of the flat, Frances with an ice pack to her bleeding temple, bruises appearing on the side of her neck, and they both stared mutely ahead, sipping beer.

"I guess I understand," Elaine said. "Him, I mean. A dealer, right? Should have guessed, should have seen it coming ages ago. I know what you get up to at night. And I'm not stupid." She sighed. "You needed money. You know, I thought at the time it seemed a bit out of the blue, asking me to move in. But, well, I loved you, so . . ."

Frances didn't say anything, just sipped her drink.

"I didn't set up the payment because I wanted to propose to you on Friday, see what you said, then I was going to sort it out Saturday if you said yes." She looked down at the ring still on Frances' finger and said, "Well, I guess I did half my plan, eh."

Frances placed the empty beer bottle on the floor.

"The funny thing is," Elaine said, "I just wanted to be like her, for you. I bought champagne because you said she liked it. I bought cookery books to fill the gaps. We went to Camden because you said that's where she liked to go. I've tried to ignore all the warning signs, tried to play happy, made myself sing and act happy, hoping it would all work out.

"I thought with enough love and sex and affection you might grow to love me back, but it would never have worked because you just use people, Frances. To numb, to get what you want, to keep ticking over in some sort of half-life, because you're not alive, not really. You're on hold, and we're all just helping to keep you there."

Frances looked down at the battered box and its contents, now indistinguishable from one another, just shadowy shapes on the floor. She picked the crumpled piece of paper up and looked at it. Then Elaine said, "You've got to sort it out, the pain that's working away in the background. Her."

"Adrienne?"

"No, for God's sake, your mother. You need to deal with it, accept it, find a better way to cope. Say a prayer, write her a letter, see a shrink, whatever, say your piece to find some peace. Because she's tied up in everything you do. She dictates everything you do. Until that's put to rest, you'll always be the hurt little kid wanting its mother."

"Easy for you to say."

"I know. But it's true."

Frances nodded and said, "I know. It's turning me into a monster."

Elaine tutted. "Not a monster. Don't exaggerate. You always exaggerate. You're not as bad a person as you think you are, you're just damaged. So's everyone. That's life. Damage control."

And Frances saw, right there, a chance to be good. She found the gear, and she went for it. She opened herself another beer, then set it on the kitchen worktop and braced herself to do something completely new. She was going to tell the truth. She was going to confess.

"What the fuck are you wearing?" Elaine said.

Leave it all behind, and face the truth: Frances told her.

She told Elaine everything.

14

Frances asked the jeweller to repeat the figure he'd just said, and when he did she whispered, "Wow."

"It is a very unusual piece," he said.

"I know."

"It always makes me sad when someone brings in an engagement ring. 'Another one bites the dust,' I say to myself. Such a shame."

"Not always." Frances grinned. "Thanks again."

"Cheerio."

Outside, Elaine leant against the window, tightening her scarf. "Well?" she said. "As much as the last valuation? More?"

"More," Frances said. "Much more."

"Oh, babes, that's brilliant. But now I've got to rush or I'll miss my train."

"I know, I know—come on, let's go."

They walked briskly along the seafront together, the lighthouse looming behind them, then turned inland, through the empty market square, past the boarded-up shops. A few people exited the supermarket, and a man in a beige jumper stepped out from the library and dragged a WE ARE OPEN sign back inside. They passed the old record shop, the café windows pasted with steam, the locked and boarded ice cream stands and fish vendors. Elaine said, "God, this place is depressing."

Frances laughed and lit a cigarette. "Not in the summer. You liked it in the summer, remember?"

"Nope," she said. "I didn't like being here then, I just liked being with you. I always thought it was tacky and depressing."

"You liked the Waltzer."

"Okay, I'll admit, I liked the Waltzer."

They turned uphill and Elaine said, "How are you feeling?"

Frances thought for a moment, then said, "Alright. At the moment."

"You're doing the right thing, you know."

"I know, I know."

"You're being a big brave girl," Elaine teased.

"Shut up."

Elaine laughed. "But I mean it. Seriously. You are being brave. It was always going to be you who had to take the first step. You're the one with a name and address. You had to do the approaching. And you did. You should be proud of yourself."

"Well, it was your idea, so if it goes tits-up I'll know who to thank."

"I just gave you a nudge. And it won't go tits-up. Let me know how it does go, though, yeah?"

"Of course."

"And send me pictures."

"We'll see. If I chicken out, there won't be any pictures to send."

"Don't be silly. Considering everything you've been through, I know you can handle this."

"You've always had such faith in me."

"It's a tough job but someone's got to do it."

They arrived at the entrance to the train station and stood facing each other. The time had gone quickly and now both were reluctant to leave. It felt too much like a permanent separation, an ending. Both stood, shuffling side to side, unsure what to say, now the moment had arrived. "Want me to wave you off?" Frances said.

"Don't be silly—you'll be late. Besides I need to go and get my luggage from the lockers. You go. I'll text you when I get there."

"Make sure you do."

"And remember, it's not goodbye, it's . . . ?"

"Good riddance?"

"Silly." Elaine sighed and said, "My Fearless Frances."

"I don't know about that."

They hugged, the slightly tighter, longer, tender hug of a farewell. Elaine kissed Frances' forehead and said, "You are fearless. Don't forget it. And don't worry."

"About a thing?"

"Because?"

"Every little thing might actually be alright," Frances sang. "I know. So you keep saying."

"Well, it will." Elaine looked down at Frances. Funny Frances, Fearless Frances, just Frances. "That goes for both of us," she said. "It's a promise. Life's about to get good. It's about to get really, really good."

Frances smiled. "I hope so. And thank you."

Elaine groaned and thumped her on the arm. "I told you, stop thanking me. Now go, or you're going to be late and I'll miss my train; then I might actually have to hate you."

Frances watched as Elaine hurried to the lockers, pulled out her luggage, then ran over to the barrier. She put her ticket in, and stepped through. Just as Frances thought it was over, Elaine turned, beaming, and waved wildly, blowing kisses into the air. She mouthed the words "Be happy," and Frances nodded, then waved back And then, despite the time and the need to hurry, she watched Elaine board the train, watched her talk to a fellow passenger, watched her store her luggage overhead, watched the train pull away and Elaine slowly and smilingly leave.

SHE WALKED ALONG the promenade with her hands in her coat pockets, head down against the wind. The tide was in, waves crashed up over the wall in ferocious arcs, and children played in them, daring one another to stand still. She walked with focus, wind-swept water spraying her shoulder. The sea was moodier now that the season was changing; autumn always brought out its angry side.

She turned onto the pier and walked under its entrance, past the arcades on her left and the carousel to her right, both vibrant with flashing lights. Past the candyfloss stall, the doughnut stand, the smell of coffee and sugar and beer. It was the tail end of the season and few people were there; soon the horses of the carousel would be halted for months of respite and frostbite until the Easter scrub and lick of paint. The pier would remain open for the winter walkers and the fishermen, and the Boxing Day crowd, who arrived happy and bloated, to take the air and sip hot chocolate, but all the rides and arcades would be in darkness, hibernating until spring. She walked past the Waltzer and rickety ghost train, out the other side into the open again, halted in her stride by a chilly gust as she headed off along the wooden slats. The sky was thick with a cloud that seemed stuffed into the atmosphere, like padding. No gulls overhead but several rocked haughtily on the waves, unimpressed. The fishermen were here, full of patience and hope, scowling along lengths of line, elbows on the barrier, cigarettes stuck in silent mouths. Frances stood a short distance away from them, mirroring the stance, and looked across the water to the lighthouse on the hill—thumb-sized from this distance—and she saw the waves that swept upon the children, flickering like white curls of hair.

Hands cold, she shoved them back into her pockets and felt the ring there. Elaine hadn't wanted it back; without a hint of maliciousness, she'd said, "It's yours now. Do what you want with it." She had handled the facts and fallout in her usual generous way, being accepting, if not understanding, about everything. Miraculously, she'd had no ill-effects in the aftermath, and reported nothing more than a general feeling of being "out of it." She had no memory of anything since the run. She had asked a lot of questions, and Frances had answered them all. She'd been appalled, of course, but also able to swiftly, easily, forgive, such was her nature; she responded to most of it with the words "Oh, Frances," and a shake of her head. It was only then that Frances realised how nice she was; it surprised her, in fact, at this late juncture, to realise she liked her. And Elaine loved Frances, despite everything, and, if anything, felt more tender towards her. She moved out of the flat two days later, saying to keep the money and she wished her well, but she needed to start her life over. She had moved back in with her parents for a while, and was now heading off across the country to a new house, a new job, a new beginning. Frances realised she would miss her. Four months had passed, and the experience, plus the openness, plus some therapy and subsequent change in Frances, had allowed them the sort of friendship Frances had never had before. One without lies and deceit. It was nice.

She took the ring from her pocket. The final valuation it had just received would cover the cost of catering college. She had recently taken her sweet onion soup into work and the chef patron had immediately put it on the specials board. The chefs had all clapped her on the back and taught her knife skills and shown her how to flair pizza dough. She still retreated to pot-wash, but less so now.

"You got skill, you know," King had said, "so don't hide it. You gotta blow your own trumpet in this life or know what happens? Some bastard gonna come along and he's gonna fuck your trumpet. I'm telling you, right in there, he's gonna fuck it. Believe in yourself, Puppy. You're better than pots and pans."

Maybe he was right.

She had recently moved to a new flat, one further away from work but with a view of a park and cheaper rent and no memories. She had briefly considered moving here, going into a house share, being a student by the sea, but she wasn't ready to live here. Not yet, anyway.

She had not worked upstairs again, partly because it was the only way they could get her to come back and partly because the staff upstairs said they'd quit if she did, but she'd been informed that Adrienne had come in several times, always with different people, always happy and looking around. Then late one night Frances' phone rang and there was that cheery voice asking if she wanted to meet "for a glass of something grape." Frances swallowed deeply, and said a very flat "No."

"Is that because you're otherwise engaged? Nobody need ever know."

Frances had hung up and cried for half an hour. Adrienne, and anything grape, needed to be gone from her life, but that did not stop her grieving them. She hadn't heard from Adrienne since but still half expected to bump into her one day and hoped she'd have the strength to cross the street if she did.

And they had all been right. The doctor, Adrienne, Elaine, they had all hit the nail on the head at one time or other. Say your piece to find some peace. Forgiveness is key. They'd all been pointing her in this direction but she had stubbornly argued, lied, deceived herself, because that was what she had always done, and so it was how she knew to be. None of them had known the truth, though. Nobody did. And now, it was time to face it.

She took the crumpled piece of paper from her pocket and looked at it, like she had looked at it hundreds of times in its box. An address, not a quarter of a mile away from this pier, only a few streets away, in fact. She had known where it was but had rarely gone there, just kept the address safely for years, like proof, like evidence of a connection. The house with the pink door. Then she removed from her pocket the letter that had arrived a few days ago, a stranger's hand, cautiously written, little more than a place and time. Such brevity was essential, she knew, but she had read and reread it, searching for more, as if perhaps it was encrypted. There was so much it did not say.

She looked at her watch.

It was not too late to turn around. She could throw both pieces of paper into the sea. She was tempted, nervous all of a sudden. All she'd have to do is walk away.

But then, she heard the sound of footsteps approaching behind her, and she recognised them.

Perhaps they resonated from a dream or a distant memory, but they felt more than merely familiar; they were known without a doubt. The footsteps that had walked through doors, had walked away, and had lived here for so long. This was why she was drawn to this place. This was why she loved it. This was why it felt like home, and why it gave her an endless sense of searching. Too afraid to knock on that door, she had scoured the faces of those who lived here, hoping for a chance encounter. This was why she had always come here in times of need, and this was why her feet had brought her here when she was not thinking. This was why she had never belonged anywhere else: because the only place—the only way—she could ever belong, was here.

"Frances?" the voice behind her said.

She looked at the blank-eyed sea birds wobbling on the waves and tried to emulate their expression, tried to look empty and cold and unimpressed. She looked down at the two pieces of paper, folded them, and put them back in her pocket. Then she turned.

It was not the face of the Gold Blend woman, nor was it Adrienne, nor anything from her imagination: The face was her own—Frances'—but twenty long years older, each regret and worry etched in its brow, with a smile, like hers, looking back at her fearfully. She felt the recognition as a sudden shock; here she was and of course it was her. She would have recognised her anywhere.

"Frances," she said again, and moved to embrace, then stopped as if caught on a gust of wind or moment's reflection, and instead drew her forefingers to her lips, palms touching, as if in prayer. "Frances," she whispered. "Thank you."

Frances stood still. The one word she had longed to say all her life formed in her mouth, but stayed there, for now. Instead, she reached out and lightly touched the arm of the woman's coat. She felt its fibres, its softness, and clasped the arm beneath it. It was real. She was real. Her heart lurched up, swollen full, into her throat.

The sea bird took off into the air; a fisherman's line began to twitch. The coat smelled like pears and honey, her hair like a bouquet. Somewhere, the world began to flood with colour; a kingfisher flew above a depthless mirror before a backdrop of brilliant green, and the colour was coming, was heading for her. She braced, and allowed it; she saw full spectrums of colour, felt full spectrums of feeling. Forgiveness tumbled out as love poured in and the two collided, combined, and became one. And as her balloon heart burst with such sudden belonging, she clung on to her mother, as a child, once again.

ACKNOWLEDGEMENTS

Deepest gratitude to my family and friends who have supported me over many years, in many ways, and whose encouragement and love helped more than they could ever know. Huge love to you all.

I'm eternally indebted to several people for launching my writing career. My amazing agent, Susan Ginsburg, who took my dream and smashed it out of the park. Her assistant, Catherine Bradshaw, who answered every one of my incessant questions and helped keep me sane. My fabulous editor, Jenny Jackson, who steered the way with such precision at all hours of the day. And heartfelt thanks to all the staff at Writers House and Knopf who turned this chapter in my mind into an actual book.

Last but not least, Tilly. My constant companion through every single page.

+

A NOTE ABOUT THE AUTHOR

Dawn Winter lives in Essex, north of London, and studied English literature at Roehampton University. She has held a variety of jobs in prisons, hospices, kitchens, and factories. *Sedating Elaine* is her first novel.

A NOTE ON THE TYPE

The text of this book was set in Walbaum, a typeface designed by Justus Erich Walbaum in 1810. Walbaum was active as a typefounder in Goslar and Weimar from 1799 to 1836. It is the slight but pleasing irregularities in the cut that give this typeface its humane quality and account for its wide appeal.

Typeset by Scribe, Philadelphia, Pennsylvania
Printed and bound by Berryville Graphics, Berryville, Virginia
Designed by Anna B. Knighton